P9-BZX-849

This Book Belongs To
Donna Clarke

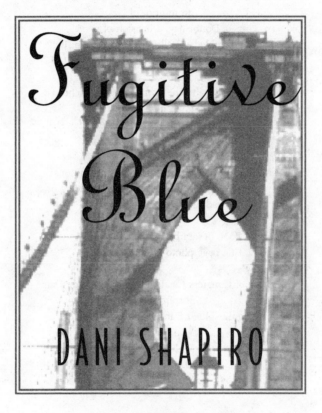

Fugitive Blue

DANI SHAPIRO

NAN A. TALESE

DOUBLEDAY

NEW YORK LONDON TORONTO

SYDNEY AUCKLAND

PUBLISHED BY NAN A. TALESE
an imprint of
Doubleday, a division of
Bantam Doubleday Dell Publishing Group, Inc.
666 Fifth Avenue, New York, New York 10103

DOUBLEDAY and the portrayal of an anchor
with a dolphin are trademarks of
Doubleday, a division of Bantam Doubleday Dell
Publishing Group, Inc.

All of the characters in this book are fictitious,
and any resemblance to actual persons, living or
dead, is purely coincidental.

Book design by Marysarah Quinn
Title page photo by Mark Garofalo

Library of Congress Cataloging-in-Publication Data
Shapiro, Dani.
Fugitive blue / Dani Shapiro. — 1st ed.
p.   cm.
I. Title.
PS3569.H3387F8   1993
813'.54—dc20   92-18253
CIP

ISBN 0-385-42107-9

Copyright © 1993 by Dani Shapiro
All Rights Reserved

Printed in the United States of America
January 1993

1   3   5   7   9   10   8   6   4   2

First Edition

FOR JEROME BADANES AND
ILJA WACHS

I confess I am only broken by the sources of things.

—ANNE SEXTON
("Said the Poet to the Analyst")

PROLOGUE

$\mathscr{E}$very night I see mirages. Beneath heaped overcoats and loosened neckties, glimmers of gold and flashlights sparking like fireflies against the theatre's black curtains, deep within the winter coughs, the rustling of candy wrappers, the clicking of handbag latches, hundreds of strangers in the audience become whoever I want them to be.

All women of a certain age and elegance become my mother. In the second row there is a woman smoothing her gray hair. She raises a hand to her lips, and for a moment I think I see her. She leans back in her seat as if she owns the place.

I am an actress by blood and necessity. I am also the director's woman. Ex-woman. We have adapted Vladimir Nabokov's autobiography, *Speak, Memory*. I play Lolita. The final moments of the play are mine. During my monologue I

1

pace in a flesh-colored leotard behind a sheer curtain as the audience wonders if I am really naked, forty blocks from Broadway.

My costume is Nigel's inspiration. After all, he directed this piece. He orchestrated my performance as well as his exit from my life. Perhaps my costume is his idea of a perfect self-torture. If he wants to have the illusion of my naked body again, all he has to do is walk through the theatre doors and join the crowd.

Nigel and I formed El Raton, a theatre company located as far Off-Broadway as you can get and still be in Manhattan. We named ourselves for the giant rats which swarmed the Chelsea warehouse where we first put down roots ten years ago, but there are no rats anymore, not unless you count the people.

Suddenly we are an overnight discovery, a precocious bunch of upstarts pushing thirty. Uptown lawyers and Wall Street types come down here in packs for their annual dose of culture, clutching torn corners of newspaper with our address, whizzing past their usual haunts in the backs of limos and Checker cabs, venturing deep into the bowels of Manhattan where bistros are scarce and meat-packers begin working before dawn.

When I take my curtain calls, I look into the shadows. I search for the faces I have loved. I stand in the center of the stage and step forward in my flesh-colored leotard. I stare the audience down. I search for them. I strip the strangers as I have been stripped. I despise the older women, the slender young blond boys, the men ogling me from the front row. I despise them precisely for who they are not.

Their applause is like the crashing of a heavy wave: here one moment, thundering, gone. I have grown accustomed to the sound. I don't take it to heart. After all, I have been encircled by a truer fame all my life. I have shivered in the cold gleaming light which has always surrounded my mother, Georgia Higgins Hirsch.

Nabokov did not believe in time. Each week I pace the stage, a ghost, an apparition, and prove his point. But I find it impossible to dismiss time, the very thing which has so intensely failed me.

He did believe in memory. He said that we live in order to remember. And what about that? No, at the age of thirty-two, I'm afraid I must impugn the master: we live in order to forget.

I.

$\mathcal{M}$y mother is packing her bags. She tosses cowboy boots, blue jeans, bras and panties into cases and trunks which are scattered across her bedroom floor. There does not seem to be a method to her madness as she flings scarves, sweaters, cotton turtlenecks, a plastic Waldbaum's bag filled with the contents of her medicine chest, a travel alarm clock and several emery boards into the jumble.

I stand in the doorway watching. She is a blur of motion, spinning, her eyes whirling, hair springing frenzied in every direction, the heels of her cowboy boots making dull thuds across the bedroom carpet as she tries to stuff her entire jewelry box into the top of an already bulging suitcase.

"Joanna," she says breathlessly.

I am mute.

"This has nothing to do with you," she says. "You know that, don't you?"

I stare at her. In the mirrored headboard I see our reflections and know the truth: she is leaving because of me. I am wearing a pink Danskin top and pants which stretch across my chubby body. I have recently developed painful mounds of breasts, and hair sprouts beneath my arms and between my legs. I am moon-faced and flushed. When I sit on the toilet I cannot bear to look at my thighs, which spread out beneath me. I think I am repulsive. I cannot imagine how I can possibly be related to the woman standing before me, whose long legs propel her around this room on her singular mission, whose blue-black hair streams behind her with all the ceremony of a flag, whose cheeks are flushed with the exertion of getting away from me as quickly as possible.

"Josie, you'll come see me every weekend," she says, "I promise."

The doorbell rings.

"That must be the movers." Her voice is muffled. She is busy unplugging the lamp on her side of the bed.

I race down the stairs, my heart thumping faster than my feet. I will tell the movers to go away. I'll tell them they have the wrong house, that we've lived here since I was born twelve years ago, and that no one we know is moving.

I swing the door open.

A man wearing a brown cap and shirt emblazoned with the moving company logo fills the door frame. He holds a clipboard in his hand. Behind him, across the street, I see a moving truck.

"Higgins Hirsch?" he asks.

I spin on my heels and run back upstairs, past my mother's bedroom and into my own, slamming the door. Through my window I see four men ambling up the front walk, carrying folded boxes and wardrobes. They are all wearing uniforms, like policemen or undertakers.

"Joanna," my mother calls from down the hall.

I stare at the curtains of my bedroom window, the ripples they make when I part them.

"Joanna!"

Perhaps she's changed her mind. I race down the hall. My mother is standing in the center of an island of luggage, and she is crying. She holds her box of sculptor's hand tools which she drops as I walk toward her and into her outstretched arms.

"I'm sorry," she cries.

The world feels unendurable.

"Georgia, don't go," I say out loud.

"I have to, Josie. If I stay here, I can't imagine what will happen."

I do not wait for my mother to leave. I know, somehow, that the only control I have in this situation is to leave first. I sneak down the back stairs and into the garage, wheel my bicycle down the driveway. I feel like I am embarking on a trip to the moon, or a round-the-world cruise. As I slowly pedal to the corner, it seems I am leaving the corpse of my old self behind.

I roll past Nottingham Way, Exeter Road, Cotswold Court. My New Jersey neighborhood has its streets named after English locales. In the distance I hear a bleating series of beeps, an unfamiliar sound, and realize it must be the horn of Georgia's moving truck as it backs into our driveway.

I pedal faster, closing my eyes first for a second, then two, then three. I aim my bike in a straight line down Revere Drive and feel the hot breeze against my lids, my cheeks as I pedal through the darkness. Each time I open my eyes I'm farther along than I thought I would be, as if by closing my eyes, I am erasing distance. I squeeze my lids tightly and pedal as hard as

I can, swearing to myself I won't open them until I count to ten.

I get to seven before I hear a whizzing nearby, and when I blink open there is a blur of skin and metal and spokes in front of me, and I yelp once, a sound louder than the moving truck's bleeps, before I crash into the gutter.

"Oh God, I'm sorry!"

A boy is standing above me, a boy with blond hair which falls straight across his forehead, wearing a white tee-shirt smudged with dirt and grass.

I wonder if I've died and this is what angels look like.

"Where did you come from?" I mumble.

"Philadelphia. We just moved here," he says.

"No, I mean just now. I didn't see you coming," I say. I look down at my knee and see it is scraped, bleeding.

"I cut you off," a quick grin, "I always do that to people I like. Consider it a compliment."

"Thanks a lot," I moan.

I stand up and dust gravel from my knee.

"I'm so sorry," he says. "Does it hurt?"

I don't answer him. We stare at each other for a moment.

"Hi," he says softly, "I'm Billy Overmeyer."

"Hi," I say back dumbly.

He has a lovely voice, a lovely name. The bearer of such a name would be entitled to a charmed life, full of intrigue and high drama. I hate my own name. Joanna Hirsch sounds crude to my ears. It smacks of dirndl skirts, sensible shoes, double chins.

"Do you want to keep riding?" he asks.

"Sure."

We cycle side-by-side back toward my house.

"We just moved in," Billy gestures to the pale brick house across the street.

"We live there," I point to the Georgian columned house at

the precise moment the moving truck rumbles down the driveway.

Billy looks at the truck, then at me curiously.

"My mother," I say.

"Where's she going?"

"Into the city."

"Are she and your father getting a divorce?"

"I don't know."

He looks at me cannily, out of the corner of his eye, as we cycle side by side. I am staring straight ahead, and he thinks I don't see him looking at me. I have unusual peripheral vision. And what I see is kindness in his face, a softness which makes me want to cry.

He races ahead of me.

"Look! No hands!" he calls.

I take my own hands off the handlebars for the first time.

"Me too," I yell.

I stretch my arms out and make airplane noises. Billy turns his head and grins at me. I pretend my heart isn't pounding in my ears. I don't know this now, but in the single motion of removing my white knuckles from the steel handlebars of my bicycle—a feat of which I have been terrified for months—I am entering into a lifelong habit of bravado which will end twenty years from now on the steaming pavement of a New York City street. I don't have that information, I can't see the future. I have no way of knowing—in all the randomness of neighborhoods and suburbs, of boys and girls who become friends in the dying light of Indian summer—that the two most important events of my childhood have happened on the same day. My mother is gone. I have met someone who will matter to me for the rest of my life.

It is the year before we become teenagers. I am twelve. I have just taken my hands off the handlebars and soared like a bird down Cotswold Court. And there is an infestation of cicadas in New Jersey. They shed their skins when they die, and the streets are littered with insect carcasses which blow around us on this late summer suburban day.

$\mathscr{F}$reudians are only too happy to point out the parallels between the husband a woman chooses and her father. I ask you, isn't there the same possible connection between a woman's best friend and her mother?

And what if this best friend happens to be a boy, a slender young blond boy with hair that hangs straight over his eyes, improbably delicate fingers, tightly muscled legs and eyes so clear you think you can see into the back of his head?

$\mathscr{B}$illy and I make figure-eights on the street between our two houses. He pedals around the corner to the driveway in back of his new home, and I pause before making a sharp left into mine.

"See you tomorrow?" he yells.

"It's the first day of school," I holler back.

"You want to walk together?"

"Okay," I wave and veer into the driveway. I have a new friend. A boy friend. A boyfriend.

I park my bike in front of my father's old Volvo, leaning it up against a winter sleigh. My knee stings, and the back of my elbow. I walk through the garage door and into the kitchen.

My father is sitting hunched over the kitchen table, hands cupped around a steaming mug of tea.

"Daddy?" I say quietly.

He doesn't answer. His head is bent, and he is looking intently into his mug of tea as if an answer might be swirling there, spelled out in the steam. When he raises his head and looks in my direction, his glasses are all foggy; I cannot see his eyes.

Dusky light streams through the kitchen window. At this hour he is usually in his office, which has a separate entrance on the side of the house and a black and white shingle: *Bernard Hirsch, M.D., Pediatrics.*

"Dad, are you okay?"

"Your mother is gone."

"I know."

"She's not coming back, Josie," he says to me, "she's moving into the city."

His back heaves as he turns away from me. I walk over and hug him from behind. His balding head is hot and smooth beneath my cheek. Until today, I have never seen either of my parents cry. The rules have changed on this late summer day, and my childhood, as I knew it, is over.

"*I* think," said Nigel, "we'll call it El Raton."

We watched as squirrel-sized rats darted from corner to corner of the warehouse floor. We sat cross-legged on the stage, a bottle of Dewar's planted between us.

I took a swallow.

"Why not La Cucaracha? We have plenty of those," I say, wiping my mouth with my sweatshirt sleeve.

"Cockroaches are small. Think big, Joanna, think lofty thoughts."

I reached past the bottle and put my hand on his crotch. "Here's a lofty thought."

"Is that any way for the co-founder of New York's most exciting theatre company to behave on this hallowed stage?"

I looked around me. There were cartons everywhere, labeled costumes, spotlights, fabric for curtains, folding chairs.

"This is a hallowed stage? Not yet, it's not. Come on, honey, let's christen it."

I sat on top of Nigel, pulling my sweatshirt off, my breasts cold, nipples puckering in the heatless warehouse.

"Watch out!" he howled, grabbing the scotch bottle and tipping it to his mouth, spilling the amber liquid all over his face and hair.

"I'll lick it off," I said.

"Which do you like better, Joanna? Me or the booze?" he asked, holding the bottle at a distance.

I unzipped his pants, grabbed the bottle and bent over him.

"El Raton," I said, "I love El Raton the best. The giant rat."

$\mathcal{M}$y father and I eat dinner together on my last night before seventh grade. The house is quiet. We are novice divers, way over our heads as we begin to explore the deep uncharted waters of life without Georgia. It is hot in the kitchen. I scrape my chair back and open the window which overlooks the backyard. A bird feeder in the shape of a house hangs from the lowest branch of our elm tree. Humid air streams in. It is difficult to breathe.

I spoon snapper creole into my mouth and focus on the television set my father has dragged, with its stand, into the kitchen corner near the cupboards, so we can watch while we eat. Now every time we need the good china we'll have to move the television stand. Perhaps he thinks we'll never use the good china again, now that my mother is gone.

We are watching the nightly news without the sound. Projected behind the newscaster is a train wreck, metal carnage strewn over the European countryside, fire trucks pulled up alongside the tracks. A man rakes his hand through his hair once, twice, as if trying to tear it from his head. There are stretchers, white sheets pulled over immobile bodies.

I glance at my father. Tears stream down his face.

"I want to read you something, Josie," he says.

He pulls a crumped sheet of notebook paper from his breast pocket, along with his reading glasses. He perches them on the bridge of his nose and clears his throat:

"Dear Bernie . . ."

His voice cracks at the sound of his own name.

"Dear Bernie,
I've always known the only way I'd be able to leave is like this. It's the cowardly route, I know, to steal off in the middle of the day without warning. I don't like myself for it. But you'd have to be blind not to know this was coming. I'm stifled here. Enslaved by this house, by this marriage, by motherhood. I somehow wandered into the wrong life thirteen years ago, and stayed. I can't stay any longer. I hope you will understand. And I desperately hope that, some day, our daughter will forgive me.
Love, Georgia."

My father looks at me above his bifocals.

"That's your mother," he says.

"Yes," the word creaks from my lips.

"She did the best she could, Josie."

"Yes," I repeat, although I don't understand. All around me I have friends whose mothers do the best they can. They carpool their children to ice skating, horseback riding, tennis and ballet. They bake recipes taken from the backs of cereal boxes.

The mute button releases on the television.

". . . casualties are predominantly from the first-class compartment . . ." intones the newscaster.

I march upstairs, a robot, an automaton. I go to my bedroom to prepare for the first day of seventh grade. I lay out my navy blue skirt and blazer, a white blouse, knee socks and penny loafers. I write my name in the top, left-hand inside corner of all my spiral-bound notebooks. *Joanna Hirsch, Joanna Hirsch, Joanna Hirsch* I write again and again, as if my life depends on it, as if my own name will confirm my presence here in this room, this house which sits in the shadow of Georgia's flight.

I get into bed, pull the covers up and close my eyes, but I know I will not fall asleep until I hear my father creaking up the stairs of our five-bedroom house, the sounds of water running, the zipping and unzipping of clothes. I will pretend to be asleep when he comes in and kisses me good night, but beneath my closed eyes I will be able to feel the sadness he has begun to carry around with him like loose change clinking in his pockets. I will not rest until I know he is safely in bed, a heavy book balanced on his stomach. My last thought before I sleep will be a prayer that my father will not somehow begin to believe that it is easier to die than to live.

II.

$\mathcal{M}$y mother lives on Broome and West Broadway, above a store which sells avante-garde hair ornaments. She has an enormous loft, most of which serves as a studio. The current issue of *Vogue* carries a feature interview with her. They photographed her at home—the artist in her natural habitat. The article is called "The Two Sides of Georgia Higgins Hirsch." One photograph shows her in a man's white shirt and paint-splattered jeans, looking up at one of her works in progress, a seven-foot-high steel telephone pole topped by abstract birds. It is entitled *Leaving New Jersey.* Another photograph shows her in a black cashmere turtleneck and elegant trousers, hair clean and gleaming, in a rare moment of lipstick and repose. At the beginning of the piece, in large red italics, my mother is quoted. *Artists have no business having families,* she says, *I am not convinced artists are truly capable of love.*

$\mathcal{B}$illy and I trudge down the noisy corridors of Tipton Academy. Locker doors slam and echo, girls' voices rise shrilly above the boys', and bells as loud as fire drill alarms clang, announcing that homeroom starts in five minutes. We find our lockers, halfway down the hall from each other, alphabetically separated by the I's through the N's. Between our two lockers is a bulletin board which lists all the different seventh-grade sections. Although it's supposed to be a secret, everyone knows these sections are ranked from the smartest students to the dumbest. From what I can gather, I am in the smartest section, and Billy is in the second smartest. I decide not to tell him this.

I know the day will be spent gathering armloads of books and enough assignments to make sure we don't see the light of day until Thanksgiving. The homework doesn't bother me as much as what comes later, the two hours after the academic day which are devoted to the bane of my existence, intramural sports.

Field hockey tryouts are set for this afternoon and I dread them. I hate field hockey, basketball, soccer, lacrosse; in short, I hate everything which makes one popular at Tipton Academy. I hate these sports because I am not good at them. No one has informed me that there is a direct inverse correlation between success at field hockey early in life and success at anything else in adulthood. No one has told me that you can always spot the former field hockey captains when they reach the age of thirty, with their lank hair pulled tightly back in headbands and thick, scarred ankles rising solidly from sensible walking shoes.

On this early September day, in the Indian summer sun, I feel the strain in my thighs as I bend my knees and try to raise the hockey stick to precisely the right angle and thwack the ball hard, following through gracefully, arms extended in a motion which might, some day, translate into a good country club golf swing. I imagine that I am thin and wiry like Mary Louise Donahue, or tall and solid like Judy Butler. I pretend that I have a mother who is waiting at home for me with a special Rice Krispies treat fresh out of the oven.

Shielding my eyes from the sun, I see Billy in the distance, in a line of boys performing soccer drills. They are all wearing blue-and-gold tee-shirts, blue shorts, white socks and sneakers, but Billy stands out from all of them. His blond hair glints in the sun, and he pushes it out of his eyes, tucks it behind his ears, lifting his tanned, lanky arms. When his turn comes to dribble the ball down the length of the field, he runs gracefully, bending his legs like a dancer's. His hair sails behind him, his arms swim through the air as he lopes toward the goal, kicking the ball with his instep. He scores easily, without breaking stride, then runs behind the goal and to the back of the line once again.

He's a good athlete; wouldn't you know it. I'm sure he's going to like Mary Louise Donahue or Judy Butler better than me.

I push wisps of hair out of my eyes, which are stinging. Strands of hair are stuck to my cheeks. There are about twenty-five girls on the bench, and we go through drills, two at a time, passing the puck back and forth between us, stopping it with our sticks, then trying to get past the goalie. When my turn comes to score, I move my stick back, close my eyes and swing as hard as I can. Small tufts of dirt spray around me, and the ball lies motionless on the ground.

Miss DiNazio claps her hands and orders us to run four

times around the quarter-mile track. The boys are also running, and I see Billy just ahead of me, in stride with one of the popular ninth-grade boys. I try to catch up with them, but my legs won't move fast enough. I focus on the backs of Billy's legs, the smooth tanned muscles in his calves, and imagine he must really be cursing his bad fortune at having his closest neighbor be me. I watch as the ninth-grader turns and says something to Billy which makes him laugh. He throws his head back, his mouth open to the sky.

I veer off the track and begin running as fast as I can. I head in the direction of the woods, where there is a secret path which leads to Buckingham Drive, which leads to my house. Just as I reach the edge of the woods, I hear my name being called.

"Joanna, wait!" yells a voice which cracks from the effort, a taut rubber band on the brink of snapping.

I turn to see Billy.

"Get out of here," I hiss. "You'll get into trouble."

"What about you?"

"What about me?" I repeat.

"Where are you going?"

"Home."

At the thought of my house, dark and quiet, a single tear trickles from the corner of my eye down my red sweaty face. I pray Billy doesn't notice.

He glances quickly over his shoulder.

"I'll go with you," he says.

"You don't have to do that."

"I know."

Billy and I walk silently through the woods. I feel lighter, somehow, knowing that my book bag, knapsack and all my textbooks are stuffed into my locker. A mosquito buzzes past our ears, then lands on my arm and Billy slaps it quickly, killing it, leaving a small trail of blood on my skin.

We look at the mosquito blood and begin to laugh.

"I hate field hockey," I say with all the weight of a true confession.

"I hate soccer," says Billy.

"But you're good at it!"

"I can still hate it even if I'm good at it," he says.

"I've never won a single award in that school," I say gloomily.

"What kind of award?"

"Most Popular, Smartest, Most Likely to Succeed, Most Beautiful," I list them as we walk along.

"Well, you should have been voted Most Beautiful," Billy says.

I stop in my tracks.

"Oh, please."

"You *are* beautiful," he repeats.

"Please."

"No, really."

I look at him and realize he means what he is saying. For a moment, looking into his eyes is like gazing into a perfectly designed mirror which shows me my most flattering self for the first time in my life.

"Last year I almost won Most Likely to Succeed," I tell him.

"Oh, how awful."

"I know. You never want to be Most Likely to Succeed."

"We should do a season consisting only of Swedish playwrights," said Nigel.

It was nearly three in the morning, and we had long since finished our shifts tending bar at Pacific Rim.

"Why not Icelandic playwrights?" I asked as I swiveled my ass over the top of the bar, pulled out the Cuervo and Triple Sec, fresh-squeezed lime juice and a shaker full of ice.

"*Are* there Icelandic playwrights?"

"Why not? There must be. We'll go there, we'll find them."

I placed our two drinks on the mahogany bar with a flourish, pink plastic dolphins wedged jauntily against the sides of the glasses. Pacific Rim was known for tropical drinks, rum concoctions with names like Sex on the Beach and Dark and Stormy, drinks which were always topped off with the small plastic animals that had become our trademark; monkeys, pandas, giraffes, elephants. In some circles, the sharks were practically collector's items. They were blood red, sharp enough to use as weapons and as long as the glasses themselves. On the windowsill of our studio in Hell's Kitchen, Nigel and I had amassed a collection; if a burglar ever broke through our window he would knock an entire jungle's worth of colorful animals to the floor. This was our alarm system.

"Can you believe it's El Raton's third season? Pretty soon we're going to stop being prodigies."

Nigel's voice was slightly slurred.

"Prodigies don't tend bar or wait tables," I say.

"It's a proven historical fact that prodigies have always been willing to starve for their art," said Nigel.

There was a sudden banging on the door. Someone was ignoring the neon Closed sign. Nigel and I exchanged glances, both of us reminded that this was New York City at three in the morning, and risky even on Third Avenue and Eighty-first Street. We were more than a bit tipsy, and the lights in Pacific Rim announced to whoever walked by that we were alone in the restaurant with a night's worth of cash.

Nigel slid off his bar stool, drew himself up to his full former-rugby player's height and walked to the door, while I stood behind the bar with my finger on the button which would set off an alarm in the police station.

I saw him swing the door open. My finger twitched.

"Look who the cat dragged in," he called. "Joanna, your favorite person is here."

"What about *your* favorite person? I'm insulted. Aren't I your favorite person?" I heard a voice as familiar to me as my own.

They wove their way back to the bar.

I stared at Billy.

"Overmeyer, what accords us this honor?" Nigel asked.

"I finished my dissertation exactly fifteen minutes ago," said Billy.

"You mean 'Neurobiological Aspects of Schizophrenic Blah Blah?" asked Nigel.

"One and the very same," said Billy.

I swiveled over the top of the bar, jumped down to the floor and threw my arms around him.

"God, Billy, I'm so proud of you," I murmured.

We hugged tightly, violently. I felt my breasts pushing against him, his arms linked around my waist.

Nigel tilted his head back and drained his margarita. A plastic shark fell to the floor.

"Here's to the three of us—Josie, Billy, Nigel—prodigies one and all."

The phone rings constantly in Georgia's studio. I am lying on the floor of the living area, my geography textbooks spread out in front of me. I am deciding where I want to live when I run away from home, which I intend to do at any moment.

I close my eyes and point. Tibet. All I can remember about Tibet is that monks live there. I close my eyes and point again. Sweden? No, I'd look pretty ridiculous in Sweden, with my black wavy hair and eyes so dark you can't see the pupils. I continue to point at different maps, my main objective being to put at least a thousand miles between myself and New Jersey.

It was late afternoon when I arrived at my mother's studio for a weekend visit, and she was nowhere to be found. Bob Marley blared from an unseen stereo system, and one of my mother's assistants was on the phone, dealing with Georgia's scheduled trip to Detroit where they have commissioned her sculpture for an industrial park.

"She's in back working," the assistant told me in hushed tones, covering the mouthpiece of the phone. We all know it's best not to disturb Georgia when she's at work.

Once, when she was still living in New Jersey with us, I made the mistake of knocking on her greenhouse door in the middle of the day. We had been let out of school early because of a blizzard, and a teacher had driven me home. It was a Wednesday, and my father's pediatric office was closed, his windows dark, venetian blinds lowered. As soon as I got out of the car I ran to the studio and banged on the door.

A moment or two passed before she flung the door open, and the air of the greenhouse steamed out into the snowy afternoon like the breath of a dragon. The studio was humid, almost tropical. My mother was damp from head to toe. Her hair fell in wisps over her forehead, and her eyes were wild beneath safety goggles. A few snowflakes blew in the door, touched her cheek and melted on contact. Her hands looked like stubs; her fingers clenched inward, covered by dust.

"What do you want?" she asked.

"It's me, Mom. Joanna."

She looked for a moment as if she didn't recognize me.

"I know that," she said, suddenly frantic. She waved her hands, shooing me away. "Joanna, listen. From nine in the morning until you get home at three, I am not a mom. This is the only time I have for my work. Can't you see I'm working? Can't you see?"

I nodded. It was the only thing to do. I looked past my mother at the steamy interior of the greenhouse. I knew she would never invite me inside, she would never explain it to me. Against the pale green glass wall was a forest of bare-branched, carefully sculpted trees, assembled from what I can only describe as trash. Crushed cans piled in a vertical line were tree trunks; tinfoil, the white, twisted fillings of pillows, triangulated bits of glass bottles tumbled in the surrounding air like branches into the sky. The whole structure was spattered with gold spray paint. It was a child's nightmare, an enchanted forest gone awry.

I craned my neck, trying to see even further into the studio, but she reached out a hand, gently stroked my face once, then closed the door without a word.

I trudged through the blizzard away from the greenhouse, and as I passed my father's darkened office on the way to the main house, I wondered: what if I needed her, really needed her at noon? Would she be there for me? Would she drop everything? I was in competition with the cans, the tinfoil, the shards of glass into which she daily breathed life and motion, all these things kept her from me. I wanted to rush into the greenhouse and smash against her sculptures until they shattered to the floor, pieces all around her. I wanted to stand in the center of the rubble, a vision rising from her ashes. I desperately wanted her to believe that I was her greatest creation.

In my geography textbook, I point to another country. The outer islands of Tahiti. Bora-Bora. Mud huts. I point my finger madly all over the globe. Rio, Caracas, Lisbon, Barcelona, Madrid.

Finally I am interrupted by my mother, who emerges from her sanctum. I smell her before I see her: the metallic bitter scent which comes from spot welding.

"Joanna, sweetness, angel," she murmurs as she kneels down and gives me a hug.

Georgia must have had a good day.

"Everyone, this is my daughter, Joanna," she calls out to her assistants, all of whom have met me many times. They are accustomed to Georgia when she's like this, as am I. Something happens to her during the hours she spends alone. There are skylights in her studio which can be reached by ladders, and on beautiful days they are often tilted to the air. I imagine when she enters her workspace she climbs up and flings the skylights open; a compartment in her head unlocks, and thousands of invisible fragments are released, flying up and out, through the skylight, into the Soho sky. They circle and fly back to her like homing pigeons, in the shapes of a bird, a tree, a skull, an angel. She cannot escape them. She is like a child, spellbound by the alien forest of her own creation. Her nightmares and dreams are one and the same.

"Come, let's take a walk, just you and me," she croons. "I have something I want to show you."

She bundles me into my down jacket, puts on a big slouchy hat and throws a soft purple cape over her shoulders.

"Georgia, you're going to be cold in that," I say.

"I'm fine, just fine," she says. "And please. Don't call me Georgia. Call me Mother, Mama, Mom. But don't call me Georgia. It's obnoxious."

"Why?"

"Because I'm your mother," she sings to the tune of "Red, Red Wine," the song which is blasting from the stereo speakers.

Then act like one, I want to say, but don't.

Georgia and I walk up West Broadway. We pass street-level art galleries, and at each one we pause and look into the windows. She always has something to say. She points to a painting that, to me, looks like a solid black canvas.

"Brilliant," she announces.

We stop in front of another gallery which has mannequin-like wooden figures in the window, bent at inhuman angles.

"Post-Modernist junk," she mutters.

"Where are we going?" I ask her.

"You'll see."

We walk past warehouse-lined blocks sprinkled with occasional cafés and restaurants, where artists sit next to ad agency executives. The twilight air smells of freshly ground coffee, Italian bread, brandy. We pass boutiques whose windows are filled with angular suits and tight neon dresses. There is a black bridal gown and widow's veil on a live mannequin in the window of a place called Wearable Art. The mannequin has shiny silver teardrops painted on her face.

"Oooh," cries Georgia, "Look at that! Feminist irony. Well, I'll tell you, Jo. There's a very fine line between marriage and mourning."

She laughs and links her arm through mine. I laugh too, the wind cold against my face.

We turn east on Houston Street. Her cheeks are flushed, and curls spill from beneath her purple hat. She is walking faster now, and I am struggling to keep up with her.

"Where are we going?"

"You'll know when you get there."

The sky is dark gray and my stomach is rumbling by the time we slow down in front of a shabby little building on East Houston Street.

"This is it," Georgia says, swinging open the front door,

ushering me inside, past a sign which says *Hellinger Galleries,* and a smaller sign announcing tonight's opening, a show called "Remembering Lithuania: Calvaria, 1941."

"What is this?" I ask her. Whatever it is, I hope they have food.

"You'll see," Georgia whispers as she enters the gallery, filled with people who don't look like they belong in this rundown building on East Houston Street.

"Look, she's here," someone calls out, and suddenly we are encircled by a crowd of people, all holding small plastic glasses filled with champagne.

"Ms. Higgins Hirsch," a reed-thin man with wireless glasses steps forward from the circle. "We didn't know if you'd really come."

"Well here I am," Georgia says brightly. "And this is my daughter, Joanna."

"The daughter," I hear a few people murmur, "the daughter."

"You see, there's no such thing as extinction," the thin man says, and the crowd nods assent, as if their necks and heads were all attached by invisible strings to a single puppeteer.

"What's going on?" I ask under my breath.

The smooth white walls are dotted with black-and-white photographs. There is ample space between each photograph, as if to stress the significance of every image.

My mother and I begin at the beginning.

"This is a piece of my history, Joanna," she says as we head toward the photograph nearest the door. The images are meant to be seen clockwise, and this is how the crowd moves, in one direction, a slow circling. "I'm not sure I'm up to this," she continues in a low voice.

The first photograph is sepia-toned, browns and grays depicting a village street.

"Calvaria," Georgia breathes.

"Where is that?"

"I was born there," she says.

We move to the next photograph, and the crowd follows. Beneath each frame is a typewritten explanation neatly Scotch-taped to the wall. This photo is of an ancient temple with ornate stained-glass windows, the front doors built in the shape of the tablets on which were written the Ten Commandments. *Kehilath Abraham,* the explanation reads, *scene of the massacre.*

"What massacre?" I whisper.

"Ssshh," says Georgia.

Tears are flowing down her face.

"Do you want to leave?" I ask.

"No."

We go on. There is an image of a small house, no more than a shack, really, built directly on a dirt street with no front yard, just a few blurry hens scratching at the stoop. The shutters are open, and inside the front window the shape of a woman can be seen. She is bending over, the ties of her apron forming a bow around her ample waist.

Georgia draws in a sharp breath.

"My God, where did they ever get these?"

The caption reads *A typical village house.*

She bends and whispers in my ear.

"I think . . . I'm pretty sure that's your grandmother, Josie."

My head snaps back. I have never heard Georgia mention her parents. I have only heard whispers, stories which have seeped like smoke from under the crack of my parents' closed bedroom door. I have heard alien, guttural words which sound like spitting, layered between tears and pledges; tales of the ocean, the forest, the extinct world of her childhood. I have never known the details. I have searched for my mother's history, sensing that the answers are spread before me like a path through a mine field. I have studied her work for the answers, tracing the veins of her marble men, sniffing for hints in the piles of waste she has always scavenged from suburban streets and scrap heaps of downtown New York. My mother learned to see before she could speak, to run before she could walk. She creates art out of tragedy—and this is the legacy she has passed on to me—I am learning to find tragedy in art.

We stop finally in front of a photograph which is all by itself. It shows the synagogue, but now the building is ravaged. The doors in the shape of tablets are demolished, riddled with holes, the stained glass shattered, and all along the ground there are men covered by black and white shawls, men with open eyes who see nothing, yarmulkes dotting the earth, limbs twisted in stiffened angles.

My mother reaches a hand around me and covers my eyes, but it is too late. I have read the caption. *On Yom Kippur, at the end of the Neilah service, the congregation of Kehilath Abraham was gunned down as they left at the end of their Day of Atonement. All the men in the village were murdered.*

"My father," whispers Georgia into the top of my head. "I was three years old, and I saw it happen."

I turn my head and look at her once more.

"I have to leave now," she says slowly.

I nod.

"We should never have come," she whispers.

She raises a hand to her lips as if to quiet herself, then it drops, a dead weight at her side.

She stares hard into my eyes as if the force of her gaze can push the last hour into the unconscious recesses of my memory.

"And we will never speak of this again."

III.

$\mathcal{B}$illy and I lie on our backs in the woods. The ground is cold and hard beneath us. Leaves fall from the trees, dance through the air and onto our bodies, but we don't move. We stare at the sky, patches of blue veiled by the dry leaves high above us, the faded brown veiny leaves which cling on for dear life, rustling like the taffeta gown of a woman hurrying to a midnight ball.

We have spread an old sheet beneath us. This has become our autumn tradition. We leave a sheet here every week, wrapped in plastic so it doesn't get wet when it rains. If it really pours, it becomes moldy and we just throw it out and bring another one. My father never seems to notice. Keeping track of sheets is the least of his concerns. Inside the sheet we wrap extra sweatshirts, a pack of cigarettes and several books of matches. This is our secret place. No one can find us here, in the woods between our homes and Tipton Academy.

We smoke and stare at the sky. Billy sticks a blade of grass between his two front teeth and pulls it back and forth against his gums.

"What are you doing?" I ask him.

"My mother told me to floss every day."

"You're gross."

"I can't help it. I'm a boy."

I roll to my side and face Billy. He blends into these woods, melding with the ground, his blond hair glinting like a particularly vivid leaf, his hands veiny and strong like the visible roots of a tree.

"What class are you cutting right now?" I ask him.

"Introduction to Algebra."

"Billy! If you cut that one, Johnson will turn you in. He isn't cool," I say.

"I don't care," he says dreamily, "I couldn't stand it in there today. What are *you* cutting?"

"Art," I say.

"Art! You, of all people, cutting art! That's just really perfect," Billy laughs.

"Fuck you."

"What's the matter?"

"Nothing."

We fall silent, chewing grass, smoking. An ant crawls over Billy's thick-ribbed gym sock. It falls into a crevice and lies there on its back, legs flailing. There is a gentle, untroubled quiet in these woods, halfway through our first year of middle school. He exhales smoke; it billows above us, a man-made cloud. Billy and I understand that we can say anything to each other, therefore we usually don't say much at all. In the distance I hear the rumble of cars as they pass over the speed bumps along Tipton Academy driveway.

"My parents are fighting again," he says. "I heard them last night."

"What about?"

"I can't tell. All I hear is their voices screaming, and then they go out into the backyard and get in the car so we can't hear them."

"They fight in the car?"

"Yeah, with the windows closed and the engine running. The windows get fogged up. Last night I even walked outside, because I got scared. They didn't see me."

I can picture Billy standing barefoot in the driveway, skinny in his pajama bottoms, rubbing sleep out of his eyes.

"They can get killed that way," I say, "carbon monoxide poisoning."

"I hope they do."

"Billy!"

"Then I can come live with you," he says.

"Billy, I'm so sorry," I say.

"I think they're going to get a divorce."

"You don't know that."

"I'm scared, Josie," he says.

I know I'm the only person he tells this to. He rolls over and presses his head into my shoulder.

"It's okay. I survived my parents' divorce," I say, though I'm not sure what constitutes survival.

I feel his head against my shoulder, his ribs pressing into my chest, his sneaker wedged between my two feet. His breath is warm against my neck, and he smells of chlorophyll and tobacco. He exhales in gentle wisps.

"What about you?" he asks after a while. "Have you recovered from Lithuania?"

"I try not to think about that," I say. I feel the earth against my back and think of the corpses, the mangled bodies of men dotting the soil near the temple steps.

He looks up at me.

"Josie, do you think it'll ever be okay?" he asks. "Do you think we'll ever be where we want to be?"

"What do you mean?"

"I mean, we hate being in school. We hate being at home. Do you think it'll always be like this?"

"Is there any place you feel good?" I ask him.

I shut my eyes tightly, hoping for a certain answer.

"Here," he says, rewarding me, "here in the woods with you."

"Me too," I say.

I roll toward Billy and we hug each other so tensely that I lose my breath. We look at each other. Our noses are inches apart.

Kiss me, I think.

He ruffles the hair on top of my head. He kisses me lightly between my eyebrows. This wasn't what I had in mind.

"Let's go," he says, "before we get into trouble."

𝒩igel left the day after *Speak, Memory* opened. He must have packed quickly, piling his jeans, boxer shorts, dirty laundry and extra contact lenses into large Hefty garbage bags. I was gone early that morning, to an audition for a television pilot in an office building on West Fifty-seventh Street. In the time it took me to get there, sign in, smile into the camera and slate my name, in the time it took me to shake the casting director's hand, then take a cab back to our Hell's Kitchen apartment, Nigel, who usually wasn't even awake before noon, was gone.

He took no furniture, no lamps, no sheets or towels.

All our belongings were mine. All he took with him was a photograph of us, carefully mounted behind glass in an old-fashioned sterling silver frame, a gift to my parents thirty-two years ago in honor of my birth. As advertised by Tiffany's in 1959, the frame was delicately etched with details regarding my sex, height in inches, weight, time and date of birth.

It would never have occurred to Nigel that the frame was valuable or important to me, as he tucked it carefully between a few sweaters and wedged it into a garbage bag. He doesn't think that way. No, I'm certain Nigel took that picture because it was one of us, once when we were happy.

He left a note on the mantel, in the empty place where the frame used to stand. The note rested on top of a pile of that morning's newspapers: the *Post,* the *Times,* the *News, The Wall Street Journal.* I knew *Speak, Memory* was reviewed in each of them. I had read the reviews standing in the neon light of a Times Square newsstand the night before.

On a pink memo pad, on top of which was printed *While you were out,* I saw Nigel's left-handed scrawl.

"This is how I want to remember you. P.S. I'll send for my books."

One of the words was blurred. I imagined, when I first picked up the note, that a single tear had fallen onto the notepad, clouding the word remember.

I am thirty-two years old. I spend each day encapsulated in a world of my own making, floating inside an invisible bubble which simultaneously exposes me to the world and keeps me sealed off. My days begin with Stravinsky on a Walkman tape strapped to my ears, riding in cabs or graffiti-smeared subway cars, taking elevators to the gleaming offices of film companies and advertising agencies. I climb onto Broadway stages and squint into the darkness at the producers who have summoned me, the nameless voices who boom out at me to take it slower, faster, who ask me to use different colors as if I were a painter in control of a palette.

As night falls I retreat to my second home, El Raton, house of rats. I sit on a wobbly stool and apply my own makeup, wet down my hair and set it in can-sized rollers to shape it into Lolita-like waves. I talk to no one. Backstage all is silent. Everyone prepares. In front of the curtain, the house is slowly filling up. First they will judge us, this audience. It is human nature to devalue the strange and unfamiliar. They will shift in their seats, they will cough needlessly, but if they are like all the rest, they will soon be won over. And for two hours and ten minutes, I will not be alone.

Billy would encourage me in the quest for solitude. He would be compelled by the need for "a private and thorough analysis of the facts."

I can almost hear him, as if his voice could cross the Hudson River where he now lives, where he will live until he dies.

It is winter. The pool of Tipton Academy is surrounded by plaques, as are the gymnasium, wrestling room and virtually every hallway. While the main halls of the school are lined with names of honor students and valedictorians of years past, the gym and swimming pool are the domain of the athletes, golden children whose days of glory were spent in these echoing caverns, coaxing muscles out of pale soft layers of baby fat.

There are twelve of us in our navy blue bathing suits standing in line to be weighed at the beginning of the swim team's season. I don't understand why we have to be weighed, much less why we are subjected to this humiliation in front of each other. But this is the way Coach DiNazio does it, and I have learned not to argue with her. I stand behind Billy in the line. We don't speak to one another. DiNazio has warned us that one word equals twenty laps. A sentence, and we'll be swimming all night.

I know I weigh more than Billy. His narrow back flexes and relaxes in front of me, smooth, golden, dauntless. I have seen him dive into the bright water of the Olympic-sized swimming pool. His body slices the surface like a knife through the soft blue roses on top of a birthday cake.

"Overmeyer, you're next," barks DiNazio.

Billy steps on the scale and looks straight ahead, avoiding DiNazio, who is sliding the metal weight back and forth like a clerk at a supermarket.

This scale is familiar to me. It is a doctor's scale; my father has the same kind in his office. At least once a day I sneak inside his office to weigh myself. If I have been drinking a lot of water, my weight can vary up to four or five pounds. I try not to drink too much water.

"Eighty-four pounds," announces DiNazio. "Hirsch, you're next."

I step on the scale, regretting the breakfast my father prepared for me this morning—poached eggs on a bed of asparagus with English muffins and Canadian bacon, and a big glass of fresh-squeezed grapefruit juice.

"What does that say, Hirsch?" asks DiNazio.

I look at her, my cheeks blazing.

"What does it say?" she repeats, a decibel higher.

"Ninety-five."

"Ninety-five *what?*"

"Pounds," I mumble.

"Get into the pool. Twenty-five laps will work some of that

off." She claps her hands together once, and the sound echoes off the tile walls.

I sit on the edge of the pool and slide quickly into the water, feeling eleven pairs of eyes focused on the back of my neck. Through the big windows which overlook the playing fields, I see the winter track team picking its way through a path in the snow, which has been cleared by a plow. I wish I could join them. I would wear my hat and mittens, long underwear and three pairs of thermal socks. I would run around the track, stripping as I ran, circling madly, leaving a trail of clothes until I had nothing left, then I would fall into the snow banked along the sides of the track; all they would ever find of me would be the outlined form of my naked body as I sank through the snow, a white gate to the other side.

The air directly above the pool smells of chlorine and urine; there is a soft mossy fungus between the tiles which never quite goes away. I begin swimming through the water, which burns my eyes and keeps them red all winter. Water gurgles through the sides of my bathing cap and into the cavities of my ears. I push my way along, scissoring my legs, reaching forward, grasping handfuls of blue, turning my head and gulping air, kicking harder, faster until I lose track of the laps and feel only the dull weight of my limbs, the bleakness of my own body.

I feel something brush against my arm, soft as an underwater plant.

"DiNazio went to the bathroom," he whispers. "Are you okay?"

"Fine," I say, water dribbling from my nose. "Just fine," I gurgle and spit, barely able to see his face through a haze of red. His caring disturbs me. I don't want Billy Overmeyer's kindness. I kick harder, swim faster. I want him to love me. And I have learned at this point in my life that love and pity are incompatible. One erases the other.

This is how I want to remember you.

I've gone over Nigel's note a thousand times in my head. After ten years, eight short words are all the explanation he had to offer, leaving the interpretation, once again, entirely in my hands.

This is how I want to remember you.

"What are you doing with him?" Georgia would ask me on the occasional foray from her loft to our studio apartment. She rarely referred to Nigel by his name. "After all, Joanna, he's a *waiter,*" she would say. In Georgia's opinion, there were those who waited, and those who were waited upon.

"He's not a waiter, Georgia, he's a director," I would answer.

"He's a waiter," she'd repeat.

"So what," I'd snap, "I'm a waitress."

"You're not a waitress, Jo," my mother would respond, horrified.

"What would you call it?"

A pause.

"You're finding yourself," she would say with a flourish.

"And Nigel isn't?"

"Nigel is thirty-four years old."

"So?"

"There's an age where it is no longer attractive to be a perpetual student who tends bar," says Georgia.

My mother would look around our studio apartment at Nigel's bookcases, which were organized according to country and language. She would glance at the black-and-white photographs from productions which had taken place ten years earlier. Georgia never had to struggle for her art, not in the material sense. Her struggle came from within. From the time she was a young woman her talent blazed a path for her, shooting through the blackness of her psyche and into the night air. It illuminated everything in its route, erasing all obstacles. I should know. One of the primary obstacles was me.

This is how I want to remember you.

Which would be less painful a memory for Nigel? Pacific Rim, the melancholy of those who *really* do something else while they work in restaurants for tips, who approach tables of well-dressed patrons and recite their names along with that evening's specials: "Hi, I'm John [Jake, Joe] and I'll be your waiter this evening!"

"Overmeyer," he might remember saying once, "what's with you? You spend every Saturday night with Josie and me."

"I like it here," Billy replied. He crossed his arms behind his head and stared up at the ceiling of our college dorm room, at shadows cast by the sun setting through the window which faced west, overlooking the campus. The hanging plant swayed in the early evening breeze, weaving shadowy spiders on the walls.

It was spring. Billy and I had almost completed our sophomore year, and Nigel was halfway through graduate school in drama.

"Get a life, Overmeyer," Nigel said.

"I have one, thank you very much."

"All you do is study!"

"That *is* what we're here for," said Billy mildly.

"I thought we were here to shack up with our girlfriends

and get laid as much as possible," Nigel said, pouncing on top of me. I was lying on the bed next to Billy. Our hanging plant produced some of New Haven's finest marijuana, and we were feeling the effects of our late afternoon joint.

The three of us formed a pyramid on the single bed. There were words unsaid in the tangle of limbs, a puzzlement and ache which went every which way and remained entirely beneath the surface. I slid out from beneath Nigel, off the bed, leaving the two of them. Nigel hopped up quickly and sat on the edge. Only Billy continued to lie there.

Nigel and I were a couple. Joanna-and-Nigel. Nigel-and-Joanna. People uttered our names as if we were one person, joined at the hip, inseparable. And Billy? Billy was constantly with us. We were rarely alone. It began in New Haven, and continued when we moved to New York. Our triumverate moved from dorm rooms to studio apartments, from warehouse theatres to the bar at Pacific Rim.

When I look back now, I see that it was not Nigel and me, but the three of us who were inseparable. And when Billy was gone, Nigel left shortly thereafter, as if dealing solely with another human being, with no shield and no safety net, was too much for him to bear.

Now that I am alone I often think of those early years at Yale. I recently came across a magazine piece advising women to have yearly mammograms; there is a photograph of an attractive woman pressing fingers into her left breast. Beneath the photograph, the caption reads: *Mary Johnson will not feel the lump in her breast for two years.* If you had seen the three of us during our college years, you never would have foreseen the way it all turned out. Who of us would become an Off-Broadway actress, who would remain across the Hudson River, and who would disappear into the boozy neon night.

Georgia and my father meet once a month at a coffee shop near the Lincoln Tunnel. It has been two years since their divorce, and the purpose of their meetings is allegedly to discuss my well-being. All I know is that when my father returns from seeing Georgia, his eyes are bleary and he walks like an old man. For days after their meetings, he becomes absentminded, leaving pots of food bubbling over on the kitchen stove, burning loaves of bread, misplacing the keys to his office and having to wait outside the office door until his nurse arrives. I have seen him standing, stooped over, as she closes her car door and strides up the walk, her key already pointed in front of her like a small weapon.

If these meetings between my parents are solely for discussing my happiness and welfare, I wish they would stop, because it makes me feel worse. My father's gloom envelops me like the steam rising from one of his bubbling kitchen concoctions.

Tonight, when I come home from school, there is a note held with a carrot-shaped magnet on the refrigerator door, where he is sure I will see it: *Gone to see your mother.* It is signed with a few xxoo's, and a crudely drawn smiling face. There is only one artist in the family, and it is not my father.

This throws a wrench into my plans to eat dinner tonight at the Overmeyers, an invitation I have been hoping for all year long. If my father is in his usual post-Georgia mood, I won't want to leave him alone. There is only one solution to this. I will bring him with me.

I call the number I know by heart.

"Do you think it would be all right if my father came to

dinner tonight?" I ask Billy, who answers the phone. "He's just gone to see Georgia."

"*Oh*," says Billy. "Are you okay?"

I am silent, biting my lip to keep from crying.

"Hold on."

I hear the phone being covered by a hand, a muffled conversation in the background.

His mother picks up the receiver.

"Joanna? Dear, we'd all be delighted for your father to join us," Lila Overmeyer says. "We'll see you at seven."

"Thanks. See you at seven," I echo, and hang up.

We'd all be delighted. The phrase bounces off the shiny white walls as I sit at the kitchen table waiting for my father. I spread my math homework in front of me. The words *we* and *all* are so consoling, so abundant. They connote a crowd, a gathering, a herd of cows, a flock of sheep. I stare at the long division assignment in my notebook. Numbers bounce. Three divided by two. Two divided by one.

The mouth of the Lincoln Tunnel spits my father out just as dusk is falling. I hear his car crunch the gravel in the driveway, the electronic rumble of the garage door. He drags himself through the kitchen, looking quickly at me, then down again at his feet. He goes straight to the den, where he turns on the television and flips channels until he settles on "The Jeffersons." He finds and lights a cigarette, inhaling deeply, as if he wants the smoke to get down into his lungs and stay there.

None of this is a good sign. My father rarely watches television, never watches sit-coms and doesn't smoke. I follow him, holding an open jar of macadamia nuts.

I plop down next to him on the ultrasuede couch.

"Look, Dad, your favorite," I offer the jar of nuts.

He waves my hand away.

"Not hungry," he says.

He focuses on the television screen. Mr. Jefferson has just said something which causes Mrs. Jefferson to break out into her deep, sit-com belly laugh. Chuckles and giggles from the docile audience follow like a well-trained orchestra.

My father does not laugh. He stares straight ahead, his mouth pulled down into creases which are always there, a reminder that sadness is never far away, faintly etched into his face like a worn map.

I watch as tears roll down his face, dribble into the creases near his mouth.

After a few moments, he turns to me. His cheek is damp. On the screen, a young woman says: "When it came time for me to use a douche, I asked my mother what *she* used. She told me her secret was Massengill Disposable Douche!"

"Ask me what it was like to see your mother," he says.

"What was it like to see my mother?" I dutifully repeat.

"Like an appendectomy with no anesthesia," he says, as if he's been trying to come up with this all day, "like pulling a tooth with no novacaine."

"Why do you do it, then?" I ask. "Why do you go see her if it's going to hurt so much?"

I have not yet learned that part of being an adult is regularly inflicting torture upon oneself, that somehow pain is an integral part of feeling alive.

He buries his head in his hands.

"I miss her, Josie," he cries.

"I miss her too," I say softly, so softly I know he won't hear me.

I close my eyes and listen to my father's quavering breath. Everything will be all right as long as he keeps breathing. As I stroke his back, I imagine what Georgia might be doing this evening. Perhaps she has a dinner date with the owner of a Madison Avenue art gallery. She rushes home from the Lincoln

Tunnel, and quickly throws on a gray cashmere dress, several strands of pearls, and wraps a long gold necklace several times around her wrist. She piles her hair into a falling down knot and steps into a pair of black high heels.

She has not worked today. She can never work on the days she sees her ex-husband. He drains her effectively, as if he plugs her arm with an invisible syringe and removes every image, every reflection, every memory from her blood, as if the very precursors of her art are malignant cells which have to be expurgated.

She will walk into La Goulue and heads will turn. People know they should recognize her, even if they don't. Even if she weren't on the cover of this month's *Artforum* Georgia would turn heads.

I wonder what my father thinks when he thinks of her. I wonder what image of Georgia impresses itself on his mind, flattens itself against his memory like a bug against a window-pane.

I met Nigel during my freshman year. He was a graduate teaching assistant in the drama department, and I was a lowly nobody. He had left Liverpool armed with little more than a British passport and a student visa. He had dedication, I could spot it immediately. I knew about dedication from my mother; it climbed its way up the sinews of his arms, it shone like a beacon on his brow.

The first time I met him, I was auditioning for a college production of *Mooney's Kid Don't Cry*. I was trying out for the role of Mooney's wife, for which I was much too young, so I had tied my hair into a disheveled knot on top of my head and, in a singularly misguided moment, had stuck a pillow under my apron in an attempt to look matronly.

I walked out on the stage and paused for a moment before beginning my monologue, and suddenly I heard a man's laughter, an unmistakable belly laugh flowing from the darkened seats.

I was confused, so startled I forgot to be nervous for a moment.

"What's so funny?" I asked the black space before me.

This created new peals of laughter.

I stood still, crossed my arms over my chest, waited.

Finally it stopped.

"Sorry. I'm sorry, love," a British accent floated at me from the darkness. "It's just that you couldn't look like Mooney's wife if you stuck *fifteen* pillows up your front."

"If you're going to speak to me, at least cut the phony accent," I said. I was furious.

The houselights came up and Nigel revealed himself, a strapping, sandy-haired man wearing a soft flannel shirt and black jeans, the beginnings of a beard covering his golden face.

"It's hardly phony, love," he said dryly. "Imported directly from Her Majesty's sparkling city of Liverpool."

I felt ridiculous, standing awkwardly in front of him, sweating under the hot spotlights with a pillow tied around my waist and my hair stuck together with half a can of hair spray.

"Do you want me to do my monologue now?" I asked him.

"Well, I can tell you I'm not going to give you the part, you're all wrong for it," he said.

"Let the acting be the judge," I said. I knew the only way I could regain any dignity in this situation was through showing him my work.

"All right, have it your way," he said with a sigh, and lowered the houselights once more.

My anger built up inside me, anchoring me to the ground as if a thick root had grown from the soles of my feet into the concrete floor of the stage, burrowing deep beneath the surface of the earth. I untied the pillow and threw it across the stage. The speech I had prepared—Mooney's wife's speech—came spilling from my lips in a mad torrent as I stood there with all the compact presence of a peasant woman. The words flew from my mouth, spattering into the darkness.

When I finished, I stood panting, disoriented. The sound of my own breath filled my ears.

This time the houselights remained dark.

"Thank you," his voice, in the darkness, "that will be all."

That night, as I attempted to study in the cross-campus library with Billy, I cursed the handsome, burly Britishman. I doodled his face on blank notepaper, drew horns on top, a tongue lolling from his mouth.

I didn't bother walking past the Drama School bulletin board the next day. It was a Thursday, my busiest day, and the sky was dark, blustery. Icy water had sloshed over the tops of my thick rubber boots, and by the end of the day I felt a burning in the back of my throat, chills coming on. It was nearly nightfall when he came running up to me.

"Where were you?" he asked.

I kept walking.

"We had a cast meeting at three."

"Cast?" I repeated, incredulous.

"You didn't know, love? You got the part."

. . .

$\mathcal{N}$ight is falling in the suburbs. The sky is purple, criss-crossed by black telephone wires and poles. Squirrels race across the wires holding acorns in their mouths like circus performers. Squirrels are frequently electrocuted when they travel the wires. People's voices kill them. I see one now, lifeless, hanging by its claws from the black wire, outlined against the smudged purple sky.

My father and I head across the street to the Overmeyers'. The white-painted bricks of their home shine in the flood-lights. We walk up the winding flagstone path to the front door, and I press the bell, which clangs six times inside their foyer, to the tune of *Oh-oh, say can you see.*

Mrs. Overmeyer opens the front door and the smell of basil fills the night air.

"Joanna," she smiles at me, "and this must be your father."

I had forgotten that my father and Mrs. Overmeyer have not met before. This would not be the case if my father and Georgia were still married. They would have crossed through the Overmeyer's front hall many times, to dinner parties and bridge games. Here in New Jersey, the only social life between adults happens, like Noah's ark, in increments of two.

She reaches out a hand.

"Hello, I'm Lila Overmeyer," she says.

My father takes her hand in both his own.

He stares at her intently.

"Don't I know you?" he asks.

She smiles and cocks her head.

"I don't think so," she says, "though I'm sure we've passed each other in our cars a million times."

"I don't mean from here," my father says, still holding her hand, "you look familiar to me. From a long time ago. Lila, Lila, Lila . . ." He repeats it like a melody as I sink behind him, into his shadow. My father had better let go of Mrs. Overmeyer's hand soon.

"Well," Mrs. Overmeyer says, looking at my father.

"Well," he says, smiling.

Our two families sit around the dining room table. Billy's father, Lloyd Overmeyer, is wearing a navy blue suit, his tie pulled loose from around his neck. His hair is slicked back and looks wet, but I imagine if you touched it, it would feel stiff and sticky. Mr. and Mrs. Overmeyer sit on opposite ends of the table, Billy and I are across from each other, along with Billy's older brother Johnny and my father.

The dining room is dominated by a portrait of Lila Overmeyer which hangs above the fireplace mantel. In real life, Mrs. Overmeyer looks like one of the Gabor sisters, a soft and cloudy blonde teetering in high heels alongside Eddie Albert in a place like "Green Acres." In the portrait, the artist was experimenting with cubism, the result angular and unsettling. I can just imagine what Georgia would say. *Suburban junk,* she would mutter, *Dilettante bullshit.*

Mrs. Overmeyer sees me staring at the portrait.

"I know," she says, "it belongs in the attic."

"I think it's lovely," my father says, looking at her.

I kick him hard under the table.

"So," Mrs. Overmeyer says brightly, raising her wineglass, "here's to Dr. Hirsch and Joanna! We're so glad you could finally join us for dinner."

There is an embarrassed clink of glasses, people reaching across the table. Finally? She never invited us before.

There is silence as we eat our salad, forks scraping against crescent-shaped glass plates.

My father clears his throat, and addresses Billy's older brother.

"Johnny, if Billy and Joanna are fourteen, I gather you're a senior this year. Are you applying to colleges?"

Mr. Overmeyer snorts.

"He'll be lucky to get into Fairleigh Dickinson," he says. He drums his fingers against the table. They are long fingers, tapered, elegant.

Johnny Overmeyer doesn't look up from his plate. He spoons tomatoes into his mouth so quickly he can't be chewing.

"Do we have to talk about this now?" Lila Overmeyer asks. "We have company."

"Oh, don't mind us," my father says faintly.

I look at Billy. He is nervously eyeing his parents, looking from one to the other.

Mrs. Overmeyer excuses herself, hurries into the kitchen and returns to the table with a steaming casserole of moussaka.

"How wonderful, my favorite!" my father exclaims.

Now I know for a fact he hates moussaka.

"Lila treats us to a new country every night," Mr. Overmeyer says. He manages to make it sound like an insult.

"You know," my father says, "Lila, I just realized why you look so familiar to me."

"Why?"

My father pauses dramatically.

"Camp Kenmont."

"Oh my God."

"Camp Kenmont, the summer of fifty-two."

"You're Bernie Hirsch!"

"Lila Morris! I didn't connect it until now," my father says.

Lila turns to her husband with a smile bordering on triumphant.

"This is the first boy who ever kissed me," she says.

Mr. Overmeyer's fingers stop drumming.

"Really," he says.

"Bernie Hirsch," she repeats, shaking her head, "I can't believe it."

"Lila," he smiles at her.

I shift my leg toward Billy under the table. I press my foot against his, but he's not looking at me. He is focused uneasily on his father, who is twirling his salad fork between his thumb and forefinger.

"Are we done with 'Old Home Week'?" asks Mr. Overmeyer. A muscle clenches in his jaw. "Can we bring ourselves back into the present tense?"

Moussaka, puréed carrot casserole, green beans almondine circulate the table in silence. I glance at my father. He is looking down at his plate happily. It seems the memory of kissing a girl in the woods at Camp Kenmont a thousand years ago can obliterate a vision which never seems far from him, the image of his lanky, wavy-haired, blue-jeaned ex-wife. *Ex.* I muse about the word. *Ex,* as if it can be crossed out in thick black ink, not quite erased but scratched out by the simple memory of kissing a girl once long ago, her lips pressed against his own like a lush, exotic fruit.

Mrs. Overmeyer suddenly laughs.

"Bernie, my God, I just remembered Color War. This is bringing back memories I didn't know I had," she says. "Do you remember we played the girls against the boys, and—"

"What about when you and I stole the rowboat," my father interjects.

Lila throws her head back.

"The rowboat! At midnight!"

"Goddamn it, Lila!" Mr. Overmeyer explodes.

"Lloyd, I was just—"

"I don't give a shit what you *think* you were doing, just stop it, goddamn it! I don't want to hear about this!"

"Lloyd, don't you think you're overreacting a bit?" asks my father, who has stopped eating and is folding and refolding his napkin.

Lloyd turns on my father. "I suggest that *you* not tell me how to act in my own home."

Billy scrapes his chair back. The sound is as loud and surprising as a shot. He pushes his palms into the table, steadying himself, and I see a vein throbbing in his neck.

"Goddamn you!" he cries. "Couldn't you just this once—"

"William, shut up," his father says.

Billy stands, and his chair topples over.

"Pick up that chair this instant."

Billy glares at his father. His arms dangle by his sides; then, as if I have seen this all before and know what comes next, I watch as Billy takes his water glass and hurls it at his mother's portrait. It shatters, shards of glass against flesh-colored cubist forms, splinters everywhere.

The silence in the room is a high-pitched hum. Billy turns and runs; runs out of the dining room and through the front hallway, flings the front door open and races across the lawn, past the dining room window. We turn and watch our own reflections in the dark of the window, barely able to make out Billy's lone figure as his legs propel him out of sight.

Lila's cheeks are bright red.

"Well," she says.

Lloyd Overmeyer picks up a fork and resumes eating.

"He'll be back," he says.

My father stares at him with a look I have never seen.

"You might not want to eat that, Lloyd," he says. "There could be glass splinters."

"I'll take my chances," Lloyd says with a full mouth.

Lila walks into the kitchen and returns to the dining room with a broom.

My father jumps up.

"Let me do that," he says gently, grabbing her hand where it wraps around the broomstick.

"No," she says. Her chin lifts and I can see what she must have looked like at fourteen. "No," she repeats, "it's my mess, and I'll clean it up."

Streetlights glare against the starry sky like syncopated half-moons. The pavement glitters, cutting a smooth path through the dark lawns which lead to the woods.

I make my way through the night, around corners and turns I know by heart, kicking a solitary stone I picked up in the Overmeyers' driveway. I tell myself that if I keep kicking the stone, if I don't lose it, I will be able to find Billy in the woods. I will follow his scent like a dog.

He is lying like a broken stone angel, dazed, arms thrown over his head. I do not smell him, but see the glint of his teeth, the whites of his eyes.

Crunch, crunch. He hears the leaves beneath my feet.

"Go away," he moans.

"It's me," I whisper.

"I know. Go away."

"They're going to come looking for you," I say.

"Let them."

I move closer.

A match flares in the dark, and I see Billy's face lit up like a Halloween mask, his skin orange against the black shadows, the way his cheeks go hollow as he sucks on his cigarette.

"Let me just sit with you," I say.

I ease myself to the ground, which is ice cold, damp, and I think of Billy's glass as it shattered against the canvas, his mother's painted face, the silver shards which flew like confetti, the pool of water which formed on the floor at Lila's feet. The portrait seemed almost to change expression, the mouth falling open.

"Are you all right?" I ask him.

A rhetorical question, in much the same way that Billy's telling me to go away is rhetorical.

He is silent. His body is shuddering, the way it was when he pushed his chair back from the table less than an hour ago. I wonder if he has been shivering ever since, whether he has watched his legs quaking with a detached interest, as if they belonged to some one else.

I grab his fingers and hold on. They flutter in my hands like a bird trapped there, then stop.

"They don't love me," he whispers so softly I barely hear him.

"Billy, of course they do. They're your parents," I say.

"They don't. They don't even love each other."

He stares straight up at the sky, the moon shining through the bare branches. Something unhinges in the silence between us, and he begins crying. The tears he has fought all night come streaming from his eyes, and I am afraid they will form icicles on his face, seal his lids together.

"Cover me, Josie."

"What do you mean?"

"Cover me like a blanket."

I climb on top of him. His body shakes beneath me. He reaches out and stubs his cigarette against the tree trunk, glowing embers fading.

Billy's lips are a pale, beautiful blue the first time I kiss them. I envelop him, pressing my thighs against his, my stomach through a down jacket against his, and I rest my elbows against the ground, then reach both my hands up and touch his face softly, wiping away the icy tears.

"*I* love you, Billy," I say. "*I* love you," pressing the words into his lips, the heat of my breath against his mouth, teeth meeting.

Kissing Billy is the solution. My physical self is the best comfort I have to offer. I run my mouth along his jaw. He wraps his arms around me and locks them there as we roll over and over.

It is no longer cold, and he is no longer shaking.

We walk home from the woods, hands entwined, our breath steaming into the night air. He takes me to my door and kisses me good night as if all this had been a normal first date. "Tomorrow?" he asks.

"Tomorrow what?"

"Walk to school?"

We can't seem to speak in full sentences.

"How about cutting school altogether," I say. "I feel like living dangerously."

"What do you want to do?" he asks.

"I don't know. Something fun."

"Like what?"

"Let's sleep on it."

He squeezes my hand, then drops it. I stand by the front door watching as he walks slowly across the street, back toward the shattered glass, the dishes still on the dining room table, the grim straight line of his father's lips.

When he reaches his front door he turns and waves, a small dark figure dwarfed by spruce trees and floodlit white brick.

"Tomorrow," he calls.

"Tomorrow," I call back. The word tastes sweet in my mouth.

The television is still on in the den. I walk into the eerie, blue-washed light and sit on the couch staring at the eleven o'clock news.

I hear my father creaking down the stairs. He pokes his head in the door.

"Are you all right?" he asks.

"Umhm." I don't turn my head around to look at him. My lips feel swollen and chapped. I am afraid my face will give me away.

"Do you want company?"

"No thanks."

He hovers by the door for a moment, then creaks back up the stairs.

I plunge my hand into the open jar of macadamia nuts on the cocktail table beside me. On television, on the news, Roger Grimsby is solemnly intoning something I cannot quite hear as a photograph of a mangled helicopter is flashed on the background. Roger Grimsby is handsome. His eyes are twinkly. He looks solid, responsible, as if there can be no doubt as to the validity of anything he says. I wonder what kind of father he would be. Perhaps I'll write him a letter. I wonder if he has any kids; maybe he would be willing to adopt a few.

I have no idea how long I have been asleep when I feel myself being scooped into my father's arms and carried upstairs to my bed. He smells of exotic spices and a hint of a sweet after-dinner drink.

"You're getting too heavy for this," he whispers into the top of my head.

I nuzzle close to him, the itchy wool of his cardigan soothing and familiar against my cheek.

"What time is it?"

"Never mind, it doesn't matter."

"But it's a school night."

"Ssshhh. Keep sleeping, JoJo."

I nuzzle closer.

"I can't sleep."

"Hey," my father whispers, "if you're happy and you know it, clap your hands."

I lie limp against him.

"If you're happy and you know it, clap your hands," he sings softly.

I don't move.

"What's the matter, sweetie?"

I wipe my nose on his cardigan.

"Is this all about those awful Overmeyers?"

"Sort of," I sniffle.

"I'll kill anyone who hurts you," my father whispers. "Do you want me to go kill them now?" he asks.

"No," I giggle.

"Are you sure?"

"Yeah."

"So maybe we'll just forget about them, and have sweet dreams tonight?"

"Maybe."

"Okay. Now sing with me, Josie."

He lowers me into bed, pulls the covers up around my chin. Our voices drift through the empty rooms of the second floor. "If you're happy and you know it, and you really want to show it, if you're happy and you know it, clap your hands."

IV.

We have all been in the news by now, Nigel, Billy and I. Nigel was news when *Speak, Memory* was reviewed on the front page of the *Weekend* section of the *New York Times*. "The Nabokov memoir translates splendidly to the stage," wrote Frank Rich, "in a rare and miraculous case where the material itself and the young actress Joanna Hirsch somehow transcend the plodding and hackneyed direction of Nigel Easden, who really should know better by now, and stick to producing new plays at El Raton, not directing them."

Billy is no longer news. He has receded into a paragraph, a statistic, a blurb in the public consciousness. And I have begun to appear between the covers of glossy magazines as my mother once did, my makeup flawless, smile radiant. *Up-and-coming actress Joanna Hirsch,* the captions read, *On top of the world and loving every minute of it.*

Though my mother has traveled oceans and mountains in order to escape, she has left something behind. She believed she could outrun atavism, the recessive gene which appears through the generations, the calcified bones of her ancestors embedded in the earth. Tragedy is a world voyager, and blood knows no geography. Her specter stays with me.

$\mathcal{M}$y father shakes me awake early in the morning.

"I have to go to the hospital," he says. "An emergency with one of the Posner girls. Can you get yourself ready for school?"

"Mmmmh," I mumble.

"Will you eat breakfast, Josie?"

"Mmmmh."

"Promise?"

"Yeah," I say with my eyes closed.

I have no intention of going to school today. Billy and I are planning to play hooky together. I lie in bed long after I hear my father leave for the hospital. Finally I rouse myself and walk downstairs in last night's rumpled clothes. My father has accidentally left the coffeepot on; I pour myself a cup. He would never let me drink coffee if he were home. Nutritious fresh-squeezed orange juice would be sitting on the breakfast table, and he would be whipping up eggs Florentine.

I take a sip of coffee. It tastes acrid and alien to me. I have noticed a similar flavor in foods I have been told are an acquired taste—caviar, beer, Greek olives, single-malt scotch —as if adulthood brings with it an appreciation for bitter things.

I pour a heaping teaspoon of sugar and a lot of cream into my mug. Now it tastes better. I open the refrigerator door and find a box of Stella D'oro cookies, chocolate and vanilla lady-fingers. This will be my breakfast.

In the front hall there is a long antique desk my parents brought back from a trip to Portugal. On top of the desk several months' worth of bills are heaped in a pile. Carved drawers are filled with mittens and earmuffs, bits of paper, half rolls of Lifesavers, train and bus schedules.

I search through the drawers, not knowing exactly what I'm looking for, but sensing I will recognize it when I find it. When my hand alights on a recent train schedule, I realize how Billy and I are going to spend our day off. We are going to do the most dangerous thing available to us at the age of fourteen in Morristown, New Jersey. We are going to take the commuter train into New York City. We are going to pay a surprise visit to Georgia Higgins Hirsch.

First there is the question of what to wear. It feels strange to pull on my jeans on a school day, rather than my navy blue Tipton uniform. I push my feet into tennis sneakers without undoing the laces, and rummage through my father's closet until I find one of his softest, nicely worn shirts. I need a good luck charm.

Now there is the question of money. I hope Billy has some. I open my piggy bank, a pink cow, and empty out several pounds of change. I stick my hand into every coat in the coat closet. I feel like a thief. In my father's yellow rain slicker, I hit the jackpot—a ten-dollar bill. Between the bill and another three dollars and thirty-five cents' worth of change from the pink cow, I am armed for the city. Thirteen dollars in my pocket seems like a fortune.

A knock on the front door.

I look through the peephole and see Billy in his Tipton uniform.

I open the door a crack.

"Why are you dressed like that?" I ask, not wanting to know the answer.

"I have to go to school," he says as I let him in. He doesn't meet my eyes, and when he walks past me, I notice he is limping.

"Billy, what's wrong?"

He doesn't turn.

"Nothing."

"Why are you walking that way?"

"What way?"

"You're walking funny."

He leans against the kitchen door, his back to me.

"Tell my father that," he says softly, "tell my father I'm walking funny."

"No, Billy . . ."

"Just drop it, Josie, okay?"

He goes down the hall to the bathroom and shuts the door. When he returns his hair is slicked back, and his face is wet.

"I'm sorry," he says. "I just can't. Some other time, when things are more normal, all right?"

He hesitates in the foyer for a moment, then reaches out a hand to me.

"Billy, come with me," I say.

The hand drops.

"I said I can't, Josie," he repeats sharply. He turns and walks across the front lawn as quickly as his limp will allow him.

The ride to the city takes forty-three minutes. When the conductor comes by to take my ticket I think he looks at me oddly, wondering what a fourteen-year-old is doing alone on the commuter train to the city, why I am not in school where I undoubtedly belong. For a horrible moment I think I am going to have to explain myself, but he just keeps walking, his metal ticket puncher leaving tiny dots of yellow paper strewn over the floor of the train.

In Hoboken I change to the PATH train, which screams through a long, dark tunnel with patches of sunlight flashing every few seconds like lightning until we are in Penn Station, or I should say *I* am in Penn Station, because suddenly I feel absolutely alone. I should never have come without Billy. I walk through narrow corridors until I reach the center of the station where there is no one waiting, no sign which says *Joanna Hirsch* waving above the crowd with all the ceremony of a flag.

I leave the station and stare frantically at all the taxis moving along, bumper-to-bumper. I realize I don't even know my mother's exact street address.

"Can I help you, miss?"

I turn and am confronted by a small man wearing a Mets baseball cap. He smiles at me. He has no teeth.

"I'm trying to get a cab," I say, hoping to keep my voice from quavering.

"I'll help you."

He sticks two fingers between his gums and lets out a piercing whistle. One of the cabs pulls over.

"That's for you, miss," he says.

"Thank you," I say gratefully, and move forward.

The man jumps in front of me.

"Aren't you going to give me something?"

"What do you mean?"

"I just got you a cab! You think I did it out of the goodness of my heart?"

"I could have gotten it myself," I say, confused.

"But you didn't, did you?"

The man is starting to make me nervous. He's standing too

close. I reach into my pocket and part with one precious dollar.

He tips his baseball cap.

"Thank you, sweetheart," he says, then moves on.

I tell the cabdriver to take me to Soho. President Carter is in town, so it takes a long time to get to a neighborhood I recognize, and costs more than I thought it would. I walk down West Broadway until I see the hair ornament store, above which Georgia lives. I stare at the row of buzzers until I spot the one marked only with her initials, GHH. I have never been given a key to her loft. Georgia has created a life for herself in which motherhood is a vaguery, something she thinks about only when confronted with her slightly sagging stomach or my eager face appearing at her door.

There is no answer when I press the buzzer next to Georgia's initials. Somehow I knew this would happen; this is what befalls children who play hooky from school and ride the train into the city, pretending they are old enough to live real lives and make their own decisions. I press it once, twice, three times and am greeted by a mocking silence, the silver mesh screen of the intercom staring at me like a face devoid of its features.

I wander along the side of the building and step into the hair ornament store. There are no customers, only a salesgirl with long white-blond hair tied every six inches with gold and silver bows, reminding me of wheat tied in bundles.

"Can I help you?"

"Just looking," I say, picking up barrettes and hair bows, examining them closely like a woman squeezing produce at a fruit market.

"Actually I'm looking for a gift for my mother," I say. I finger a red velvet bow and imagine it adorning Georgia's dark curls. I picture Georgia pulling her hair into a bunch at the nape of her neck, ringlets escaping like wisps of smoke. Her white arms rise above her head, angled, awkward, as she fixes the bow in its proper place.

"That one's fifteen dollars," the salesgirl says.

"Ah," I murmur, as if I had anything close to fifteen dollars to spend on a hair ornament.

She studies me, head tilted.

"You aren't, by any chance, Georgia's daughter?" she asks. I turn to her.

"How did you know?"

"You look just like her," she says, "and I saw you come out of the vestibule."

I am so relieved to have made contact with someone who knows my mother that, for a moment, I forget to be terrified by the comparison.

I imagine her fifteen years ago, poised before a canvas, back when she was still painting, when color was a prelude to shape and form. I can almost see her heavy with me, filled with her own power, saturated with images of angels hovering over bare branches, of amniotic sacs. I imagine a faint smile danced like a shadow across her face as her wrist flicked circular trickles of paint onto the canvas, layered swirls of white and twilight blue. The result was pure motion, as vast and unbearable as a cloudless day. I have one of these canvases hidden in the back of my closet, under several blankets and my winter boots. Georgia considers these paintings immature, and would kill me if she knew. During those years she frequently painted with Prussian blue, the color Picasso used during his Blue Period. Perhaps Georgia thought of Picasso as she stood before her canvas. Perhaps she dreamed of long summers in Golfe-Juan, winters spent in Paris; painting quickly, furiously, racing against the dying afternoon light.

Prussian blue is a fugitive color. It is made from potassium cyanide, and over time it bleeds into other colors surrounding it. Sometimes, when I miss her particularly, I pull the canvas out, I put it on my dresser and stare at it when I have trouble falling asleep. This makes me feel close to her. At least I was close to her once; I turned inside her, I kicked my feet against her rib cage, blood streamed from her heart to mine and back again. It was the only time I did not stand between Georgia and her work. It was the only time that my existence was not, by definition, erasing hers as surely as if my presence were a noxious, fugitive blue, bleeding into her, changing over time, her limbs my legacy.

"So what are you doing here? Do you have the day off from school?" the salesgirl asks. Now she's being nice to me.

"Yeah," I say. Then casually: "Do you have any idea when my mother will get home?"

"Oh, she's probably at Vishna's," she says. "Usually she's there if she's not here."

"Vishna's!" The image of Georgia's new assistant, her twenty-five-year-old cancer-stricken assistant, races through my mind and I suddenly realize what I have already known: my mother has a boyfriend.

"So my mother is at Vishna's," I say to the salesgirl, trying to sound matter-of-fact. "I guess I'd better go there."

We look up Kripalu in the Manhattan white pages. There are not too many listed. With my vague knowledge of the city's geography, I figure out that Vishna must live at 34 Gramercy Park East.

"I have a favor to ask."

The salesgirl looks at me warily. She's afraid I'm going to ask her to baby-sit or something. She has underestimated me.

"I'll need five dollars to get to Vishna's apartment."

She stares at me.

"What's with you, kid? You can't walk around this town with no money in your pocket!"

I dig my fingernail into the fleshy part of my hand in an attempt not to cry. My policy used to be never to cry at all. Now it is simply not to cry in front of strangers. I don't believe in crying in stores, on city streets, in restaurants. Yet here I am, feeling tears well up in my eyes.

"Okay, sweetie, okay."

She digs into an enormous black bag larger than my father's medical kit, pulls out a wallet and hands me a couple of bills.

"Just in case Georgia isn't there, you come right back here," she says. "Your mother would kill me if I lost you."

Lost me. What a concept. As if I were a stray earring or a missing glove. As if I were a commodity, merchandise that could be lost, found, perhaps even replaced. I crumple the bills in my pocket until they are as small as worry beads, thank the salesgirl and head back to West Broadway.

There is a mural on the side of a building across the street from Georgia's loft. Purple angels fly through a bright green sky toward a distant door adorned with wreaths and ivy. The creator of the mural is an artist who paints only in public spaces. I have seen his work on uptown sidewalks, downtown buildings and occasionally on lavatory walls. I read an interview with him once in an art magazine which featured Georgia; he said that he chose to paint on public surfaces because it gave his audience an opportunity to "engage directly with his art." I'm not sure what he meant by that, but I have seen his work stepped on by rush hour crowds, stained with urine on the walls of Penn Station, and now, as I look across West Broadway at his mural of the purple angels, I see that someone has spray-painted red horns on each angel's head. The green door is also covered with bright red-painted words: *The road to heaven is paved with blood.*

. . .

The cab stops in front of a brownstone on Gramercy Park. Georgia flings the door open. She is wearing her usual work-day stained coveralls, and steel-toed construction boots. There is an enormous gold earring dangling from her ear, this time in the shape of a dolphin. Each time I have seen Georgia for the past six months, a different animal has been hanging from her ear. Now I wonder if they are all gifts from Vishna. Behind her, near an urn filled with fresh gladiolas, he stands in her shadow.

"Josie," she says, drawing me into her arms, "your father called a little while ago. He's been worried sick about you. He said the school called his office. What are you doing here?"

"I missed you," I say.

She hugs me tight. I feel my heart pounding against hers.

"I missed you too, pumpkin."

I burst into tears.

"Jesus, what are we doing to you?" Georgia murmurs, pulling me closer. I smell patchouli and plaster dust.

"Vishna, put up some tea," she says.

He moves soundlessly away. Georgia leads me to a pink circular couch in the center of the living area. She swivels so she is facing me, then takes my face into both her hands. These are the hands which created Georgia's most famous piece, which is in the sculpture garden of the Museum of Modern Art. It is almost as if these hands cupping my face do not belong to her. I feel her calluses against the sides of my face, and think they are sacred instruments. Her gift is on loan to her. She knows she can only keep it as long as she puts it to use. I imagine if she closed her eyes and concentrated deeply, she would be able to see every age through which I will pass until she would witness her own daughter become an old woman before her eyes. Perhaps she will sculpt me one day. It would be the only way to her heart.

She looks into my eyes and I think I will disappear. "You look tragic. You look like you're in mourning," she says.

I sit perfectly still, hunched over. I hear the distant whistling of a teakettle.

"Joanna, are you that unhappy?"

I nod mutely. I want her to take care of me.

Vishna appears, carrying a silver tray and tea service for three. In addition to tea there is a plate piled with Italian biscuits, and another with scones and jam. He stumbles over the edge of a rug, almost sends everything flying. The tray looks as if it weighs more than Vishna.

"A little something Italian, a little something British," he says as he places the tray on the coffee table, then sits next to Georgia on the couch.

He pours tea ceremoniously and passes the biscuits, which Georgia and I both decline.

We sip tea in silence.

"Vishna, sweetheart, I think that my daughter and I need to spend some time alone," Georgia says. "I've decided to take her on a little day trip."

Vishna glances at her, wounded.

"I'm sorry," she says.

"I don't suppose you want me to join you?" he asks.

Georgia shakes her head.

"Not today."

He brightens as if he hadn't heard her.

"We could go to the circus! The circus is in town."

He looks at me to see if this idea appeals, I want to glare at him, but his face is sad and deformed, like that of the thin man, the fat lady, the midget. Perhaps we all belong in the circus, Georgia, Vishna and I. We are all, in one sense or another, curiosities.

"So, Josie. Are you ready for our adventure?"

Georgia's voice breaks my reverie.

"Where are we going?"

"You'll see."

It is that hushed, motionless time of day in the city, the middle of the afternoon. Offices are filled with people back from their lunch hours, children are not yet out of school, mothers and infants have strolled home for afternoon naps. My mother places a soft tweed overcoat on my shoulders, and wraps her favorite purple scarf around my neck.

"My clothes almost fit you," she smiles, shaking her head. "I can't believe how big you've gotten. You're almost a woman, Josie."

The sleeves of her coat fall around my knuckles, but I know what she means. The irony has not escaped me; as I try with all my might to make myself disappear, my physical, tangible growth continues so quickly I can almost see the hairs on my head lengthening, my bones stretching as I stand before a mirror. Just in the past two months my rib cage has puffed out, my breasts have grown. I need bras, but have been too embarrassed to ask my father to take me shopping, and talking to Georgia about anything so dreary has seemed out of the question. I like to imagine she never went through adolescence, that she sprang beautiful and fully formed, an ageless goddess, from her mother's womb.

She hails a cab, her arm already outstretched as we walk through the front doors of Vishna's brownstone.

We pile into the backseat.

"The Brooklyn Bridge, please," she says.

"The bridge, lady? Just the bridge?"

"Yes. Thank you," she says, then sits back, pleased.

The cabbie tilts his rearview mirror so he can see us better. He weaves his way in and out of traffic, speeding up at the yellow lights. He slams his fist down on his horn as a station wagon tries to cut him off.

"Jersey drivers," he mutters, then looks at us. "You ladies aren't from Jersey, are you?"

Georgia laughs, delighted.

"No, we're not."

We're not? I glance at her, and she winks at me. When I'm with Georgia the rest of my life doesn't exist. There is no Tipton Academy, no Billy Overmeyer, no sad stooped-over father whose only solace comes from the runny noses of children and the shadow of Lila Overmeyer's smile. There is only this: my mother's feet are kicked up on the footrest of this Checker cab, the tips of her black cowboy boots splattered with dried mud. Her arm is flung around my shoulder, and my head rests against her. Every time the cab passes over a pothole on Second Avenue, the half dozen bracelets on her wrist jingle in a melody which is soothing to me, a sound I must have heard as an infant when she rocked me to sleep. Her profile, looking straight ahead at a destination only she can see, is both comforting in its familiarity and the most frightening sight imaginable, a harbinger of my life ahead, a beautiful courier of things to come.

We inch our way onto the FDR Drive through heavy traffic caused by an accident we can see a few hundred yards ahead of us; an old white van has hit a guardrail and there is steam pouring from its hood. Several dark-complected men in turbans stand behind it, their white robes billowing in the wind gusting off the East River. As cars swerve into the next lane, the turbaned men signal frantically like exotic, demented traffic cops.

Finally we crawl past the accident and the cabbie presses his gas pedal to the floor. I feel the car's muffler vibrating, straining with effort as we sail down the FDR Drive. We accelerate all the way to the Manhattan side of the Brooklyn Bridge.

"Right here?" he asks, his hand hesitating on the meter.

"Yes," Georgia responds, "right here."

She grabs my hand as we exit the cab. Horns blare when we dash across the wide expanse of pavement until we reach a steep stairway leading to a path which runs above the center of the bridge. We climb the stairway, Georgia taking two steps at a time. When we reach the top, I see a few joggers in the distance, as small as stick figures in a child's drawing.

"What are we doing here?" I ask as I huff and puff, stopping at the top of the stairs. Clearly, all of DiNazio's punishing laps have done little for my stamina.

"You'll see," says Georgia.

"Why does everything have to be such a big secret?" I ask.

"Some day, Josie, you'll discover that the most interesting part of life exists in secret," she says.

She glances around her and takes a deep breath.

"Come on," she says, taking my hand once again.

We head toward the center of the bridge. I can feel the walkway swaying slightly beneath my feet. I shrink back in fear, imagine the bridge falling like a Lego set into the East River, churning its polluted waters beneath us. Georgia squeezes my hand tighter. She would hold me even if we fell all the way to the bottom of the river. She would hold me as we drifted past floating debris and drowned Mafia corpses.

"It's the suspension on these bridges," she says; "all bridges give a little. Don't be frightened, angel."

When we reach the midpoint, Georgia stops. Cars race below us, exhaust fumes vanishing into the frosty dusk like breath into the night. She whirls around and looks at me, flushed, breathless.

"What do you think?" she asks.

"About what?"

"About *what?*" she repeats, smiling indulgently. "I've brought you to see the eighth wonder of the world! Close your eyes, Josie."

I shut my eyes tight, scrunching my face into a knot. I feel

Georgia wrap both arms around me, pulling me in front of her.

"Keep them closed," she says.

I feel as though I'm flying through air, but the air is thick and heavy like water, and time seems to have slowed down. Georgia turns me around once, twice. She spins me around and around until I am dizzy. The traffic roaring by us on the bridge sounds far away, as if heard from under the surface of water, a distant ripple.

"Okay, open your eyes now," Georgia says.

Slowly I relax my face and open my eyes. What appears before me is an artist's sorcery, the white magic of the Manhattan skyline set against a flawless pink sunset and a flat grimy sky. The pollution blanketing this city is what creates the beauty of its sunsets, but I am unaware of this today, at fourteen-going-on-fifteen. I lean against my mother's shoulders, the proud, aching shoulders of Georgia Higgins Hirsch. I expand my field of vision until I see the whole panorama of the skyline spread out before me in all its splendor, a wide glittering turn-of-the-century necklace encased under thick glass in a museum. It is far away, and I know I cannot touch it, but by looking at it from this vantage point, I am convinced it belongs to me.

We stand still for what seems like hours, my mother and I. The cars have slowed to a dense rush hour crawl, and the sun has disappeared behind the west side of the city. Lights emanate from windows starting at the World Trade Center, past Sutton Place, all the way up to Spanish Harlem; they flicker like candles along the city's edge.

"Extraordinary," breathes Georgia. "Just look at the colors. You can almost see the energy. The whole city is vibrating with it."

She pulls me close, wraps her arms beneath my chin and

cups my head against her chest. A few stars begin to populate the sky. She points to them.

"Did you know there are some stars which we are never able to see? They are hidden from us until they explode in the sky and pieces streak down like meteors. They are invisible until they fall."

As I watch the sky for any telltale movement, Georgia bends forward and whispers in my ear.

"Joanna, this is why we're here. If we don't look with pleasure at the sky, if we aren't awed by the sun setting behind the greatest city ever built, we have been created in vain."

It is the longest speech she has ever given me. I have the feeling she brought us all the way out here to the middle of the Brooklyn Bridge just to say these words to me today.

She swivels me around so I am facing her. Her eyes are filled with tears.

"Do you understand?" she asks.

I look at her. The tension in her face frightens me, and I say nothing.

"Do you understand, Jo? I want to be a good mother," she cries, "but this is all I have to give you. I live for this. If I don't live for this, I will die."

V.

*M*y mother stopped answering her phone six months ago. I have not boarded a plane and flown to Rome in search of *La Nordamericana*. I have not rented a Fiat and raced along the autostrada in fifth gear, curving along the edge of the Umbrian mountains, then up, higher up into the peaks in search of her.

I have waited.

I have decided that if any harm came to Georgia I would know it. It would be front-page news, an item tucked into the bottom left corner of the *New York Times*. There would be an outdated photograph of the beautiful sculptor; they always referred to her this way. As if beauty and art are antithetical, as if the smooth planes of loveliness must hide a certain vapidity, or at the very least, an unwillingness to investigate the truth.

Undoubtedly, she was given too much. I wonder if this is

what saved her from certain death at the age of three in Calvaria, Lithuania. I wonder about the profusion of curls ringing her head, the elegance of her hands—all these things protected her as she was lifted and placed beneath the loose floorboards in her neighbor's attic. It is a miracle that the light emanating from her small body did not attract the attention of the Nazi search dogs, that they did not sniff out the pale sweet scent which I can detect across a room.

Georgia Higgins Hirsch, the only artist *Harper's Bazaar* has ever put on its list of the world's Ten Most Beautiful Women, has become a solitary figure, her cape sailing behind her like a heroine's from a nineteenth-century novel as she walks alone down the crumbling stone path from the rectory where she lives, into town, where she is respectfully known only as *La Nordamericana,* where her requests for steel girders, quarry stone and special marble brought from Carrara are met with bemused smiles by her protectors, ancient toothless *artigiani* who will ride to the other side of the country in search of whatever she needs. They have seen the inside of the barn she has converted into a studio.

She has stopped answering her phone, acknowledging telegrams or perhaps even responding to knocks on her front door. I know she is working, and that is all I can hope for. When Georgia stops working she may stop breathing as well. From time to time a truck shimmies its way through the narrow mountain passes in order to reach her. Several of her pieces are loaded in back, then dispatched by freight and air to her galleries in Paris and New York.

I received a call from her gallery last week.

"Where is she?"

"Who?" I asked, annoyed. I hate when people don't identify themselves on the phone.

"Georgia. Who else? Where is she?"

"Who's this?"

"Sorry, Joanna. I apologize. I'm rather worked up. It's Ward Knowlton speaking."

Knowlton has been Georgia's gallery dealer since I was a teenager.

"You should know better than I," I say.

"I have no idea. We sent a truck up there, but no Georgia. No Georgia anywhere."

"I'm sorry, Ward. I haven't spoken to her in over six months."

I say this as casually as possible. My hand is cold around the phone's receiver, my legs are shaking. Nigel is gone. Billy is gone. And now Georgia. I'm sure she's alive, hanging over the edge of a Sardinian cliff just to feel the air swirl around her, the endless drop beneath her feet.

Or perhaps she has flown to New York. She will be in the audience tonight. During El Raton's seventy-third performance of *Speak, Memory,* Georgia will be seated in the back row. She will wait for me at the stage door, her arms outstretched, eyes gleaming with a new understanding of the solidarity between us. She will have aged during the past months, her hair braided behind her, the color of day-old snow.

"Joanna," she will say, "darling, I am home."

The rehabilitation center rises above the hills near the Jersey Turnpike, a five-story masterpiece of sandstone and smoked glass. The U-shaped visitor's parking area is filled with large shiny German cars. My orange Volkswagen bug looks misplaced among these cars, as if it had somehow wandered here from the coast of California. In the lobby there is a wall of mirrors. I am wearing a pair of faded jeans torn at the knees; a printed scarf woven through the belt loops; a man's undershirt. I have pulled my hair into a french twist. Turquoise earrings dangle from my ears, a thirtieth birthday present from Billy.

I enter an elevator large enough for several wheelchairs and take a few deep breaths to calm myself. The doors open to the long-term care unit. I silently count: I have both eyes, one nose, a mouth, ten fingers and toes. The only part which concerns me is my heart. It seems to be missing. I don't feel it thumping in my chest. I raise my hand to my tee-shirt and a nurse looks at me curiously.

"Are you all right?"

"Yes. I'm looking for Overmeyer," I say.

She stares at me with watery blue eyes.

"Down the hall, room 638," she says. I watch as she walks away squeakily, rubber-soled shoes, opaque white stockings. There is something manageable in the way she moves, a solid custodian of magic potions, guardian of life, death, and what exists here, in the median.

At the door of room 638 I hear a television inside, the theme of "All My Children."

I push the door open a crack and see Billy propped up in a mechanical bed. His head is shaved. His arm dangles atrophied over the side of the bed. But his eyes startle me most of all: they are dark blue and empty as those on the stuffed boar's head which hung in the basement of his parents' home. As children we used to stick cigarettes in the boar's mouth, drape scarves and toilet paper over its antlers. We couldn't believe something so lifelike could really be dead.

The nurse's aide is raptly watching "All My Children." She doesn't notice me standing in the shadow of the door. Cliff and Nina are having a fight. Nina is pregnant with Cliff's baby, but he doesn't want her to have an abortion because he's dying of leukemia and this is his last chance at posterity. I recognize the scene. I will appear any moment as Nina's evil sister Samantha. Samantha is a lab technician who used to go out with Cliff and has faked his test results to make him think he's dying.

There I am. I rarely see myself on television when I do soap operas; the shows are broadcast two weeks after we tape them. Besides, Nigel has so turned me against this work. "Prostitution," he calls it. On the screen my hair is frozen into a mass of waves. I am wearing a navy blue skirt and white silk bow-tied blouse. This is how lab technicians dress on soap operas.

I speak my first line.

"How dare you?" I hiss at Nina. "You should *never* have told him you were pregnant, you fool!"

"He's mine," says Nina, "and you'll never take him away from me. You want to take him hostage, but you can't have him. I know all about you, you conniving bitch. You always want what you can't have."

Suddenly there is another sound in the room, a noise at once savage and profoundly human. If you have ever heard anyone in excruciating physical pain or at the brink of death, this is what it sounds like: it comes from the bowels and escapes through the throat, and there is no self-consciousness in it, no hypocrisy. The thin membrane of skin between the body and the surrounding air becomes, for a moment, inconsequential. There is no *I*, no *you*. There is only the pain of the moment.

He is staring at the television set. His neck jerks back and forth, his head rolls around as if attached by a string.

"I'll get you," I say on-screen. I am holding Cliff's picture in my hand. "You'll be mine. You think you have a choice in the matter?" I look at the picture and laugh a demonic soap-opera laugh.

"Billy! Billy, what's wrong?" his aide asks, rushing to his side. It is a silly question. He cannot answer. The aide should know this.

The sound continues, a low-pitched guttural wailing.

The aide presses a small button by Billy's nightstand.

Before the doctors come rushing in, I take one last look at him. The pain in this room is so palpable it shimmers around objects, making Billy's body extend beyond itself in a ghostly metaphysical way. His hand grows larger, becomes a claw. It reaches out toward me.

My face on television causes him to cry out in agony, to open the black hole of his mouth. The doctors think he cannot understand; they think his mind is as dead as his body.

I know better. I know that Billy understands every second of every minute, every minute of every day. And he knows that the prognosis, as they say, is somewhere beyond the region of hope.

I walk down the hall, past an electronic wheelchair holding a woman with no legs or arms, a woman howling, her mouth stretched wide; I retrace my steps to the elevator, through the mirrored lobby and revolving doors, back into the heavy New Jersey air.

If I were on trial here what would the charges be? He is not dead, so I would not be accused of murder. Willful negligence? Gross misconduct? Assault with intent to kill?

The porch light is burning when I finally return home from Georgia and the Brooklyn Bridge. The front door is open as I trudge up the front walk, and I smell meat cooking, cumin, a hint of coriander. My father must be going through his India phase. Everything he cooks is a bright saffron yellow. In the morning, when he doesn't have hospital rounds, he prepares the marinade for that evening's meal. He likes slow-cooking things. A pot simmering on the stove helps my father to believe we are still a family.

I enter the hall and look through the house into the kitchen, where my father is sitting at the round oak table. He is still wearing his white lab coat and is bent over a book, talking to someone I cannot see. A cup of coffee sits too close to his elbow and I watch as he knocks it to the floor just as I knew he would. He bends to pick it up and sees me approaching.

"Look who's back! My daughter, the intrepid traveler!" he exclaims joyously.

I glare at him. I am not in the mood for sarcasm.

"Look who's here, Josie," he says.

I walk toward him and see the last person I expect to be sitting at my kitchen table. A pencil is stuck behind his ear and an Introduction to Biology textbook is open in front of him.

"Hi!" he says with a smile.

I look from my father to Billy and back again. They are both wearing the same beatific grin.

"I'm helping Billy with his biology," my father says.

"I can see that," I reply faintly.

"Your father knows this stuff inside out," says Billy.

"I should hope so."

"Dr. Hirsch, would you excuse Josie and me?" Billy asks politely.

My father nods.

"Just be down for dinner in fifteen minutes," he says.

"I'm staying for dinner?"

"I hope so. I'm making lamb Muglai," my father answers.

Billy pulls me out of the kitchen and upstairs to my bedroom. His left leg drags behind him. His fingers dig into my
arm. He takes me by the shoulders, sits me down on the bed
and stands facing me.

"Look," he says, then stops. I gaze at him directly for the
first time, and see his face is bruised.

"Look," he repeats, "I'm sorry. I'm sorry I couldn't go with
you today. I'm sorry I yelled at you earlier."

The tip of his nose is pink against his face, his eyes are
bright, and I can't help thinking he looks like a rabbit: frightened, gentle, endearing.

"It's okay."

"No it's not, Josie. Nothing's okay."

He stares intently at a piece of lint on the rug.

"Did your father hurt you?" I ask softly.

I see a muscle fluttering in his jaw like the pulpy heartbeat
of something newly born.

"We don't discuss that," he says.

"Billy—"

"Talking about my parents makes it worse, Josie. You understand, don't you?"

A knot of sadness travels from my stomach, through my
chest, up into my throat, like a displaced vital organ.

"Yes," I answer.

He sits on the bed and puts his arm around me. I suddenly
feel much older than I am, like we are both adult versions of
ourselves sitting on the white ruffled bedspread.

"Your parents love you, they really do," he says quietly,
stroking my hair in a gesture he must have learned from his
mother.

"My parents are children," I say.

"So are mine," he says, and thumbs a tear away from my
cheek.

My father's voice floats up the stairwell.

"Joanna, William! Food's on the table!"

We look at each other silently, then lean forward until our lips touch. Billy's eyes are open; seen from this close, they are like bright blue marbles, the kind with magic swirls inside. His nose bumps against mine, and I feel his breath on my upper lip. We break away and hug tightly, almost violently.

Flushed, quiet, we smile at each other. I think of last night in the woods, the way I covered his body with mine like a blanket. For the rest of his life, when anyone asks Billy about his first kiss, mine will be the face which will flash before his eyes, these twenty-four hours, the memory of the icy ground, the leaves and now this moment—a white frilly bedspread, the redolent smell of coriander drifting up the staircase, the cool cheeks and hot breath between us.

"Joaaaana!" my father calls again.

We clasp our hands together. There is no need to cut our fingers open the way we would if we were both boys exchanging blood vows. A pact has been sealed between us.

Billy loves me.

I can taste it on his lips.

My father is ladling curried vegetables into bowls on the kitchen table. I inhale deeply, thinking of the Brooklyn Bridge stretched out like an opulent necklace in the night, the exotic Indian smells permeating the air outside our kitchen window, and for a brief fleeting moment, my life almost makes sense.

"Wait," said Nigel, "wait just a minute. Everybody stop. Joanna, lovey, you're doing it all wrong."

I peered at him from the stage. I could barely make him
out in the ninth-row center, where he always sat during rehearsal.

"What's the problem?" I asked.

"What's the problem? *You're* the problem, dear heart."

Nigel, please don't do this, don't do this, don't do this, I repeated to myself, eyes closed, a mantra.

"Excuse me," faltered the actor playing Nabokov, "but the
scene is going just fine, I think—"

"How dare you?" thundered Nigel. "Hasn't anyone ever
told you never to fuck with the director? Never!"

"Nigel, what can I—"

"Just follow the fucking notes I gave you, Joanna," he
growled, then stalked toward the exit sign. "Fifteen-minute
break, everybody."

I knew where he was going. O'Malley's, around the corner.
He would order a double, down it, rap his knuckles on the bar
and do it again. By the time he returned to El Raton his eyes
would be filmy, hands flapping the air senselessly. "Let's play
games," he'd say, "let's do theatre exercises." He would have us
down on our hands and knees and instruct us to act like
various animals. "Act like a dog, Josie," he'd say, "not a pedigree, a mutt. Or better yet, this: a mutt who thinks she's a
pedigree."

Cruelty, in some of us, is exposed only when we are
drunk. Nigel drank in an attempt to summon his cruelty, to
find it under a thick layer of Johnnie Walker Black. He didn't
know about the airline bottles of vodka I kept in my knapsack,
small syrupy weapons of my own. When he went to
O'Malley's I sat cross-legged on my dressing room floor. Three
Smirnoff bottles later, I was ready to face my lover the director. I was equipped to do whatever he required. I knew that—
despite himself—he was coaxing out of me the performance of
a lifetime.

. . .

$\mathcal{L}$ately I have begun faking. I have faked a sprained ankle, held a thermometer in a cup of warm water, pinched my cheeks so hard they glow. I do not want to go to school. Some mornings the fear of walking into homeroom, then trotting at the sound of the bell like Pavlov's dog to Math, English, Biology, Spanish and American History only to be faced, after classes, with Gloria DiNazio, is too much for me to bear.

And then there is Billy, who I see in homeroom, pass in the halls between classes, whose name I doodle during study hall. The question of whether or not I will sit next to Billy at lunch dominates my day. Seeing Billy in a crowd makes me lonesome; I want him to myself. I know where he is at all times. I make it my business. I know whether he's in the lab, at lacrosse practice, in the Fiske Garden smoking cigarettes. Keeping track of him tires me out, and some mornings I need to hide in bed.

I can fool my father the doctor. When he sees my flushed cheeks his concern for me overrides all his pediatric knowledge. He tucks me into bed, turns on the humidifier and leaves me a breakfast of citrus sections before he heads across the lawn for his morning appointments. He checks me during the day, hurrying home between patients. He supplies syrups and pills. I see no way around drinking the syrups, which make me drowsy, but flush the pills down the toilet.

This morning I am having a hard time faking it. I pace my room, not wanting to be here, not wanting to be in school. I walk from window to door, door to window. I am not sure what causes me to look outside at the precise moment my father ambles down the walkway. He is headed in the opposite direction from his office. I do not know what predestined scourge nudges me as I throw on my bathrobe and a pair of pink fuzzy slippers adorned with black beetle eyes, bound down the stairs and out the back door, sneaking around the side of the house to follow him.

He walks with purpose. His hands are thrust deep into the pockets of his raincoat—it is not raining—which flaps behind him like an undercover spy's. When he reaches his destination he pauses, looking quickly each way. I duck behind a brick pillar at the entrance to our driveway. My terry-cloth robe is not warm enough. Now I really will catch the flu.

He rings the Overmeyers' bell.

Perhaps he needs something, a cup of sugar, a pint of milk. Perhaps Mr. Overmeyer will answer the door, slap my father robustly on the back and invite him inside like an old friend. I feel like I do at the movies when I know the scary part is coming up. I don't know whether to cover my eyes or keep them glued to the scene. I opt for total exposure. Knowing is better than imagining.

Lila Overmeyer opens the door. She smiles when she sees him; it is not her contained, familiar smile, but something wider, unfastened. She, too, looks both ways before she grabs his hand, laughing, and pulls him inside.

I race across the street. If anyone were looking from a second-story window of a neighboring house he would see a white and pink blur dashing through an opening in the bare forsythia hedges.

Terry cloth catches on the brick wall as I slip toward the kitchen window; perhaps they will sit at the Formica counter and have coffee and danish, reflecting on Camp Kenmont days of long ago.

Sneaking around back, I pass the television room where Billy and I used to watch "Hogan's Heroes" after school. The

floor is covered by a pale shag rug so thick if you walk barefoot your feet disappear. There is a large white couch, a glass
coffee table and a red lacquered bookcase filled with Mr.
Overmeyer's golf trophies.

A shadow, a hint of movement caught out of the corner of
my eye, makes me stop. Leaving the kitchen behind, I back-
track and peer over the windowsill into the television room.
Lila Overmeyer is standing in the doorway; she is wearing a
long shiny robe the color of sand.

I close my eyes and count backward from twenty-five. By
the time I reach zero she will be gone. I will be back in bed
across the street, pretending to be sick. This may turn out to
be a self-fulfilling prophecy. My stomach feels queasy, and
there are chills roaming my spine.

. . . four, three, two, one. I count slowly. When I open
my eyes my father is in the room and has his arms around Lila
Overmeyer. His head is buried between her neck and shoulder, and she is stroking his back. Perhaps this is not what it
seems. She may be comforting him. After all, she is a very old
friend. He may be talking about Georgia, his heartbreak. I
strain to listen. Through the double storm windows, I cannot
hear them.

I close my eyes and count again. This time from fifty backward. I say the word *Mississippi* between each number as
slowly as possible.

. . . four-Mississippi, three-Mississippi, two-Mississippi,
one. This time, when I open my eyes, there can be no mistak-
ing what is going on. Mrs. Overmeyer is enveloped in my
father's arms and his mouth covers hers. Her body has gone
limp, feet dangling as he pulls her toward him.

I don't belong here, but feel paralyzed, rooted to the spot. I
am afraid they will see me; they can see out better than I can
see in. I have to press my face against the pane to get rid of the
glare. My heart pounds. The likelihood they will look out the

window is small. They are absorbed in each other, in the sacred rite which has begun between them.

My father pushes the top of her robe from her shoulders and it falls around her waist. Her breasts spill out, heavier than Georgia's. He bends down and runs his tongue over her nipple. *Oh,* he seems to be saying, his mouth open like a child's. He pushes her gently to the thick shag rug. Her knees sink into the carpet, she leans back, then he kneels next to her and touches her breasts reverentially, skimming the surface of her skin like a faith healer.

I close my eyes again, and keep them closed for a long time. It is cold enough to see my breath, but I feel light-headed and sweaty. I have been standing so still a sparrow hops over my slipper on its way to some spilled birdseed under a nearby bush. When I open my eyes my father is naked. Lila Overmeyer is sitting on the edge of the couch holding him in her mouth, her head moving rhythmically.

When she pulls away, I gasp. I have never seen this phenomenon. I know it is called an erection, and now I see why. It looks like something stronger than the sum of its parts; rugged and yielding like the neck of a strong docile animal. Seeing Greek statues in Georgia's art history books has not prepared me for this. The penises I have studied at great length look more like exotic vegetables or bunches of ripe fruit.

My father lies on the floor. He lifts Mrs. Overmeyer and plants her on top of him. Her silk robe covers her stomach. She wraps her legs around him and they roll through the room, crashing into the coffee table, knocking against the television stand. For a perilous moment the television looks like it will fall, but they don't notice. I see the long muscular line of her thigh as she strains against him; her breasts heaving. Unwittingly, I reach a hand up and feel my own budding chest;

my palms are damp and there is a new tense strain in my groin.

I don't belong here. I have never belonged anywhere less in my life. I think of my father stooped over the kitchen stove, a stethoscope still hanging around his neck, an old apron of Georgia's tied around his waist. I can almost see him stirring one of his stews in a large cast-iron pot, his slow, wistful smile when he tastes his own concoction. I wonder if I will ever again be able to believe in his fragility.

He lies her down on the couch. I stand in the brambles, watching as he moves on top of her. Lila's neck is turned, eyes shut tight. My father lifts himself on his elbows and stares at her with an expression I have never seen, a certain expectation, his jaw thrust out, hard, decisive. He raises one hand and pinches the nipple of a breast between thumb and forefinger. I can see all this. I am that close. Lila Overmeyer's head tosses from side to side. I wonder if he is hurting her.

The sound of a car crunches against gravel. I hear it before they do. Just as Mr. Overmeyer's station wagon pulls into the driveway they are moaning together, their groans becoming louder and louder, hipbones grinding against each other's so hard I wince. Then, with one last arc of Lila's back, it is over.

I slip around the side of the house. I notice my thighs are shaking with a detached interest, as if they belong to someone else.

"Hi, Mr. Overmeyer!"

"Joanna! What are you doing here?"

"I just came by to see if Billy was home."

"Billy's at school," he says, "where you should be, young lady. What are you doing in your bathrobe?"

He doesn't wait for an answer. He strides toward the house, briefcase in hand. My heart lurches. I imagine at this very moment that my father and Lila are strewn naked across the couch in the television room. What will Mr. Overmeyer do if he discovers them? I have noticed the rifles hanging on the walls of his study.

I run after him.

"Let me come in with you," I say. "I'm really thirsty. Do you have any lemonade?"

The screen door slams behind us.

I keep chattering.

"Are you sure Billy isn't home?" I ask.

"Billy! Billy, are you up there?" I yell at the top of my lungs.

"Joanna, what are you doing?" Mr. Overmeyer asks, annoyed. "I told you he isn't home."

I hear faint rustling from the other end of the house. I walk slowly to the front hall and peek out one of the long vertical windows on either side of the door. I see what I had hoped to see. My father is racing across the Overmeyer property as fast as he can. He is barefoot, carrying his shoes. His shirt is unbuttoned, raincoat flung over his shoulders.

I hurry back to the kitchen. I don't want to take any chances that Mr. Overmeyer will follow me. I should not have feared. His back is turned, and he is pouring a healthy splash of vodka into a water glass. He hands me a lemonade and raises his glass in a toast.

"It must be cocktail hour somewhere," he says with a weak smile.

In a few moments, Lila Overmeyer comes into the kitchen. Her color is high, and her beige robe is tied too tightly around her waist.

"Ah, the lady of leisure arises!" Mr. Overmeyer says. "Darling, have you been lying in bed eating bonbons?"

He makes the word *darling* a humiliation.

"No," Lila says in a strained, high-pitched voice, "I got a slow start this morning. I'm not feeling very well."

"It seems everyone around here is sick," he says.

She turns to me.

"Josie, dear, are you ill?"

I stare at her.

"Cat got your tongue?" she asks, reaching out a hand to ruffle my hair as if I were an errant, beloved pet.

I duck away.

"Josie! What's wrong?"

I stand transfixed, trembling.

"You know what's wrong," I whisper. The words force their way out of my mouth.

I don't wait to see the color drain from Lila Overmeyer's face. I spin and race out of the house. I run as fast as I can all the way down Exeter Road, past all the sad suburban streets with their British names, faster and faster until I reach Katz's corner deli, where I sit on the stoop and concentrate on counting Cadillacs.

"We're not leaving until we see five Cadillacs," Billy used to say.

"No," I'd respond, "let's wait until we see one Rolls-Royce."

I had never seen a Rolls-Royce.

"Okay."

We would sit as twilight fell, watching at least six Cadillacs drive by, their owners propped up straight, squinting grimly into the distance.

"If I owned a Cadillac I wouldn't look so miserable," Billy once said dreamily, "I'd play the radio as loud as I wanted, I'd smoke cigarettes and flip them out the window."

"Look, there's another one."

I'd pointed to a black car making its way toward us, headlights bright though it was still daylight.

"That's not a Cadillac, that's a hearse," Billy had said. "There's a dead body in there."

We'd watched silently as the hearse rolled by, windows darkened, black glaring orange against the setting sun.

I see one El Dorado, then another. Then a third goes by, or is it a Buick Skylark? I can't tell. I am crying so hard, everything is smudged. I concentrate on the blurry cars parading Knightsbridge Avenue. I can no longer distinguish between Chryslers and Cadillacs, trees and sky and the gray stone stoop beneath me.

I have never sat here on Katz's stoop alone. I think of Billy, who is probably in Algebra class right now. I cry harder, thinking of what I will say to him. Does what happened between his mother and my father make us brother and sister? I can't help thinking it wedges something silent and irrefutable between us.

I know this is a day by which all others will be measured. I will hold this secret beneath my tongue, owning it, stashing it as if it were a ticket to an imminent voyage. I will keep this information from Billy. And in doing so, I believe that our world will remain frozen, arrested, that nothing will change from this moment on. If I swallow the image of Lila and my father in the television room, if it burrows deep into the soft tissue of my belly, it will die inside me. It will go no further than this day.

The perfect crime, I once heard, is an invisible one: stab your victim with an icicle. The blade pierces his heart and dissolves instantly, melting on contact, ice water pooling with blood, fingerprints no more than memories, the body an irredeemable blue. The weapon thaws even as the wound remains. It is of little consequence, you see; because even if the weapon is imaginary, the wound is real.

. . .

"What on earth do you talk about for fifty minutes at a clip? Don't you get sick of yourself?" Nigel asked Billy. "Anyway, how can you speak honestly with someone who's going to decide your professional fate?"

We were seated around the book crate which served as our dinner table in our studio. The table was littered with half-empty plates of spaghetti primavera, an overturned bottle of Spanish wine and a pair of silver salt and pepper shakers which Georgia had sent us from Italy.

"Why do you have to be so negative about everything?" Billy replied.

"Analysis is an indulgence of the upper-middle class," Nigel announced.

For Nigel, *upper-middle class* was an unflattering description. He would sooner be called anything other than bourgeois.

"What do you think we all are, with our Ivy League degrees and our privileged professions?" Billy asked.

"Speak for yourself," said Nigel.

Billy sighed. "Even if I didn't want to be in analysis, I'd have no choice," he said. "It's part of the training. I can't get my doctorate without it."

I got up to do the dishes. Sundays, I cooked. I combed the Italian markets on Ninth Avenue and bought fresh pasta, thick hunks of Pecorino Romano, freshly marinated olives. I pretended we lived in Paris as I slung a colorful string bag over my shoulder and stuffed it full of fresh fruit and vegetables. I bought things we didn't need and couldn't afford. I spent half a night's tips on groceries.

"Why are you doing all this?" Nigel raged.

"Doing what?" asked Billy.

"You've just spent ten years of your life in school, school, school. And now you're almost finished with your dissertation, and all you're interested in is advancement: 'Is it going to be published? Will I be able to join the institute?' All this hierarchy, William. I can't believe you really care so much about your own image."

Billy got angry.

"Not everyone can do things the way you do, dearest," he said.

"What is that supposed to mean?"

"Some of us not only need to love our work, but also to make a living at it. Some of us don't want to starve and struggle and live on Ninth Avenue, and slave until two in the goddamn morning while we pretend to be working in the theatre which is something we're not even really doing!"

Billy paused, catching his breath. We all looked at the red-checked tablecloth in silence.

The teakettle began to wail in the kitchen, fogging the window overlooking the street. I walked away from the table, dishes in hand, glad to remove myself from the tension between them.

In the kitchen I set three mugs on the counter. I made a rum toddy for Nigel, hot water with a slice of lemon for Billy and instant coffee for myself. I stretched, arched my back and looked into the dark of the kitchen window, the metal gates as heavy and secure as a prison's. In the black of the window I saw the lighted room reflected behind me. I saw Billy lean forward, quickly looking up to see if my back was turned, stretch his taut neck across the red-checked table and mouth "I'm sorry." Then he grabbed Nigel's chin and pulled him forward, kissing him firmly, openly on the mouth.

Nigel stiffened and turned away. He hunched his shoulders and hissed at Billy. *"What the hell are you doing?"* Billy rocked back on his heels and began to laugh. Neither of them seemed to find it odd that I didn't turn around to witness this sudden change in atmosphere. They were too absorbed in the stormy air between them.

I angled the bottle of rum back into Nigel's drink and poured him a second shot; then, although I had promised myself I wouldn't drink that night, I tilted my head, my open mouth the most willing of receptacles, and poured cognac down my throat.

When I get home from Katz's corner deli, my father is in his office. Around the side of our house I can see several cars parked on the street; he must be in the middle of office hours even though today is Wednesday, normally his day off.

A mother wheeling a double stroller walks down the side path toward her car. I smile at her, and she looks at me oddly. Suddenly I remember that I am not really dressed to be out-doors. I had forgotten all about my attire. She glances at me again and walks faster. Dressed in my terry-cloth robe and fuzzy slippers, my hair disheveled, my face swollen from crying, I must look like I belong in the doctor's office, not outside on the front lawn.

I see my father's nurse, Mrs. Queely, peering at me from the office window, her efficient hand parting the drapes. I know I should go inside—the office, the house—it doesn't matter where. I know I shouldn't be standing here on the lawn, in full sight of passing cars and my father's patients, but I can't move.

A moment or two passes. I am as motionless as a papier-mâché Christmas statue on an expanse of grass. My father opens his office door.

"Jo?" he calls to me through the screen. "Joanna?"

I look up at him. Behind the screen mesh of the door he is a shadow; divided up by an accumulation of thousands of tiny squares.

I am silent. I just watch him as he begins to dissolve. The squares lift and sway like columns of dust. Shadow and door become indistinguishable. The lawn heaves as if it were a green blanket being aired in the wind. I watch it all as if it is happening on a stage and I am sitting in the audience, removed and intent, hands folded comfortably in my lap. I watch even as I feel my knees buckle, and for a moment the blue of Georgia's earliest paintings, the spattered white of the winter sky swirls over me before everything fades to black.

"Josie," I hear my father's voice gently in my ear, "you fainted, sweetheart," he says in a murmur at once worried and professional.

"Come on, open your eyes. Open up."

There is a stinging smell in my nostrils which makes me snort and shake my head.

Before I open my eyes I feel the hard leather of one of my father's examining room tables beneath me. My head rests on something soft, perhaps a pillow from the office couch.

I wince in the fluorescent glare of the examining room. We are alone, my father and I. We are surrounded by the tools of his profession: the little rubber hammer which tests reflexes, tongue depressors in plastic wrappings, several stethoscopes coiled together like mating snakes.

He strokes my forehead with his hand. My hair is clinging to my scalp. I must have broken into a sweat when I fainted. I've never fainted before.

"Are you all right?" he asks.

I turn away and face an eye chart which I can read from the top all the way to the tiny letters at the bottom. I inherited many traits from my parents; twenty-twenty vision is one of them.

"Josie," he pleads, "why are you like this? I don't understand."

I read the top line of the chart out loud.

"A. F. D. C. B."

"What's the matter with you?"

"W. M. L. E. R," I continue with the next line.

"Joanna!"

"Z. U. P. Q. G." The letters are as small as bugs.

He picks me up under my armpits and sits me on the edge of the table, holding my shoulders.

"Look at me."

There is a lesson I will learn some day, long from now. It has to do with the look on a man's face when he has just made love. You can tell when you watch men walk down the street. Sit on a Fifth Avenue bench and observe them, the armies of men, newspapers tucked under rain-coated arms, and if you watch carefully it becomes obvious in the slack of their jaws, the looseness with which their legs swing from their hips. It is the study of character, something to which I will devote much of my future life.

Today, sitting on the cold examining table and looking into my father's eyes, the eyes which so recently traveled up and down Lila Overmeyer's lush body, which closed as his lips moved down her neck, low, lower, I see a certain hard comfort, a door which was open and is now shut.

"Josie, talk to me," he pleads.

Finally I meet his eyes.

"I saw you."

"What do you mean?"

"I saw you today."

"Saw me . . . What are you saying?"

"With Mrs. Overmeyer."

"Oh God. Oh, Josie," he says. He runs a hand over his face harshly, violently. He rubs his eyes, and when he looks at me again, they are red.

He opens his palms in my direction, a plea, an offering.

"What can I do?" he asks.

I shake my head wordlessly, my eyes on the chart.

"E. W. G. O. Q," I whisper.

The black letters dance before me, rearrange themselves into words. They tell me that when my mother left I thought life had changed, but I hadn't been able to foresee the larger shifts which were to follow like a house of cards falling one on top of the other, or the aftershocks of an earthquake. My mother left, the Overmeyers moved across the street, now Lila and my father are falling in love.

I beg the chart for answers. I ask what else will shift in the wake of Georgia's departure, what other calamities will befall. The third line of the eye chart rearranges the five letters until I can read them in a straight line. *Billy,* it spells, *Billy,* and I know this plan has been triggered like a mutant gene flowing through the generations. It is the fate of my family to reach out —to let go of handlebars, of frail winter branches—and in doing so we lose our balance. Loving is dangerous, but we are a stubborn lot. We create attachments so fierce they can kill us. We search for the one most impossible for reasons of character, temperament or fate. My father and Georgia. Georgia and Vishna. Now, my father and Lila.

And what of me?

I ask the eye chart. *Billy,* it answers. The name drifts before my eyes, black letters weaving against white.

VI.

I know Nigel is still working behind the bar at Pacific Rim. I have called a few times and hung up on hearing him answer the phone. "Pacific Rim, can I help you?" he asks in a tone designed to convey just the opposite. The gruff Britishness of his voice would put off a caller asking for help of any kind. I imagine his hands curved around an icy beer bottle as he places it on the polished mahogany of the bar and looks its recipient in the eye; "Three quid," he'd say.

I wonder where he's living. He can't afford the steep rents charged these days for Manhattan studio apartments the size of closets. He could barely afford to pay his share of our rent-controlled Hell's Kitchen studio. Perhaps he has moved to one of the other boroughs, or Staten Island, though I can't quite imagine it. I can't see Nigel riding the subway into Manhattan every afternoon on his way to work at Pacific Rim. For all his snubbing of the upper-middle-class barflies he serves, Nigel could not imagine himself part of the masses, one of the pale, moon-faced denizens of the underground, newspapers tucked under arms, shoes black and beady like the thousands of cockroaches swarming beneath the city, pouring up through the grates near Time Square and Bloomingdale's, infestations behind refrigerators and sink pipes.

No, he has not moved far.

Still, where does he go at the end of his nightly shift? I know he knocks back a few before he goes anywhere. I used to join him in this ritual, one of the few givens of tending bar. We never went home sober. Watching investment bankers with their thick wrists, blue-white cuffs pushed back and weighty gold watches rap on the bar and order drink after straight drink—it did something to us, the sheer predictability of it. These men and women were the pillars of society, the people who made things tick. In the backs of taxis, we sometimes heard reports on the radio about the Dow Jones Average, and it was in another language, the language of up and down, of stock prices rising and falling. Things were "bullish" or "bearish." We had no idea what any of this meant, nor did we care, but it blistered our egos to see people younger than ourselves, just out of college, with their gold and platinum credit cards and their brash manners which came from four years in Ivy League hothouses, dining in private clubs where they were waited on by black men old enough to be their grandfathers.

"Let's open the Johnnie," he'd say, reaching for the large-size bottle of Johnnie Walker Black. Nigel always grabbed the largest, the strongest, the top-of-the-line. He'd place as many shot glasses on the bar as there were staff members left in the restaurant. Then six or seven of us would sit around the bar at two in the morning while the dishwashers finished their shifts, and we'd pitch bottle caps at the mice darting between the tables searching for bread crumbs. During dinner hours the mice hid, but became bold after the customers went home.

This is a fact few people know about New York, or want to know. It doesn't matter where you are. Lutèce has them. La Grenouille has them. I've seen them on Madison Avenue in the wee hours, and I've seen them near Wollman Rink in Central Park. The city has an entire small, furry underground army, very egalitarian in choosing their haunts. Hell's Kitchen, Sutton Place, the wooden floor of Pacific Rim.

When you've been to the beach for the day, the sound of waves crashing often remains in your ears for hours. It is the same with the sound of a restaurant. When I worked at Pacific Rim, all night in my dreams I would hear knives and forks scraping against plates, tiny claws against floorboards.

Success has bought me silence. I no longer hear the sound of glasses clinking, bells ringing, dishes clattering on metal sinks. When I turn over in the middle of the night, I hear only the barren hum of the air conditioner. I don't think my own thoughts; the jumbled words of playwrights and screenwriters rove through my head, and I feel a cool absence; what is missing lies flat, invisible against the soft white cotton sheets that Nigel left behind.

I stopped drinking eighty-seven days ago. The sickly sweet possibility of a blackout no longer tempts me at the end of the day. Oblivion no longer lures me in the shape of a bottle or a tall wintry glass. I am no longer able to choose at what point my consciousness ends and the hot trail of alcohol begins, poured delicately at first, wetting my lips, then flowing down my throat, through my esophagus, into my bloodstream.

Billy has been in a coma for over six months. Even though his eyes are open, the doctors describe his physical condition as "obtunded" (to make less intense; dull, deadened).

Nigel has been gone seven weeks. Georgia has retreated to

the Umbrian mountains, where she no longer answers her phone, where she makes paper airplanes of her correspondence and sends unread legal documents, letters and potential contracts, like homing pigeons, out the high tower windows of the rectory. Perhaps she imagines herself as Rapunzel. She will grow her hair until it reaches the ground, and she will speak only to the first person who climbs his way up this gray ladder, into her self-imposed quarantine.

I am the only one left. The days have lapsed into a peculiar monotony. When I rise in the late morning, I am still jolted by the discovery that Nigel is not with me. His absence has taken on a shape which stalks the apartment like a demon, a long-dead ancestor claiming his rightful space. I see him swirling in the steam when my teakettle boils, I hear him in the fluttering of pigeons on my windowsill.

In the afternoons I have taken to walking the streets of New York. I pull on leggings, a sweatshirt, sneakers and a baseball cap, and head out the front door into the teeming traffic of West Forty-sixth Street. On Tenth Avenue, if I turn left and walk the thirty blocks downtown to Chelsea, I pass stores selling colorful muscle-tees, thick cotton socks, jeans which are more expensive because they are already torn and faded, horn-rimmed glasses with plain lenses for those who have perfect vision but want to look cultured.

If I continue past Chelsea into the West Village, I pass windows full of black leather and other exotica: penis key chains, small circles of elasticized leather "cock rings." I see men sitting side by side on the benches near Sheridan Square, princely bearded men who look like soap opera uncles, young compactly muscled men with three earrings and multiple tattoos.

At night, in this part of town, there are plenty of places for those who are drawn romantically toward members of the same sex. I see women flock together at the quiet entrances of bars with no names, men walk boldly alone or in pairs into cafés where they will dance together, put their arms around each other, kiss against the walls. AIDS has decreased the private and increased the public. Perhaps the only gift of Billy's condition is that he has escaped this strange choleric time when young people read the obituaries to see which of their friends has succumbed to "complications arising from pneumonia," or "carcinoma," or sometimes it is named, AIDS itself. The acronym jumps from the newsprint under names too young to be famous, names attached to ages such as twenty-eight and thirty-nine.

Sometimes I head in the opposite direction. I walk east to Madison Avenue, then uptown, past midtown office buildings and people with purpose, past hotel awnings and shops full of a different kind of leather, soft supple clothing purchased by tourists on credit card binges, or the very rich. There are nannies here, pushing blue British baby strollers, women in designer suits whose necks are heavy with ropes of pearls, jewel-encrusted buttons lining their jackets like medals won in war. Even the homeless in this part of town, holding empty coffee cups jangling with a few loose coins, do not ask for something to eat: *Please, I'm trying to send my kid to college,* they'll say, or *You should have seen what I was like before the Wall Street crash of eighty-seven.*

Billy's office was in this neighborhood, on the first floor of a brownstone between Fifth and Madison. One afternoon I walked by and saw that the bronze plaque had been replaced with another name, another Ph.D. I wanted to press the buzzer and have the door click open; then walk inside, lie on the couch, close my eyes and pretend I was talking to Billy. I wanted to tell him all the things I had never told him when he could hear me. And then, in his professional capacity as a psychoanalyst, I wanted him to explain the psychological implications of unrequited love.

$\mathcal{W}$e are fifteen years old and there are almost no virgins left. Even Miranda Posner, who was once the prettiest girl in the school and now has pimples and twenty extra pounds, was found last week in her parents' bedroom with Rick MacIlwain, captain of the lacrosse team. Her mother walked in and caught them stark naked, Rick's pale behind mooning her from the creased surface of her new mauve chenille bedspread. Miranda has been grounded, rumor has it, for life.

I am still a virgin, and Billy is too. We have done every other illicit thing available to us in Morristown, New Jersey, in 1975. We have hidden quart-sized bottles of beer behind bushes on our way to parties, we have rolled our own joints, expertly licking the sweet gum on the thin edges of rolling paper, twirling them deftly between our thumbs and forefingers. We have cut school and sneaked into the city, our destination the brightly lit shops on Forty-second Street which sell fake identification cards; four dollars apiece has bought us adulthood.

I haven't lost my virginity because there's no one I want to lose it with. I've had lots of boyfriends, but none have lasted more than three consecutive weeks. The most recent one, Chris Boswell, got to third base. I don't know why I let him touch me. It seemed like a good idea at the time. We were in the basement of Tipton Academy during a dance, and I could hear the sounds of the Jersey Jukes, a group of teachers who had gotten together with the supremely misguided notion of forming a band. They wore powder-blue polyester suits, carried screeching microphones and sang the best of the Eagles and America.

Chris and I had successfully evaded the chaperones. I went first, saying I had to go to the bathroom; Chris followed a few minutes later. We met in the boiler room, the only place in the basement which hadn't been discovered by the whole sophomore class. As I walked toward the red sign of that area, I heard low rustlings and moans coming from the closed doors of the janitor's closet and the gym equipment room.

I know Billy watched me as I left the dance. He knew where I was going, what I was doing, and with whom. I could feel his eyes against my back as I walked through the double doors of the gym; I imagined he could hear the squish of my foam-soled shoes as I made my way down the corridor and, after looking sneakily left and right, darted down the staircase.

Chris and I didn't waste time. He kissed me twice. His lips were dry and chapped. He squeezed my breasts mechanically, nonchalantly like they were fruit left on a windowsill, then—the whole point being the discovery of how far you could go—he pushed his hand into the waistline of my jeans. His fingers fluttered over my stomach for a moment, waiting to see if I was going to slap them away. There was just enough room to wiggle down until he reached the elastic of my panties; he plunged his hand into the white cotton with eyes closed tight the way a diver's eyes might be as he arcs off a cliff into uncharted waters. His fingers made a sound, *squish, squish* as he wriggled around for a while. I spent most of my time wondering what this boy I barely knew was doing with his hand down my pants.

When I returned to the gym, I thought I smelled of sex. In the dark, the room seemed more cavernous than usual, with the sound of the Jersey Jukes screeching from the microphones, wormy shapes of boys and girls attempting to dance, and the sticky sweet smell of spilled Coca-Cola spiked with rum.

Billy was alone in the bleachers. I sat next to him without

saying a word. He kept cracking his knuckles, pulling on his fingers, the snappy, bone-crunching sound nearly drowned out by the music. He was wearing a hat, a Clint Eastwood tough guy kind of hat tilted low over his eyes.

"Don't sell yourself so short, Joanna," he said quietly.

The words stung.

"What do you mean?" I asked, knowing full well what he meant.

"Chris Boswell, Adam Shaw, John Freedman." Billy listed my three most recent boyfriends.

"What about them?"

Billy tilted his hat up and gazed at me directly. As his eyes met mine I became aware of the complicity between us, the unsaid words and unnamed gestures of the past two years. My cheeks burned at the inequity; he had known all along that I wanted him. He knew that given the choice of any boy in Morristown, New Jersey, given the option of being in the boiler room with a hand down my pants, finding its way around like a car lost in a foreign country, I would have chosen him, Billy Overmeyer. The one with whom there would be simply, utterly, no possibility.

We are gathered here in the study adjacent to my father's office. We have come to witness the wedding of Lila Overmeyer and Bernard Hirsch. There are six of us in attendance: my father and Lila, Johnny and Billy Overmeyer, the rabbi and myself.

It is June. Yellow jackets swarm the rosebushes outside the window, occasionally knocking into the glass. I can hear their muted buzzing in the silence of this room. My father and Lila have planned their wedding around the school year, hoping that the disruption will be easier on Billy and me after we've finished with exams. The wedding also coincides with the end of Johnny Overmeyer's first year at Fairleigh Dickinson.

My father and Lila believe the world can be kept manageable according to schedules and dates. They don't seem to realize that their relationship has been the talk of Morristown, almost since the day my father crossed the Overmeyers' lawn for the first time, three years ago.

This is going to be the new arrangement: Johnny, who is busy doing his best to flunk out of college, will live with Lloyd Overmeyer in a condominium in Scotch Plains. Billy and I will live with Lila and my father in the house on Exeter Road. Billy's new room, which used to be the spare bedroom, will be across the hall from mine. He's already moved in. Heaps of dirty laundry piled in a corner, a windowsill full of home-grown pot, an unmade bed with grainy sheets, a few posters, curled around the edges, stuck up on the walls with thumbtacks: Thurman Munson, Freud, Al Pacino in *Serpico*.

The rabbi clears his throat. He presses a button on a cassette player next to the Bible, a glass wrapped in a cloth napkin and a silver goblet of wine. The tape begins, the opening bars of Handel's *Water Music*. Lila enters the study holding a small bouquet of roses picked from the rosebush outside. She is wearing a white silk suit and her hair has been sprayed into a chignon. Billy and Johnny flank her as she walks toward my father, who is standing next to the rabbi, a serene smile on his lips, eyes brimming. Billy looks like a grown man today, with his slicked-back hair and brand-new suit, silk tie, pocket handkerchief tucked neatly into folds.

Johnny, Billy, Lila, my father and I gather around the rabbi. He looks at all of us in the half-moon semicircle surrounding him and beams a smile at us as he clears his throat once more.

"You are about to become a newly created family," he says. "Every family is a gift from God, a gift of hope . . ."

He continues to talk as I watch Billy standing on the opposite side of his mother, directly across from me. He is focused on the rabbi, intent, his blue eyes unwavering. His face has matured over the past three years. He has lost most of his little boy delicacy, and in its place has acquired a real handsomeness. He has cheekbones now, a strong jaw, Lila's full lips.

I cannot control my thoughts. It is my father's wedding to Lila Overmeyer, the rabbi is droning on and I am thinking of Billy's chin, Billy's lips, of tracing my tongue around his mouth slowly, running my hands down the new muscles in his back.

He looks away from the rabbi, and over at me.

"A family is a sacred thing . . ." the rabbi continues.

We hold each other with our eyes.

". . . and in the same way we say, 'what God has brought together, let no man put asunder,' I would include in that prayer the fervent hopes that this brand-new family will grow and flourish through the years, as husband and wife, father and son, mother and daughter, brother and sister . . ."

Brother and sister.

I close my eyes, and in my mind I see Billy, naked from the waist up, wearing a pair of blue jeans partly unzipped. He walks down the hallway to the bathroom where I am taking a shower. He pretends he doesn't know I'm in the shower. I pretend I don't know he knows. He pulls the curtain aside and stares at me. My body has fully matured, and is the lushest it will ever be. He reaches out a hand . . .

"Will you all please join hands," the rabbi says.

The six of us connect, cold fingers on this June day.

"I want you all to participate in the marriage vows. If you'll repeat after me . . ."

Brother and sister.

"I, Lila, take you, Bernard, to be my lawfully wedded husband . . ."

I open my eyes. Billy is still staring at me.

$\mathcal{I}$ am attending an opening at the Ward Knowlton Gallery for a very distinguished sculptor. It is winter, the beginning of a new decade; the ensuing ten years will some day be referred to with either disgust or nostalgia as the Age of Greed.

Georgia's prices have sky-rocketed. As I walk around the spare white rooms of the gallery, I think of Picasso and the squiggles he used to throw on random sheets of paper as he approached his death, when he knew the power of his pencil, even on a restaurant napkin.

Georgia is approaching middle age and I am approaching my twenties. This year, time has stood still for us, and like the slow mechanical crawl up a roller coaster, the few seconds which elapse on the top of the curve before the screeching plunge, this is the year that men will look at Georgia and me the same way: we are objects of desire. A few years ago, I was too young to know the glances which ride up and down my body like sneaky hands on a crowded subway. And a few years from now, Georgia might be too old.

She is making her entrance, arriving just as the crowd swells, with elevators full of people who have been sent the simple gray card enclosed in the announcement of the show, a card which admits them to this opening, although there is no one at the elevator door to check invitations as dozens of people flow in.

In her twenties and thirties, Georgia was too busy for more than a glance in the mirror. She was absorbed by images other than herself. Now, in this showing of self-portraits, we see the artist's fascination with the planes of her own face, as if only just realizing that in a creative journey, it is essential, no matter how far one runs, to examine that which is closest to home.

I am in a whitewashed room surrounded by images of my mother, the self-portrait artist, the con artist, the disappearing artist. Here, a piece entitled *The Long View*, a series of frames within gilded, ornate frames, each containing a part of an eye: a pupil, elliptical egg white, a kaleidoscopic blue iris, fake eyelashes, twisted and discarded, all found where Georgia still finds much of her material, the trash can. These frames are large enough to walk through. They are set up as an installation, so it is hard to tell whether the viewer is watching or being watched. There, a collage of snapshots, all of different parts of the artist. They are cheap photos, probably shot with an Instamatic, jumbled together in pastiche, an elbow next to an eye, a breast in place of a mouth, the arch of a foot where the ear should be. This piece is entitled *Self-Portrait: Schizophrenia*.

As I walk from corner to corner, I feel my mother pressing in on me—eyes, elbows, feet, lips—in a senseless jumble until I begin to think the very air I'm breathing is being supplied by Georgia, that I am living for the moment in a world completely of her making.

She is in front of me.

"Josie, darling!" she cries, extending her arms in a clatter of bangles.

I go toward her. I prefer watching Georgia from across a room, when the space between us allows me to consider her as a being separate from myself, remote and distant. Up close, she frightens me. The world thinks Georgia is arrogant but I know better. When I study Georgia closely I see myself.

She holds me by the shoulders, and presses her cheek first to one side of my face, then the other.

"My beauty," she says, "my sweet daughter."

She looks me up and down. I am wearing black leather jeans and a white silk blouse which was once hers. My hair is shoulder-length, pulled back with a fat red bow she bought me from the hair ornament store beneath her loft. I am wearing red lipstick. I look older than I am.

"Come, let's get us a drink," Georgia says, pulling me through the crowd in the direction of the bar.

"Two white wines," she says. It would never occur to Georgia that I am under the drinking age in the state of New York.

When she picks up her glass the ice rattles, and I see her hands shaking.

"Are you all right?" I ask.

Behind her I see another self-portrait, this one created from shards of glass—garbage glass, the amber remnants of beer bottles, cracked mirrors, reflecting sunglass lenses—all formed in the shape of a skull. It is surrounded by a clear lucite box, a safety precaution, I presume. The pieces are organized in a way that viewers cannot help but see fragments of their own shattered faces. Under the piece is a title: *Self-Portrait: Catch Me If You Can.*

"Are you all right?" I repeat.

Georgia is dressed in black. She wears an armload of ivory bracelets and an African pendant set against a black bodysuit, black trousers, black boots. Her hair is pulled back with no less than five ribbons, black velvet ribbons from the same ornament store. Her eyes are rimmed with kohl, and when I look closely I see she is wearing false eyelashes, top and bottom.

"I'm divine," she says brightly.

She raises the glass to her lips and downs her white wine in a few long swallows. She taps on the bar, asks for another, then repeats the gesture. She holds out her glass to be refilled a third time. The bartender raises his eyebrows at me, as if to ask my permission. What does he think I am? An adult? I watch, paralyzed, as the wine gurgles from his bottle into Georgia's lipstick-rimmed plastic cup. My mother, the cynosure of this room, the eye of the hurricane, is barely able to stand up straight at her own opening, and I am powerless over her, my meager understanding of this moment broken into distorted fragments and reflected back at me. My mother is supposed to be here, but I have lost her—and there is nothing, absolutely nothing I can do about it.

VII.

$\mathcal{E}$l Raton's three-month run of *Speak, Memory* has now been extended indefinitely. Last week there was a write-up in *New York Woman,* and *Vogue* is planning a feature story for its April issue. The back of the theatre continues to be filled nightly with standing-room-only crowds, men and women who have not stood for a performance since high school, the women's alligator purses set gingerly beside them, the men's wallets stored safely in inside jacket pockets before heading downtown.

Outside the theatre, on a street known as one of the city's busiest crack blocks, radio cars and an occasional limousine wait for those brave souls who have ventured below Fifty-seventh Street and are afraid of searching for a cab when it's over. I don't blame them. Sometimes when I leave El Raton late at night, I walk several deserted blocks before I see the white light of a taxi moving toward me. When I am alone, the longest key on my key ring pushed between my second and third finger like a corrugated knife, I curse Nigel. I have been advised, if mugged, to whip my key upward, straight into my attacker's eye. If I saw Nigel skulking by, I'd want to blind him as well. He must have known, as he quickly packed his bags, that leaving me silently would be the cruelest gesture, the ultimate revenge.

I could have accepted broken dishes, slammed doors, voices shrieking in the night. I would have preferred violence to this silence, the unbearable quiet which fills the apartment; I have known since childhood that silence has a sound, a high-pitched hum, and I will go to any lengths to avoid it.

I perform six times a week: Tuesday through Saturday nights, and a Sunday matinee. From Sunday at five o'clock when the applause dies down until Tuesday night at ten past eight when the curtain rises, my primary purpose in life is to avoid a nervous breakdown. Silence, the humming silence which fills my studio, is not drowned out by fitful sleep, television or the incessant sirens and shouts which seep beneath my window.

It has now been one hundred and twenty-two days since my last drink. Alcohol once helped me through this silence, this absence. A few drinks after the show would warm me as I strode the empty streets until I found a cab to take me home. In the theatre's Green Room, in the small refrigerator littered with half-finished sandwiches, cans of V-8 juice, plastic deli containers of tuna salad, I used to place a paper bag on the back shelf, my name marked with red ink on masking tape. The bag was filled with airplane sample bottles of liquor: small brown bottles of Tia Maria, blue and white Sambuca Romana, clear silvery Beefeater Gin. I treated that rumpled paper bag the way a child might handle her mother's jewelry box filled with the most ravishing, intricate possibilities. Every time I opened it, I knew I possessed the greatest power in the world: the power to change my state of mind in a few short swallows.

Nigel was my drinking buddy. Once he left it was impossible to ignore the thirst which accompanied my climb upstairs to the Hell's Kitchen studio, thoughts centered on the clear, syrupy vodka which waited inside my freezer door. When Nigel and I were together it was easy not to pay attention to my drinking; it seemed since both of us had the same craving, we must be normal. I imagined most couples poured themselves drinks before removing their overcoats when they arrived home at the end of the evening; most couples had bars stocked with bottles of neon green Chartreuse, 120 proof, flammable as gasoline.

Billy worried about me during the Nigel years.

"You should really do something about the drinking," he'd say, "your tolerance level is one of the signs of alcoholism."

I didn't pay attention to Billy's prophecies. I thought he was experimenting with any disease he studied, running it by me to see if it would fit. I had heard him talk about manic depression, panic disorders, borderline personalities. I figured alcoholism was no different.

"Really, Josie. I'm serious. After all, look at Nigel," he'd say.

"What about Nigel?"

Billy would just watch me patiently, with the same warm, tolerant expression, I imagine, that he used on his patients.

"There's a reason both of you are tending bar," he'd answer. "It takes one to know one."

I wish Billy could see me now, after one hundred and twenty-two days. And though Nigel has been gone all this time, I still hold out the hope that I will open the studio door and the air will be acrid with the lingering smell of Gitanes, the only brand of cigarettes he ever smoked. Nigel never cared that he was broke and Gitanes cost twice as much as other brands. As if he had never left, he would be where he always sits, sprawled in the wing chair he found abandoned on the sidewalk a few years back, reading Calvino in the original Italian.

"Hello, lovey," he'd say with open arms, his book falling aside as I flopped onto his comfortable lap. We would kiss for a while, his hands covering my whole face, his mouth exploring mine.

"Calvino is such a fucking genius," he'd say when we broke apart, "I'm thinking of staging a few of his one-acts for the Summerfest in New Paltz."

I'd attempt to nod and smile, fearful of yet another production which would never see the light of day.

"I got that guest spot on 'Magnum, P.I.,'" I'd tell him.

"Josie, *no*," he'd say. "That script was the worst piece of shit I've ever seen! You're a classically trained actress!"

He would light another Gitane, offer it to me, the filter pinched tightly between thumb and forefinger. He would wink at me once, smiling wistfully, as if to let me know that he only had my best interests at heart.

Will Nigel spend the rest of his years licking his wounds and pouring drinks down other people's throats as well as his own? Will he ever forget the words *plodding, hackneyed,* on the front page of the *New York Times Weekend* section, insult added to injury by the years it took him to receive that first review, and by the words *enchanting debut* in the very same paragraph, alluding to the woman who was good enough to fuck every night, but not necessarily good enough, in his opinion, to be making her debut in a play he was directing? Poor Nigel. They should test people on the verge of entering any creative field for the percentage of steel in their spines.

And what about my fate? Is fame hereditary, did my

mother pass on her propensity for the limelight? Will I some day stand in the center of a room with forty dollars' worth of makeup on my face, knuckles white around a wine-filled plastic glass?

I am not the one who should be succeeding. There is only one of us who did not spend life running away from his own face in the mirror; Billy, who did hard time, the solitary trek uptown five mornings a week, the fifty-minute hours spent on his back, staring at the blank ceiling.

What I would give to have crouched behind Billy's analyst's couch, to have hidden under the chrome legs of the brown leather Eames chair. Often I tried to imagine what Billy talked about. He was assigned an analyst when he entered the training program at the institute; he was not given his choice, and I wonder if he would have chosen the same analyst, given the opportunity.

"What does he look like?" I asked Billy once.

"Who?"

"The mysterious Doctor X," I answered. Billy never told us his doctor's name.

"Short. Slim. Dark hair and blue eyes. Glasses," he answered elliptically.

Once when Billy was visiting on a Saturday night, he and Nigel were out buying wine and I stole a look at his address book. In all the years I lived with Nigel I never rifled through his belongings, but Billy was a puzzle whose clues and answers were essential to me. He had a thin black book which would fit into a jacket pocket. In the front there were listings of New York restaurants, museums, hospitals, libraries. In the middle there was an inch of space allotted for each day of the year, and in the back there was room for addresses.

I looked through the black book quickly, careful not to leave any signs. I wondered guiltily if Billy had a method of knowing whether anyone had tampered with his book: a strand of hair between the first and second weeks of May, a turned-down corner, a blade of grass wedged into the back. I had pulled the datebook out of his jacket, which was flung across our bed. I imagined Billy and Nigel bursting through the door, catching me red-handed. "Oh, this just fell out," I would say, holding it flat, a delicate parcel. "Here," I would offer it with an outstretched hand, "I think this is yours."

In the back section there was an address of a doctor on Central Park West: *Maria Josephson*. Then I realized, in all the times Billy mentioned his analyst, he had never used a proper pronoun. His analyst was a woman.

It did not take long for me to arrange for an appointment with Maria Josephson, Ph.D. I used the name "Nina Leeds," a character from Eugene O'Neill's *Strange Interlude*. When Dr. Josephson wanted to know who referred me, I told her I had asked the institute for the most senior analyst on their faculty.

That Monday I found myself on the Upper West Side. I wandered down the shady side of Central Park West, cobblestones beneath my feet, horses clopping just on the other side of the stone wall; I slid slowly past old women sitting on benches, kerchiefed, stooped-over witnesses. On the other side of the avenue, doormen stood behind thick glass doors fitted with dull yellowed brass. Whistles blew for taxicabs. A homeless man shook a paper cup which rattled with one loose coin. I sat on a bench opposite 275 Central Park West. I focused on the office just to the left of the elaborate front doors; I was interested in the smaller, more discreet entrance, the plaque with the name Maria Josephson, Ph.D., engraved in brass so that a blind patient in need of psychiatric help might be able to lift his fingers and feel the name, the impressive letters of the degree, and ring the buzzer with assurance.

I was two hours early. Anticipating this, I had packed a lunch in my knapsack of an apple and a slice of cheese. I often had hours to kill during the earlier years of El Raton. This was my worst kind of day, with no auditions scheduled, no rehearsals, nowhere to be. Usually I wandered the streets of New York accompanied only by the constant prattle of my own mind, but this day I had a purpose. As people entered and exited the office at a few minutes before the hour, I studied them. Was there a thread of commonality between the patients of Maria Josephson, Ph.D.? Was there a synchronicity which came from lying their heads on the same pillow, staring at the same ceiling? Did she have a method, a kind of cognitive restructuring which would cause them all to think similar thoughts, like transparencies laid one on top of the other, as they roamed the city streets, good analysand soldiers?

I wanted to rest where Billy had spent hours and hours; I would be safe in the sanctum where he spent his mornings; countless times I had imagined the quality of sunlight drifting through the closed venetian blinds, the subtle click of an answering machine as it received calls during the fifty-minute hour, the furious scratching of the doctor's pen against a yellow legal pad.

It was almost time for my session. I packed my belongings, threw the apple core, paper bag and foil wrapper into a garbage can on the corner of Eighty-seventh and Central Park West. I heard roller-skaters whiz by inside the park, wheels rumbling. A car alarm sounded in the distance, a single startled wail.

I rang the buzzer for Maria Josephson. The locked outer door clicked open and a young man wearing a baseball cap strolled out without meeting my eyes. He walked lightly on the balls of his feet, weightless, as if temporarily relieved of a burden which would doubtless return. I knew the feeling: it was what I sought nightly in the proper mix of tequila and Triple Sec, a splash of lime.

As I walked into the waiting room, I had the sense of being

on a casting call for a part I wanted badly; I craved her attention. Flipping through month-old copies of *The New Yorker,* a
dog-eared issue of *Modern Maturity,* I felt my heart pounding,
adrenaline pumping the way it does before an audition. I had
pulled my hair back in a twist and was wearing glasses as part
of my "Nina Leeds" disguise, just in case Billy had ever shown
Dr. Josephson my photograph, on the off chance that she
would make a connection between her analyst-in-training and
the young woman seated before her.

The door opened soundlessly, and I heard her call my
name.

"Nina?" she asked softly. "Please come in."

I looked up and saw a small woman with dark hair, ornate
Indian earrings dangling, wire-rimmed glasses magnifying her
blue eyes. This was the keeper of Billy's secrets, his unruffled
confidante. As I walked into her office I wanted to wander
through this inner sanctum, run a finger over the dust settled
near the Freud first editions in her bookcase, touch the ornate
carved feet of the Victorian couch.

She settled into her Eames chair. On the floor next to her,
precariously wedged in the thick ply of the oriental rug, was a
half-empty bottle of Evian water. On the shelves which lined
one wall of the office, I noticed children's toys, some colorful
rubber balls and boxed games. Original letters were hung on
the walls, the correspondence between Freud and Jung side by
side with vintage photographs of the legends framed beneath
protective glass.

Dr. Josephson reached for a pad on the table next to her,
then thought better of it, folding her hands in her lap.

"How can I help?" she asked the usual question.

I stared at my feet.

"I'm not sure," I said faintly. "I don't know why I'm here."

She allowed silence to settle between us. The only sound
in the room was the distant bleating of horns muted by sound-

proof glass, the silvery chime of earrings as she ran a hand through her long dark hair.

I focused on the Victorian couch. A Moroccan tapestry was folded where a patient might lay his head, draped in order to spare the rose-colored velvet from the sweaty drippings of the unconscious. Billy's head had rested on that tapestry. I squinted, imagining him there.

"What are you thinking?" the doctor asked.

I was silent, the whole script vanished from my mind, an actor's worst nightmare.

"Nina?"

I gazed at her vacantly.

"That's not my name," I said.

She blinked, cleared her throat.

"What do you mean?"

"Nina Leeds is a character from *Strange Interlude.*"

This was not what I had planned to say. I intended to be perfectly controlled in this hour of clandestine glory, my secret invasion of Billy's world. But entering this room forced me to recognize that Billy led a life entirely separate from my own, private and mysterious, a life to which I would never be admitted. It was unthinkable that these walls heard his words and would not give them back to me.

"The O'Neill?" Dr. Josephson asked.

"Sorry?"

"*Strange Interlude.*"

"Yes."

I stared at the couch again and suddenly it became a claw-foot tub and I remembered sitting on the smooth curved edge —the year our parents got married—washing Billy's hair after he'd sprained his arm and couldn't do it himself. The suds trickled down his neck and into the deep hollow of his spine, stopped only by the bathing trunks he wore. I kneaded my fingers into his skull and imagined I could shape the rigid bone into a proper vessel for my desires. I pushed my thumbs into his backbone, slid them low until I reached the elastic around his waist, hovering there, slipping one soapy finger beneath the wet cotton, then another, until I caught his reflection in the bathroom mirror; his eyes were squeezed together, forehead knotted as if in prayer. *Don't do this*, he seemed to be saying. *Please, God, don't do this.*

"I'm sorry," I murmured to Dr. Josephson.

I grabbed my knapsack, pushed myself out of the chair and dashed to the door, praying it would be unlocked. I turned the knob, swung the door open and stood still for a moment facing the wall, my back to her.

"I'm sorry. This was a terrible mistake."

"Wait. Who are you?" Her voice rang out.

I turned to Maria Josephson. Tears spilled from my eyes, coursed under my fake glasses and down my cheeks.

"You can't help me," I whispered.

"Let me try."

"You can't," I repeated. "No one can."

I stumbled through her waiting room.

"Who are you?" I heard her voice behind me.

I wish I knew, I wanted to say.

𝔐y father and Lila will be in the audience tonight. They will drive into the city, safe suburban voyagers in their Acura Legend; I can almost see my father squinting into the setting sun as he negotiates the ramp, then turns on his parking lights in the darkness of the Lincoln Tunnel. When they head downtown on Ninth Avenue their car doors will be locked, windows sealed; Lila's bag will be stored under her seat, diamond engagement ring turned in, sharp stone against fleshy palm.

Speak, Memory has been reviewed in the local Morristown paper, along with a photograph of me in Lolita garb and the caption, *Local Talent.* The piece was written by a friend of Lila's.

When I make my entrance in tonight's performance of *Speak, Memory,* I think of my father and Lila. I am breaking the cardinal rule of theatre and seeing past the fourth wall; the audience is not allowed to exist in the actor's mind.

Billy was fascinated by this process.

"How does it work?" he asked me once.

"What do you mean?"

"The actual mechanism of it, Jo. How do you wipe your mind clean? Don't thoughts come sneaking in during a performance, thoughts about what you're going to eat for dinner, or who's sitting in the third row—"

"No," I responded simply.

"How is that possible?"

"You should understand better than most people," I said.

"Why?"

"The power of memory, Billy. Everything I'm feeling on stage comes from a corresponding place in my past. My memories live in my body, and they are released through the playwright's language, through unconscious physical gesture. My motivations are all carved out of my history."

"Sounds like therapy," he said with a smile.

. . .

I wandered the Upper West Side after leaving the office of Maria Josephson, Ph.D. I circled the blocks, feeling crippled, having no idea what to do next. Heading first to Broadway, I allowed the crowd to carry me, following the surge as if it were an undertow. I walked this way for a few blocks, past Korean markets with lavishly displayed vegetables and bunches of flowers, a photography store with a life-size cut-out of Ronald Reagan in the window. *Have your picture taken with the President!* I wandered aimlessly past gourmet shops, windows exhibiting large barrels filled with cashews and jelly beans, gummy bears and dried apricots, the Manufacturer's Hanover Trust building where I saw a poster featuring an actress friend of mine posing as a businesswoman. "Hi, Sarah," I heard myself say to the poster as several people sidled away from me on the street.

I walked east to Columbus Avenue, unable to leave the neighborhood. Getting on the subway was too much to bear—the crush of strangers—and though empty cabs drifted by me, I simply couldn't hail one. I didn't know where to go. Stopping at a pay phone to check in for messages was a mistake; there were no phone calls from my agent, no auditions to prepare for, just the vast emptiness of days which stretched, bottomless, punctuated only by bar shifts at Pacific Rim where the most excitement I could anticipate was getting my rear pinched by a drunken yuppie.

Now it was twilight, the hour I could respectably have a drink. I bought *Backstage,* just out, and meandered up the avenue, the empty tables of cafés suddenly warm and inviting. I would drink Campari and soda, circle casting calls for open Equity auditions held in churches and recital halls, announcing roles in Broadway plays which had probably all been filled.

At this moment I saw her. She was seated in the last remaining patch of sunlight at Bazzini's, drinking cappuccino. A plate of Italian biscuits was crowded on the table along with a sugar dispenser and a pile of fluttering papers. I ducked into the doorway of the deli next door. The breeze was blowing in my direction, so I could hear her ask the waitress for a glass of water. Her voice carried by the wind was low, beautifully modulated. This was the voice which soothed Billy. I could hear this voice telling him to stop punishing himself, that it is no more our fault whom we fall in love with than who falls in love with us. *Explain this to me, William,* I could hear her saying, *how is it possible for you to think all this is your fault?* I imagined her handing him a box of Kleenex as he lay on the couch, placing it on his stomach, the delicate professional offering.

I became a bit braver, standing in the shadow of the awning, watching Maria Josephson. She pulled the rubber bands off the sheaf of papers, closing her eyes protectively.

My name was in those papers.

No doubt about it.

My name, as surely as if I were a witness at a trial, or a correspondent in a divorce case. I was the demon, the fiend who haunted gentle Billy, the creature perched on his shoulder.

The sun was beginning to set, and I knew Nigel must be wondering where I was. Monday night was, for us, like a weekend night. We didn't work at Pacific Rim Mondays or Tuesdays, and usually did our drinking in near-empty restaurants where friends tended bar. Just as I began to think about calling Nigel, a series of high beeps pierced the relative quiet of the café. Maria Josephson reached into her handbag and turned off her beeper. She got up from the table, quickly grabbing her papers. She strode inside, unwittingly leaving several black cassette tape boxes on the black glass table. I retreated further into the shadows and watched as she went into the café, leaving patients' innermost thoughts encased in plastic, wound tightly around sprockets.

I walked slowly past two empty wrought-iron seats to her table, unobtrusive and languid, as if I belonged there. I wished she had left the sheaf of papers, and that I had a James Bond camera which would flash and click over the pages, recording it all on tiny spools of film. My heart pounded as I focused on the three cassette tapes. I leaned forward, looked closely. *B. Overmeyer* was penciled on the cardboard inside the container.

There are times in one's life in which the moment takes over, in which action supersedes logic, morality or consequence. One of those moments in my life occurred at that Columbus Avenue café as I came upon the tapes of Maria Josephson. It suddenly occurred to me that I had to listen to these tapes and there was nothing, absolutely nothing to stop me from slipping them in my handbag and walking quickly away from the café, faster and faster until I was running.

I did not feel guilty as I rode downtown on the subway, the cassettes safe in my bag. I was out of breath, and my only concern was that Dr. Josephson would somehow connect my mystery visit with the stolen items. I imagined her asking Billy, *What does Joanna look like?*

Maria Josephson would have a few sleepless nights. The thought did not fill me with remorse. I had spent countless nights wondering what Billy talked about each morning, eyes closed at her behest as she unraveled his mysteries. I thought I had more of a right to Billy's secrets than the small, dark-haired stranger.

Tuesday, January 27. William Overmeyer, initial visit. Assigned by the institute, currently completing dissertation. (Neurobiological Aspects of Schizophrenia.) Resistant to process. Needs for comple-

tion of doctorate, or wouldn't be here. Was concerned with my qualifications. Anxious about confidentiality. Wouldn't answer questions; stared at the floor. Concerned that I would disclose contents of the analysis to other members of the community.

Says he does not remember his dreams.

$\mathcal{I}$ lost my virginity during Easter break. The boy who assisted me in this venture, Dean Gregory, had asked me to the Senior Prom. I didn't want to go off to college still a virgin, but the real reason I chose Dean Gregory on that chilly April night was because Billy was in the next room. I suppose I unconsciously wished that if it couldn't be Billy next to me on the mattress, at least he could be under the same roof; there would be a collusion between us, a sense that my loss of innocence was a joint effort.

We were at a party at Jill Baxter's house. Her parents weren't home. Dean and I used their bedroom, sprawling on top of the orange and brown quilted bedspread, our clothes pushed up and down, jeans wrapped around legs. The bedspread had a wet spot. Mary Anne Flaherty and Jeff von Rollenhagen used the room before us.

Ask anybody to recount the loss of their virginity. Ask anybody, and see if they have a pretty story to tell. There's a reason it's called a loss.

Dean bounded out of bed, pulled up his jeans and was out the door before I knew what was happening. He flew back in a moment, wielding a small foil packet triumphantly in his hand.

"Where'd you get that?" I asked.

"One of the guys," he said.

"You're kidding."

"No," he said, pulling off my pants, "ssshh."

Billy told me later—years later—that he had heard Dean Gregory's squeaky, matter-of-fact voice rising above the Grateful Dead, asking if anyone had a rubber. Billy left the party, convinced he could hear the bedsprings creak above the lyrics to "Sugar Magnolia." He jogged all the way to Route 24 and hitched a ride home.

At the moment Dean Gregory's white speckled back arched, at the instant he pointed his way into me with some sort of atavistic knowledge, Billy was no longer in the next room. He was pushing against the April wind, racing through backyards, flailing against branches, hoping, perhaps, to blind himself to the image of his stepsister spread out behind the closed bedroom door.

I didn't bleed on Jill Baxter's parents' bedspread. I don't know whether it was my tree-climbing as a child or the frequency with which I touched myself beneath the sheets in the dark as Billy lay across the hall from my room, but not a drop marred the orange and brown pattern. I imagine that instead of being expelled, the blood of this experience was somehow intact, inside me, a second heart floating around my body, an internal reminder that even from my very first sexual encounter, I closed my eyes against the man on top of me and felt Billy's lips on my own.

I watched the Baxters' digital alarm clock. Dean's thrusts came every two and a half seconds. Precisely three minutes and it was over.

When Lila Overmeyer Hirsch drove me home late that night, my father's raincoat thrown over her nightgown, I wondered if she could smell the episode on me. I wondered if she did smell it, whether she would just assume that the scent was wafting from her own body.

Billy was waiting up. He sat at the kitchen table, pretending to read the newspaper. A nearly empty box of Ritz crackers was overturned next to a round container of cheese triangles, the kind wrapped in tinfoil covered with pictures of smiling cows. He didn't look up when we walked in. He didn't say a word until Lila left the kitchen and walked upstairs to the bedroom, where my father was sleeping.

As Lila's steps receded, Billy lit a cigarette, something we certainly were not allowed to do in the house. He was shirtless, wearing only a pair of white gym shorts and thick cotton blue-and-white striped socks; when he leaned back, cupping his head in his hands, I saw hair beneath his arms.

He looked at me. His eyes were bright, and his nose was red.

"How was it?" he asked.

"What?"

"Your sexual initiation."

"What makes you so sure I . . ."

"Oh, stop it, Joanna," he interrupted me. "Don't you think I have eyes in my head, and ears? Don't you think I know?"

"It was fine," I said to him.

He was trying to stare me down, but kept blinking.

"It was better than fine," I lied, "it was great. Stupendous."

"Good," he said flatly. "That's great."

"Great," I repeated.

"Great."

He scraped his chair back from the table.

"Well, I'm going to sleep," he said unsteadily.

I watched him walk out of the kitchen, down the narrow hall to the foyer, where I knew he would turn left and head up to his room, where he would close the door against me. And the rest of the world.

A sound came from my mouth, a word I wasn't expecting.

"Wait!"

He turned around.

"What, Josie?" He looked tired.

In what seemed like one motion, I stood and ran toward him, smacking into him so hard I am surprised we didn't topple over. I buried my head into his neck, leaning against his shoulder, which was now a strong shoulder, a seventeen-year-old man's shoulder, broad and built for this purpose. I wiped my eyes, my nose against him.

We had known each other five years.

I felt his arms slowly creep around me.

"It's okay, baby," I heard him say. "It's okay, Josie. This is the beginning of growing up."

"Then I don't think I want to grow up."

"Was it that bad?" he whispered, and some part of me knew the answer he wanted to hear.

"Yes," I said. "It was awful."

"Come on," he whispered into my hair, "come upstairs."

He held my hand and I followed him up the stairs, slightly behind him. We passed our parents' bedroom, quiet as thieves. We passed the tiny red light of the alarm system. The doors were locked, windows closed. We were all safe, tucked in for the night.

Neither of us said a word as we entered Billy's bedroom, as I sat down on the bed and he closed the door behind us. The silence crackled with the lifting of shirts, the unzipping of jeans, the pulling off of boots, the creak of the bed as we lay down together on the white sheets, our bodies pale and naked except for the white cotton underpants each of us still wore, the only restraint between us.

I was on my side, facing him. I folded my arms over my breasts, embarrassed. Gently, he placed a hand on each of my wrists, and pushed my arms down to my sides.

"Let me look at you," he whispered.

I pulled the sheet up.

He pulled it down.

"My God, you're beautiful."

I felt his eyes travel over me. I watched him as they started with my neck and wandered downward, over my clavicle, down until he was staring at my breasts, his pupils pinpoints on my nipples. He stayed there, never touching me, his lids heavy.

For a while I was self-conscious, aware only of Billy's eyes on me, unable to look at him. Of course I was familiar with the parts of his body which emerged from the sheets, his bare arms, his chest, his smooth, flat stomach. I saw blond curly hair pointing downward from his navel like an arrow, and felt something uncoil in my stomach, my panties wet, as they had not been earlier in the evening.

His scrutiny was physical to me, his eyes like the soft palms of his hands, fingertips brushing against me, thumbs against each of my nipples, deliberate, unquestioning.

"I love you," he said.

"I know."

He grasped my hand in the heat between us.

"This can never happen, Josie."

"I know that too."

"Do you know why?"

I stared at the hollow in his neck.

"There's more than one reason," I whispered, "isn't there."

"Yes."

"It's not just our parents."

"No."

"I love you, Billy," I said, squeezing his hand tighter.

"I know."

"I always will."

I turned over, my back to him, and faced the room. He

curled up behind me like a snail. My eyes were open, and I tried to steady my breathing. I looked around the room at the piles of clothing, and wanted to bury my face in them, inhale Billy's scent, draw it into my lungs where it would stay forever.

After a while, I heard him whisper.

"You asleep?"

I didn't answer.

"Josie, are you sleeping?"

I felt his hand on my waist, turning me slightly until I was lying flat, exposed.

"Sleeping?" he whispered once more.

Then I felt the back of his hand on me, and it was just as I had imagined it would be, brushing below my neck softly, reverentially, down until his fingers touched my breasts and it was all I could do to keep from moaning, blinking, because this was the collusion between us: he could touch me if he believed I didn't know it.

He was leaning up on one elbow now, and I felt the narrow bed sag slightly between us. The flat of his palm moved down, past my stomach, lingering, down until his fingers reached the elastic of my panties and hovered there for a moment, like a hand wavering before turning a doorknob into an unknown room. He ran his hand over the top of the white cotton, and rested there, between my legs, the heat so strong I was sure it steamed between us into the cool night.

This is what we each would remember from that last year we could properly be called a boy and a girl, Billy and I, the year before voting and legal drinking and leaving home. Before the language of men and women set in and changed us: there was a safety that night, an indestructible acceptance which we would each try to replicate with every lover with whom we shared our beds for the rest of our lives. The softness of the fall, the surrender that took place between us until we finally fell asleep in each other's arms.

Tuesday, February 17. William Overmeyer, fourth session. Arrived late. Mood and affect shifted dramatically during the hour. Disassociative. It is sexual in nature. Homosexual but lifelong attachment to stepsister. Made reference to erotic relationship which developed when they first met (next-door neighbors) at age twelve. Became agitated when asked if the relationship had been consummated. Said the relationship was never consummated, that he has never had sexual relations with a woman.

He does not remember his dreams.

*I*n the morning, Lila finds us.

There is a sharp rap on Billy's door, and then the turning of the knob, as if knocking were a perfunctory gesture. She walks through the blue shaded darkness of early morning, picking her way around piles of clothes, some of which are mine.

"Billy," she singsongs, "time to get up."

She doesn't see me at first. In her squinting and stumbling, she doesn't see that there are two shapes in Billy's small bed, twisted together, curled around each other like sea urchins floating through their dreams on the soft ocean floor.

She reaches down, intending to awaken her son. Instead she sweeps over my hair, the curly mass of it, and her hand falters for a moment, bewildered, before she blinks the sleep from her eyes, and the sharpness of her son's bed, the two figures in it, comes fully into focus.

She screams.

We both bolt upright, the sheet falling away from our bodies. Lila stares at me, and my bare breasts stare back. My nipples contract like shameful eyes.

My father appears in the doorway in striped pajamas, panting.

"What's wrong?" he asks.

"Can't you see?" Lila screams. "Look at your daughter."

I pull the sheet up around me.

"Joanna?" He takes a step forward.

I can feel Billy's heart pounding, his chest against my back beneath the sheet.

"What are you doing in here?" my father asks quietly.

"What do you mean, what is she doing in here? What do you think she's doing in here?" Lila shrieks.

"She's not . . . We're not . . ." Billy whispers, but no one hears him.

"Your daughter is a whore," Lila says to my father as shedraws her own nightgown tightly around her, "a little whore."

My father turns as white as the pale stripe of his pajama top.

"Get out of here, Lila," he says. His hands twitch by his sides.

"What do you mean?"

"Just get out of here."

"How dare you talk to me like that?"

"How dare you talk about Joanna like that?"

"But she . . ."

"She, nothing."

They stand within inches of each other, our parents, and

the smell of adults, of warm musty bodies, night cream and liniment hangs in the air.

"Billy, get up," Lila says briskly. "Get out of that bed right this minute."

Billy stays where he is. I feel him shaking.

Lila takes two strides over to the bed.

"Get up, young man."

He doesn't move.

As if in slow motion, as if watching two cars careen toward each other on an otherwise deserted street, I see Lila's hand rise in the air. I watch as it soars down until it smacks against Billy's cheek with a sound like a bone snapping, then she drops it.

"I told you to get up," she says wearily.

The actor who plays Nabokov in *Speak, Memory* is out sick tonight and there is no one to replace him. Understudies do not exist in theatres with bleachers instead of seats, theatres where rat control is written into the company budget. Often the members of the company rehearse two parts at a time, but in the case of the Nabokov character, the role is too complex for any actor to understudy.

Speak, Memory is, in a sense, a one-man show. Nabokov is onstage the entire two hours; the rest of us play characters within characters, shadows from his fiction, figments of his imagination. As Lolita, I have the biggest female role in the piece. I am the locus, the most identifiable of his characters, his nymphet heart. I move across the stage with the simple clarity of one who does not think. I hit my marks, the glowing

X's which are taped to the stage floor, my psyche as transparent as my costume, my body, the sheer glowing curtains.

But not tonight. Tonight there is a knock on the dressing room door where the five female cast members are getting dressed and made up. The stage manager tells us that Timothy is ill and the performance is being canceled. Tonight we are committing the cardinal sin of the theatre, whose axiom is that, no matter what the circumstances, the show must go on.

The company manager goes onstage at five minutes past eight and makes the announcement. There are groans and shufflings, conferrings among spouses, a swarm at the box office to exchange tickets. From my dressing room window I can see a line form at the pay phone just outside El Raton. Audience members hunt through their Manhattan Diaries or call Directory Assistance in search of the perfect little bistro which serves interesting food and a good Cabernet Sauvignon. After all, this is New York City. There is nothing worse than a wasted evening, and even in neighborhoods which are owned by the rats, there is a bistro on every corner.

Now I have the evening off; I am edgy, not sure what to do next. Each night, when I slip on the transparent skin of Lolita and empty my head of all voices except one, the part which has been written for me and memorized so that the words now seem my own, I lose myself for a few hours into the only peace I know.

I take my costume off carefully. It is made from panels of nylon hosiery, and one snag will ruin it. I do not remove my makeup with the heavy cold cream in the jar on my dressing room table. I step into jeans, pull a turtleneck over my head, then brush furiously through my hair to get rid of the spray which holds it laquered in place. I lace my sneakers, not bothering with socks although it is raining outside, grab my knapsack and leave the theatre so quickly that I run directly into the crowd still milling around the small lobby of El Raton, waiting for their radio cabs to arrive, deciding what to do with the rest of their evening.

One woman stops me.

"Aren't you Joanna Hirsch?" she asks.

I smile at her. A Georgia smile. A noblesse oblige smile.

Aren't you Georgia Higgins Hirsch?

"Why yes," I say.

"I recognized you from your photograph in *Harper's Bazaar*," she says.

She glances at the bulletin board which rests on an easel near the entrance to the theatre. Professional photographs of all the actors are thumbtacked to the board; there are eight black-and-white glossy pairs of eyes, dimples and shiny teeth.

The woman walks up to the board and pulls the thumbtacks off my photograph, sinks the tacks back into the cork and approaches me once more, wielding my eight-by-ten.

"Would you . . . ?" she asks, holding it out while she simultaneously fishes in her handbag for a pen.

"What's your name?" I ask her, poised and ready, pretending this isn't the first time in my life I've been asked for an autograph. I imagine Georgia standing in the doorway, watching me, rain teeming behind her. She would gaze at me steadily, proud witness to my rise out of isolation; my triumph would mean more to her if she realized I had ascended—as she had—alone.

"Thank you," the woman says, "my name is Jane."

"Here you go, Jane," I hand the photograph and pen back to her. I make a mental note to bring new publicity stills to the theatre tomorrow.

She grabs my elbow just as I am about to escape through the door and into the rain.

"I just love . . ." she starts, looking into my eyes.

"Thank you," I murmur, desperate to leave.

". . . your mother's work," she says; "pure genius. Such a role model to women my age, you know. She's changed my life."

The cabdriver's dashboard is covered with photographs of his family. There are high school graduation snapshots of a brother and sister—frizzy-haired, dark-eyed twins—their arms thrown around each other, blue tassled caps tilted on their heads. There is a collage of toddlers, infants, backyard swimming pools, picnic blankets thrown on public park grounds, skinny men in undershirts and ample women wearing aprons, holding paper plates piled with steaming hot dogs. There are fuzzy dice dangling from his rearview mirror.

I have given the driver my home address, but as we head up Eighth Avenue in the pouring rain, I change my mind.

"Make that Eighty-first and Third," I say, trying to sound powerful and convincing. The words seem to have crept up my throat and through my lips inadvertently. They have been lodged somewhere in my larynx for so long that their expression is, I suppose, inevitable.

I get no response.

"Sir?"

He slides back the plastic partition and tilts his head.

"I'm changing my destination to Eighty-first and Third," I repeat.

It doesn't matter to the driver. This time he nods his head slightly, then raises the volume on his radio. There seems to be some correlation in his mind between my new destination and the decibel level of the salsa music, as if the Upper East Side requires a greater assault on the senses than Hell's Kitchen.

I sink down in the seat and do breathing exercises in an effort to slow the beating of my heart. This is a discipline I learned from my vocal coach, a way to combat stage fright. I close off one nostril, breathe slowly, then close off the other and repeat. The driver is looking at me through the rearview mirror, which he has tilted so that he can see my whole body. The dice dangle between his eyes.

We pull up in front of Pacific Rim. I pay the fare without making eye contact, and tip him too much. Then I stand beneath the pink awning for a few minutes, watching couples huddled under umbrellas dash across Eighty-first Street and into the restaurant. They don't give me a second glance. Anyone crazy enough to be standing outside in this weather in New York City does not deserve to be noticed.

I need cigarettes. To do what I am about to do, cigarettes are necessary. I think of Bogie and Bergman in *Casablanca*; sharp angles, pursed lips, pounding, unrelenting rain. My life has momentarily turned into a movie, and there is a soundtrack in the background. A receding salsa beat is fading into mournful cellos, violins.

There is a magazine store two doors down from Pacific Rim. I buy a pack of Marlboros, and on my way out I glance at the magazines. *Harper's Bazaar* is displayed in the front rack, the heavily made-up eyes of a young movie actress staring at me. This actress is featured in many magazines this month in an attempt to clear her name from a scandal involving horse manure delivered to a former leading man.

I pick up a copy of the magazine, flipping through the pages stealthily, knowing what I will find on page seventy-eight. I have been doing this compulsively during the past month, since *Bazaar* hit the newsstands. I am used to opening magazines and seeing my mother's face, but am still unaccustomed to seeing my own. Yet there I am, despite my continued surprise, in full color, seated on a stool in the middle of an empty stage, a minimalist portrait. My face is pale, my lips red, and my hair, after at least an hour's work, looks appropriately tousled as if it got that way naturally. I am wearing jeans and a man's white shirt; Nigel's shirt. I wondered, during the shoot, if Nigel would see the photograph and remember the rips in the elbows, the soft white collar.

Under the photograph there is a caption: *Talent runs in families,* it says, *proven by the up-and-coming actress daughter of Georgia Higgins Hirsch.*

I have not been in this part of town since I quit working at Pacific Rim a year ago. There is no reason for me to venture north of Fifty-seventh Street, particularly to the East Side, which holds nothing for me but memories of late night stumbling down Third Avenue in search of one more bar, one more drink. Nigel and I had friends on every corner, burly men with hairy knuckles curved around beer taps, men with watery blue eyes, flushed noses and a tired air about them.

It is rare to find a woman tending bar in this neighborhood, though I did it at Pacific Rim for years. Women who tend bar must appear inpenetrable or they won't last more than a shift or two. When I first started at Pacific Rim, before leaving home, as I put on my makeup at the bathroom mirror, I'd practice my stares: my I've-seen-it-all stare, my you-must-be-joking stare, and, most importantly, my don't-fuck-with-me stare. This one involved a practiced stillness, as if dark brown marbles had momentarily replaced my eyes. I couldn't let them see any transparency, any vulnerability. The Upper East Side bar scene was like the call of the wild, and a woman bartender was exposed, moving back and forth along the endless row of bottles, visible from the hips up. A perfect target.

I never drank when the bar was busy. My first drink usually came near the end of my shift, after the crowd had thinned. I would pour myself a Johnnie Walker Black on the rocks with a twist. If Nigel was working on the floor, I'd pour his drinks during the course of the night, shot glasses waiting on the end of the bar for him.

When Nigel worked the bar, he drank all night and couldn't tend bar without it. He could drink four or five scotches and still function flawlessly; the only noticeable change would be a distinctly more clipped Cockney accent, as if alcohol brought him closer to Liverpool, to the pubs of his youth. When Nigel drank like this, he always wanted to go out for a few more after the restaurant closed. By the time we got home I often had to help him, holding his arm tightly in case he took a spill down one of the five flights of stairs leading to our apartment. If Nigel fell, chances are he'd take me with him.

Nigel and I alternated our excesses, an unspoken agreement. Neither of us lost control on the same night, one of us was always there to help the other up the stairs, or nurse a hangover the next morning. On the nights Nigel drank, he'd often try to seduce me once we got into bed, but was never able to follow through. The alcohol pooled in his head, his liver, his stomach, leaving his extremities empty and lifeless.

"Tomorrow, baby," he'd mumble and turn his back to me, ashamed. Within moments he'd be asleep, one heavily muscled leg tucked between mine, snoring as he only did when he'd had too much to drink. I would lie awake for a while, wishing I were also drunk enough to pass out, wondering what images floated beneath his closed eyelids.

I would raise up on an elbow and watch his face, his neck, his shoulders. Under the mild puffiness beginning to develop as Nigel got older, the bloat around his jaw which came straight from the bottle, he was still rock solid, a rugby player's body residing just beneath the surface of his florid skin. His arms were thick and ropy, his chest was large enough to get lost in. I would push him on his back, as if he weighed nothing at all, then stretch against him until I felt safe, small enough to believe our dreams were the same. Small enough to fall asleep.

. . .

I step into Pacific Rim, flattening myself against the vestibule wall as two couples push past me. They are young, privileged, very giddy. The women have short hair and the men are wearing ponytails. They are on their way home to their apartments not far from here, where they will set their alarm clocks for six in the morning, thin rows of white powder lined up next to the clocks, in case the blaring of the early radio isn't quite enough to rouse them from the night's revelry.

The bar is to the left of the entrance, a long mahogany one with the requisite mirrored wall behind it, shelves of bottles, six different kinds of vodka and every conceivable after-dinner drink from mint flavor to orange. We kept the blender half-hidden in hopes that customers would not order frozen drinks, which were time-consuming and messy to prepare. Besides, we couldn't understand how anyone would prefer a sweet drink; we liked our liquor straight.

I see him from behind. He is standing with his back to the restaurant, holding four mugs with one hand as he fills them with draft beer. His hair is longer; it curls around the base of his neck and into—can it be?—a small ponytail, which looks incongruous against his wide shoulders. He looks like he may have lost weight. His jeans are sagging slightly, and his forearms look pale below the rolled-up sleeves of his blue oxford-cloth shirt.

I stand at the entrance unnoticed, watching Nigel. He turns and places the mugs of beer in front of a group of securities analysts, then asks a tall blonde wearing a leopard print mini-skirt what he can get her. I can't hear her answer, but it must be good because he laughs and winks. He turns his back again and pours from a few different bottles. The resulting drink, which he places before her with a flourish, is a spectacular shade of green. I don't move for a moment or two, standing quietly as I realize what's so different now about

Nigel: he used to look like a director who tended bar. Now he looks like a bartender.

I walk toward the bar, smiling at Terri, one of the waitresses who has worked here for years. She raises her eyebrows and cocks her head in Nigel's direction, as if asking what I'm doing here. It's a good question. I wish I knew. Someone has just vacated a stool at the end of the bar, closest to the window overlooking Third Avenue. I slide into it quickly, avoiding the irate glances of those who have been standing, undoubtedly, for a long time. There are other single women at the bar of Pacific Rim, but none are sitting down. A woman who comes here alone prefers to stand, her narrow hips more fully on display, her unlit cigarette loosely held between second and third fingers of a manicured hand as she fumbles in vain, like a damsel with a flat tire daintily waving a white handkerchief, for a match in her enormous leather handbag. She knows this is a game, the "May I?" game, the tan stubby fingers, the French cuff shortened so the gold Rolex is visible, the lighter proffered with a click and a flame. The next click she hears may be a lock snapping shut in an Upper East Side penthouse, the snaps and zips of clothing which leave a trail over the shag carpet to the bed.

Nigel has yet to notice me. He is a man who winks and laughs at blond women wearing leopard print mini-skirts. In that wink and laugh I saw the painful truth that all lovers eventually face about one another: he is able to exist without me. He has spent a lifetime reading Strindberg in the original Swedish, Calvino in Italian, Molière in French, yet his classifiable skills reside in mixing a mean margarita, or creating creamy green cocktails.

He turns around.

"May I please have a tonic and lime?" I ask.

"My God," he says.

His face does not change expression.

I light a Marlboro and blow the smoke through my nose.

"Since when are you smoking?" he asks.

"Since when have you had the foggiest notion of what I'm doing in my life?" I answer.

He turns away, and in a moment is back with a bottle of pepper-flavored vodka and two small glasses.

"No, Nigel. Just the tonic."

I can't believe we're having this little exchange. This, after he sleepily kissed me good-bye as I left home one morning, then packed his bags, called a taxi and walked away from thirteen years without a word.

He pours ice into a tall glass, then fills it to the rim with tonic water from a spigot beneath the bar. He embellishes the glass with two slices of orange and lemon, as if we were on a Caribbean island and this some sort of exotic cocktail. Then he pours himself a healthy shot of vodka. All the while he is looking intently at his work; looking everywhere but at me. Nigel is biding time. There is tension in the center of his forehead, so palpable, a wrinkled knot has formed there.

I have seen this tension before, during the third week of rehearsal for *Speak, Memory,* when it seemed the show would never come together.

"Joanna," he would say to me, lips tight around a cigarette, "where's your motivation? What's the one concrete thing that happened to you before?"

We'd have arguments in front of the whole cast.

"Cut the Neighborhood Playhouse shit," I'd yell back, at my wit's end.

It seemed he always waited until there were other actors around before he'd criticize my acting. He needed an audience.

"Everyone," he announced three days before the show

opened, "I want you to know that Joanna Hirsch was not my first choice for this role. The playwright insisted. I fought him. But then the producer insisted, and money talks. Working with my girlfriend," he drew the word out as only the British can, "was not my idea."

Opening night was on a Thursday. There were at least a hundred people crowded into the cramped quarters of El Raton, spilling into the lobby, sitting on the edge of the stage, balancing precariously on bleachers in back. The stereo was playing a Rachmaninoff symphony too loudly, and Nigel had arranged for an elaborate nineteenth-century Russian punch, complete with rented crystal punchbowl and hundreds of small paper cups. The theatre people and friends who were attending the opening night party were having a good time, but everyone involved with *Speak, Memory* was on edge. At a few minutes past midnight, Nigel's assistant came running in with an armful of Friday's *New York Times*.

"Front page of the *Weekend* section," she said breathlessly.

Nigel grabbed a newspaper and stalked to a corner by himself. I was sitting in the first row of bleachers, drinking my eighth cup of punch, too terrified to look. The assistant director, who had been sympathetic during rehearsals, brought the *Weekend* section over and dropped it in my lap.

"Be brave, Joanna," he said, "just take a peek."

I held the paper in my lap and thought of Georgia's first review in the *Times*. "*When Alfred Stieglitz first laid eyes on the work of Georgia O'Keeffe,* wrote Clement Greenberg, *"he exclaimed 'Finally, a woman on paper!' Much the same may be said of the latest Georgia, the remarkable young sculptor Georgia Higgins Hirsch. Here is a woman whose painted structures will change the shape of American sculpture.*"

I held the newspaper up to my face. All around the room I thought I could feel eyes on me. I scanned the page, noticing the photograph, which was of a stark moment near the end of the first act: Lolita and Nabokov downstage, Humbert in the background. I looked frail in my white nightgown, like an ethereal Wendy in *Peter Pan*.

I glanced at the review quickly, as if it were a sort of Rorschach test, to see if any words in particular jumped out at me. There were a few: *criminal, plodding, mechanical* were the first words I saw. When I read the name to whom these referred, I dropped the paper back in my lap and looked across the room for Nigel. Moments earlier he had been standing in the corner with his back to the room. Now he was gone.

I pushed myself up to go after him and started out of the theatre, into the lobby. By now he would be heading up Tenth Avenue, into one of the dozens of bars which lined the streets. As I made my way through the crush of people I felt a hand on my shoulder.

It was May Castile, our stage manager. She was the sort of woman who didn't even pretend to like women, unless they could do something for her. The fact that she was the stage manager gave her some degree of control over me, and she never let me forget it. She was never even civil to me unless Nigel was around. Now she was smiling; a large, beaming, generous smile.

"Congratulations," she said.

I thought this the ultimate insult.

"Go to hell, May."

She took a step backward.

"What's your problem?" she asked. "Is it every day of the week you get a rave review in the *New York Times*?"

"What are you talking about?"

May held up the newspaper, neatly folded so that the lower half of the page, which was filled by the review of *Speak, Memory* was easily visible.

She read it to me.

" 'Speak, Memory,' the newest production of the newest theatre company in New York, is a tour de force, an extravagant display of the possibilities which arise when the penetrating intellectual instinct of a young playwright is married to some truly extraordinary acting talent. This fledgling company has accomplished what amounts to a miracle in bringing the memoir by Vladimir Nabokov to life. Nabokov is played by Timothy Hayes, who previously has appeared in . . ."

May trailed off, then scanned the article with her forefinger until she found the part she was looking for. Her voice raised excitedly, and a few heads turned in our direction as she continued.

" '. . . and this production introduces a young actress who has somehow been in hibernation until now. The lovely Joanna Hirsch plays Lolita, and what a Lolita she is. Perhaps not since Geraldine Page first graced the theatre has innocence been portrayed with such intelligence. Miss Hirsch is a luminous actress. When she takes center stage in the final scene of Speak, Memory, with no adornment other than a flesh-colored leotard and a radiant face, one realizes that center stage is exactly where Miss Hirsch is destined to spend her life. One can only hope she will be better directed in future productions than she was in this one. It borders on criminal . . .' "

May faltered.

"Read the rest of it," I said.

" '. . . that such a fine adaptation by the playwright and such a brilliant debut by young Joanna Hirsch should be staged by a plodding, mechanical director, Nigel Easden,' " she finished weakly.

We stared at each other, and in that split second I knew that the rules had abruptly changed. I was no longer on safe ground. I wondered who could be trusted. Then I wondered where Nigel was.

The next morning he was gone.

. . .

Now, many months later, he stands here in front of me. The bar of Pacific Rim is a mahogany barrier between us; I am reminded of the partitions which separate inmates from visitors in prison, though I'm not sure which one of us is the prisoner. Or which one will be able to walk freely away.

He has downed one shot glass of vodka and is starting on another. He looks at his watch, a colorful, plastic band encircling his wrist.

"What are you doing here?" he asks me. "Why aren't you performing?"

"They canceled the show tonight. Timothy's out sick," I answer. "Nigel, where have you been?"

He ignores the question.

"Why aren't you drinking?" he asks.

"Do you really think I ought to?"

He pauses for a moment, then lets out a hollow laugh.

"No, I suppose not."

I don't tell him it's been one hundred and sixty-three days since my last drink; I don't tell him it's been fourteen months since Billy entered the world of the waking dead; and I don't tell Nigel I've lost count of exactly how many days it has been since he walked down the stairs of our apartment and out of my life. There are too many dates to remember.

Nigel seems to have degenerated. In the planes of his face there is new evidence of age and alcohol. Thin lines of broken capillaries run from the sides of his nose like red roots of a delicate tree, and there is a puffiness around his jaw. Nigel is only thirty-five, but the destruction in his face is what one might see in a man decades older. I have a sense, watching him now, that he feels his life, or certainly the best parts of it, to be over.

"Are you working on anything?" I ask him.

"I'm staging some readings of a new John Bishop play at

Circle Rep's Lab. They say if it goes well they'll consider a main stage production."

"Great," I say, trying to sound enthusiastic, knowing that perhaps one in fifty Lab pieces ever get anywhere near the main stage of Circle Rep.

"Really, Nigel. That's great."

"Yeah," he says.

There is a long pause, awkward for two people who have shared a life together.

"I'm also thinking about moving back to Liverpool," he finally says.

"Liverpool? You always swore you'd never go back," I say, despite the promise I made to myself not to stir up trouble.

"Please, Nigel, is this all because of some lousy reviews? They were wrong! You can't just throw in the towel because a few critics took pot shots at you."

My words flow faster and faster. I can't help it. I'm watching Nigel disintegrate before my eyes. First Georgia, then Billy, now this.

"Don't leave," I stammer, reaching across the bar, "there's everything for you here."

"How the hell would you know what's left for me here?" he asks. "You've had everything handed to you on a platter, dear heart. And don't you think that somewhere in the back of his mind, Frank Rich knows who your mother is? He might as well have said it: 'Talent runs in families.' Didn't I read that somewhere recently? Joanna Hirsch. Daughter extraordinaire of Georgia Higgins Hirsch."

He spits out the words, slinging them across the bar at me.

"So. There isn't really anything left for me in New York, is there, now?" he asks, his eyes dangerously close to welling up. "There's no one who's going to give some overgrown kid from Liverpool a break, is there now? Besides, I don't have a famous mother who's going to make up for my glaring lack of talent."

He stops to catch his breath. Even Nigel knows when he's gone too far. I have never, in all the time I've known him, seen him cry.

A male voice calls from the other end of the bar.

"Excuse me! Bartender! Stop flirting with the lady and take my order!"

Nigel slowly turns around.

"Fuck you," he says. He makes it sound elegant.

"Fuck me? Fuck you," says the customer.

Nigel picks up a tin shaker; from where I sit, I can see it is half-full of the remains of a banana daiquiri. Before anyone can stop him, he has taken three long strides to the other end and has gracefully tossed the pale, creamy contents all over the young man's face. I watch thick globs of banana travel, in slow motion, down the man's chin, onto the lapel of his navy blue double-breasted suit.

Then I watch the man grab Nigel by the front of his shirt and try to drag him over the bar. He is drunk, which is, of course, what allows him to hurl insults to begin with. When he is unable to actually drag Nigel over the bar, Nigel grabs the man's hair and slams his face down. I hear the man's forehead hitting the bar, clear and loud, like the crack of a rifle. I hear this once, twice, before I blindly, gropingly, find the door.

B. *missed his session today. Didn't call to explain. This kind of acting out is unlike him.*

$\mathcal{B}$. arrived twenty minutes late, in a state of extreme agitation. Looked ill and was sweating profusely. Hadn't been home for twenty-four hours. Wouldn't reveal his whereabouts. Dissembled, incoherent.

Concerned about B.'s stability. Although he has at no time been suicidal, I think his current condition needs to be closely monitored. I don't rule out the possibility of hospitalization.

There is something here. Something I do not know.

VIII.

$\mathcal{I}$t is our senior year. I am sitting in the Fiske Garden smoking a cigarette, watching a couple of sophomores toss a Frisbee. They laugh uproariously when the bright orange disk soars over the stone wall and into the woods behind the school. They must be high. The Fiske Garden is usually permeated with the heavy sweet smell of marijuana.

I finish my cigarette and grind the butt into the soft spring earth with the heel of my sneaker. I have taken to wearing sneakers with my navy blue uniform; shoes are the only form of subversive attire possible at Tipton, whose strict dress code does not include the feet; students wear red cowboy boots, moccasins, high-tops. Today I am wearing a pair of white sneakers, upon which I have painted rainbows with acrylic paints from Georgia's studio: red, orange, yellow, green, blue, indigo, violet. In charcoal, I have also drawn my best version of the skeleton of a foot.

I follow the Frisbee into the woods behind the school. In the pocket of my blazer, I carry a small tin box which once held fancy English lozenges, a gift from my father. It now contains approximately twenty hand-rolled joints, sealed and packed perfectly. I like getting high by myself. When I grow up I will like drinking by myself, the sweet, private burn of vodka straight out of the freezer bottle.

It is a blue suburban day and spring is in the air. Dead winter branches crack beneath my sneakers as I make my way along a well-trodden path, into the woods. During my years at Tipton I have dispensed with many rites of passage in these woods. I smoked my first cigarette here, I drank my first can of Coors. I know these trees. I know where names are scratched and bottles are buried. The pot makes me expansive; I think I can actually see the air, the soft underbellies of newborn birds lodged in nests, the shifting particles of mud beneath my feet.

My vision is sharp, prophetic. When I glimpse a white naked body moving on the ground like a small animal among the leaves, I don't for a moment wonder whether I am dreaming. I know that it is Billy, and, as I push my legs forward, I know what I am about to witness will alter part of me irrevocably, like the burnt-out eyes of a child who, in a moment of random curiosity, stares directly at the sun. There will be other times, other torments between us, but this is the season of consequence, the unraveling of a silence which becomes, in one single instant, no longer possible.

He is lying on his back like some sort of toppled marble statue. There is someone kneeling over him, and, for a moment, I am crouching again beneath a windowsill five years ago, absorbing the sight of my father standing perfectly still, holding Lila Overmeyer's head as she moved gently, rhythmically below his waist.

The mouth which moves quietly over Billy's stomach is a boy's mouth. The hard limbs of the boys are twined together, and I think I am seeing double until the one who is kneeling over Billy lifts up his head and I recognize Todd Wanamaker, a lacrosse player with furtive green eyes and a full mouth, a mouth currently concentrating on Billy.

I stand frozen for an instant, and in that instant Billy tosses his head from side to side. He turns his head to the left, opens his mouth and groans, then opens his eyes and sees me. Our eyes meet, then I am running, running straight through the branches, shielding my face with arms and elbows, doing a sort of breaststroke through the air. I hear the cracking of branches under my feet, I hear Billy's voice screaming my name, but I keep running.

Sometimes on this couch I feel as if I am floating. The velvet cushion begins to move beneath me and suddenly I am on a raft at sea—and Josephson?—no one is in sight. You are behind me, your pen scratching, spools of tape spinning into each other, turning with the sound of my voice as I drown, the last gasps of Billy Overmeyer as he cracks through the ice of this couch and into the frigid darkness from which there is no return.

I'll tell you a fantasy, Doctor. You like fantasies. Even the sound of the word—fan, like fantastic, fan like fanatic—who can resist the shrouded cognitive gyrations?

So I was telling you about—

I lost my train of thought—

Ah, yes, Todd Wanamaker. I know I've told you about the woods, the strange illusory sense of creating in the flesh what I had fantasized all my life.

But did I ever tell you Joanna saw us?

I didn't think so.

Now listen, this happened. This is not a fantasy.

I don't know how to tell you about it. I can't find the words. Sometimes on this couch I feel as if I am skimming the surface of the ice and if I crack through, you will not be there, Josephson. You will not be able to save me.

Todd was giving me a blow job. Sorry, does that clarify things? He was going down on me. Giving head. Sucking cock, if you will. I don't know how long she was standing there. My eyes were closed, and when I opened them there she was.

She was like a wraith, an apparition. For a moment I thought I was hallucinating, because the very same image which had been floating before my eyes moments earlier, that of my stepsister Joanna, was now in front of me, but this vision was fully clothed, her mouth open, tears streaming down her face. I immediately went limp, yanked up my pants, and without even so much as a backward glance went tearing through the woods after her.

You see, while this boy was working his tongue over me, in my mind's eye I saw Josie, Joanna, Jo, and she was naked as I had imagined her, spread out on the leaves like some sort of pubescent goddess, ripe and lush and entirely unattainable.

This is the tragedy of my life. Small, I suppose, as tragedies go: I require a hard body, sculpted out of stone, flat from clavicle to penis, ridges of muscle pressed cold and smooth like a mirror against mine, the cruel wrenching of soft pink tissue, hands touching me strong enough to mutilate, strong enough to cradle my neck and to kill. And what I see beneath my closed eyes all this while is Joanna. Only Joanna. Always Joanna.

. . .

*I*t is April of my senior year and I have stopped eating. This self-starvation is a source of worry to everyone but me. My father continues to cook his culinary concoctions, hoping I might be tempted by dishes such as cream of shiitake mushroom soup or sole Véronique. His strategy is enticement. My stepmother, Lila, doesn't believe in enticement. She believes that punishment will force me to eat, therefore has cut off my allowance and use of the family car in hopes that I won't be able to stand deprivation on all fronts. And my stepbrother, Billy, ignores my shrinking body. I frighten him. I am slowly turning into a boy. He hangs his head during meals, shoveling food quickly into his mouth so he can escape from the table, from the spectacle of me ignoring the food on my plate.

After three weeks of water and an occasional cracker, my father decides to put me in the hospital. Perhaps he thinks the threat of the hospital will be enough to encourage me to begin eating. He thinks I am, like many other people, afraid of the hospital. He doesn't understand. Nothing could possibly be more appealing to me than the gray monotony of a quiet room, a curtain pulled between me and the world, television for which the controls are by my bedside at all times, the images before my eyes superseded by daytime programs, talk shows and the lineup of blow-dried blondes on soap operas.

The nurse wheels in a tray of food three times a day. She asks me if I have any special requests, but I am silent. There is nothing, no form of torture which could possibly make me ingest even one tiny morsel of the colorless, odorless muck they call food at Morristown General Hospital.

Days pass in this medical bliss before they send in the psychiatric residents. They sit by my bedside with notepads and charts, these earnest, sleepless young men and women. They ask me questions.

"Do you think you're fat?"

"What do you see when you look in the mirror?"

"Do you feel you have lost control over your life?"

They don't look up during their inquiry. Their eyes are focused intently on clipboards, as if the real answers are written on sheets of paper in invisible ink, and will, at any moment, appear and resolve this dilemma once and for all.

I know they think I have anorexia. I have read about this disease. When a teenage girl stops eating, this is the likely diagnosis. They are sure of this, and do not feel compelled to go any further. I have looked the disease up in my father's *Merck Manual*. Symptoms of anorexia:

1. A distorted view of the emaciated body.

2. An obsession with control over food and bodily functions.

3. Other compulsive disorders such as excessive hand-washing, constant weighing, obsessive lists of foods eaten and calories consumed.

So they come to interview me, these psychiatric residents, but I know they are wasting their time. I am not anorexic; I have none of the characteristics. I don't think I'm too fat. I don't think about food at any point during the day; all I'm really interested in is lying in my comfortable hospital bed watching television, waiting for my body, if starved long enough, to become flat, muscular, elongated.

I no longer want to be a girl.

If they asked the right questions I would tell them this. But they persist instead with their own boring ideas. They bother me with their lists and data. They have also begun to feed me intravenously. I wonder if the sugar water will spill directly into my curves, whether it will plump up the cellulite beneath my skin. The thought of all my hard work going to waste appalls me, so twice I remove the intravenous, pulling it neatly out of my arm. I stop doing this when the head nurse threatens to tie me to the bed if it happens again.

I eventually lose track of time. I know it is April, I know it is my senior year, but I no longer know whether it is Monday or Thursday. Days spill into one another, differentiated only by the shows on nighttime television. I have been here about ten days when, one morning, I hear the click of cowboy boots against the linoleum hospital corridor, then a quick, purposeful rap of knuckles on my half-open door. An unmistakable scent drifts toward my bed with the force of a sensory memory. My sense of smell has increased with lack of food; I am sharp and vigilant, a scrappy animal. I hear and smell Georgia before I see her.

She approaches my bed and looms over me, larger than I remember her. Her hair falls around her face as she leans down, looking at me.

"So what's all this?" she asks, not unkindly.

I smile weakly at her.

"What?"

"I get back from Tokyo. I have jet lag beyond belief. And when I open the door to my loft, my answering machine is blinking so much I think it must be broken. I play back my messages, and what am I greeted with? Fifteen messages from your father on my machine, telling me that Josie is starving herself to death," Georgia says without a pause.

"I have no intention of starving myself to death," I tell her.

"What then, Joanna?"

Georgia runs her hands through her hair. I see tiny particles of marble dust falling on her black sweater like dandruff.

"I want to be a boy," I tell her.

She stares at me. This she was not expecting.

"A boy," she repeats.

We continue staring at each other in silence. I try to keep my gaze as steady as possible, calm and limpid. After all, I do not think this is the most ludicrous idea. Ludicrous is falling in love with Billy Overmeyer, my stepbrother. My homosexual stepbrother. That's ludicrous. This starvation, this hospital stay, is simply an attempt to rectify things. Perhaps, as long as I'm already here, I'll be able to convince them to perform a sex-change operation. I'm not entirely sure if there is a sex-change operation to change a woman into a man, though I know that men can be transformed into the opposite. Another of life's small injustices.

Georgia has been talking, but I have not been listening to her, absorbed, instead, in my potential metamorphosis.

". . . so would you consider speaking with Dr. Bach-man?" she asks.

"Who?"

She taps her foot impatiently.

"Haven't you been listening? Dr. Bachman is one of the best analysts in the city. I know him well and I'm sure he'll see you. I think it might be really helpful, Joanna," says my mother, the healthiest woman alive.

Before I can answer Georgia, the door swings open and my other parent walks in. He freezes in mid-step when he sees her. My first instinct is to look behind my father, making sure that Lila hasn't accompanied him on this visit. My two parents in the same room is enough of a disaster without the well-meaning, nauseating buoyancy of Lila Overmeyer Hirsch. Fortunately for us all, he has arrived alone.

"Hello, Bernard," Georgia says faintly.

"Georgia."

He turns his face slightly away, wincing. He looks at her for a moment this way, sideways, the way people in movie theatres turn their heads during the scary parts.

"Hi, Dad," I murmur, my mouth beneath the soft, ammonia-scented sheet. I wonder if he remembers I'm in the room. I wonder if he remembers this is a hospital, and the reason we're all here is my hunger strike. I look at my mother and try to see what he sees.

She is dressed in black, head to toe; black cowboy boots,

black jeans, a black cashmere sweater. The only color on Georgia is the silver glint of her belt buckle and the new white streaks in her hair. They say that hair is dead, but Georgia's is alive. She has lines in her face now, but they are superb lines, full of depth and character. They say we get the face we deserve. Georgia's face grows more beautiful with each year, as if the placid perfection of her youth had always been, somehow, a lie. This woman's face, this ravaged beauty, is her true self. The face she has carried around inside her since the age of three.

"You look . . . well," my father tells her.

"Thank you. And you, Bernie," Georgia lies.

My father has taken up golf. Beneath his hospital whites he is wearing blue golf pants and a green sweater emblazoned with a small wreathlike emblem. He has gained weight, and his middle bulges softly under the green sweater. He is wearing white bucks, and his balding head has been covered by a crafty toupee, courtesy of Lila, who likes her men hirsute.

I look from my father to Georgia and back again. If a stranger were to wander in, I would be hard-pressed to explain that these two were ever married to each other. I am the only living proof. They barely look like they'd inhabit the same street corner.

Georgia is incongruous in this setting, this hospital so cheerful it seems unlikely that anyone would ever actually be sick or die here. She has appeared in a blaze of glory, between trips to Tokyo and Barcelona, to see whether she can instantly cure her starving daughter. Perhaps she can pad me with plaster, encase me in steel. And if all else fails, she can use her influence to send me to Dr. Bachman, good shrink and good friend.

It suddenly dawns on me that my father should not be here at this hour of the day. It is two o'clock, because "One Life to Live" has just appeared on the television. I have the sound off, but at this point I recognize the characters: Dorian Lord, wealthy divorced businesswoman, is gesturing angrily at her handsome, much younger boyfriend.

"What are you doing here?" I ask my father. "Why aren't you at work?"

"I came as a messenger," he smiles at me. "Something came in the mail I thought you might like to see."

He hands me a thick envelope. The return address in the upper left-hand corner says Yale University. I think I know the contents of the envelope before I open it, and my heart begins to pound. If Yale were rejecting me, the envelope would be a sliver, containing a few well-chosen, perfunctory words.

I open it, then read out loud.

"Dear Ms. Hirsch," I read, "we are very pleased to inform you of your acceptance into the class of 1980 . . ."

I look at both my parents, and they are grinning wildly. I let out a squeal, which causes the head nurse to poke her head inside the door.

"Everything all right?" she asks.

"My daughter is going to Yale," my father says proudly.

"Your daughter had better start eating or she's going to heaven," says the nurse.

"Delightful woman," Georgia says to the door which closes behind the nurse.

I am relishing this moment. It is the first time I have been with both my parents since the age of twelve, and I am the cause of this celebration. Then a thought occurs to me, the one which is never far away.

"What about Billy?" I ask my father.

"What about him?"

I am in no mood for teasing.

"Did he get in?"

My father pauses.

"Yes, Josie. He got in."

The nurse wheels in a tray of food and parks it at the side of my bed. It contains dry scrambled eggs, Saltines, a container of orange juice and a cup of red Jell-o with marshmallows on top.

Georgia looks at the food and wrinkles her nose. "How can you expect her to eat that?" she asks.

"Ssshhh," the nurse and my father both hiss at her, but I am not paying attention. I pull the tray nearer so it hovers over my stomach; if I close my eyes I can almost imagine that this is a special occasion and I am eating breakfast in bed. Mechanically I raise forkful after forkful to my mouth. I eat the eggs, drink the juice, eat every last morsel of Jell-o and marshmallows, and it all tastes divine, better than any of my father's Craig Claiborne recipes. My stomach swells beneath the bedsheet, and I wonder if I am going to get sick. I open my eyes and they are all staring at me: Georgia, my father, the nurse.

"I'm cured!" I say, smiling at them. I taste bits of egg in my teeth.

Billy and I are going to New Haven together. And whatever has existed in the past, we have a chance to create a new future. Four years. It seems like a lifetime.

We are scattered like ashes strewn from a plane, drifting through the air, landing wherever the wind takes us. We are bone sliding down a mountain, a smattering of dust at sea. There is a design to all this, a higher order: no matter how far we run, we always end, in an incongruous, interminable circle, where we begin.

Nigel has gone, or will go, back to Liverpool. He will tend bar there, as his father and grandfather did before him. He will marry some thick-waisted Irish girl and have many children. He will treat those children the way he was treated as a child: with condescension, bemusement and vague disbelief. Those children will grow up and go to Oxford or Yale, or any grand ivory tower farther away than they can imagine, in an attempt to put academic distance between themselves and their own pasts. They will read Flaubert in French, they will know the best translation of *The Brothers Karamazov*, and with each new language learned, each library shelf mastered, they will believe they are rising above their father when, in fact, what they are doing is repeating history. Nigel will die fairly young, and his children will bury him alongside generations of Easdens in a cemetery outside the Liverpool city limits. When they first find his body outside a bar early one morning, they will discover inside the frayed pockets of his jacket a yellowed newspaper clipping, decades old.

Georgia has gone off to Italy. This is also somehow fitting for the woman who was born in Eastern Europe in a time of war, raised in the south of the United States and, after a mistake in the New Jersey suburbs, settled in downtown New York City. She belongs everywhere and nowhere. I see her on deserted mezzanines, huddled outside stage doors, folded into business-class seats on midday flights. I see her everywhere, yet I know exactly where to find her. If I dial a long series of numbers I will be connected to her instantly. I almost see her hand reaching for the phone on the other side of the Atlantic. The wires which link us travel beneath the sidewalks of New York City along the bottom of the sea, encircling the ruins of Rome until they twist up the Umbrian mountains to the highest peak, a fifteenth-century rectory which has been converted into a home. There is no mailbox, no listing in the phone book, but locals know that the fortress belongs to *La Nordamericana,* the expatriate Georgia Higgins Hirsch.

Billy is the only one who is not drifting, but still I see him everywhere, as if he were dead, as if his ashes had indeed been scattered across the ground on which I walk, rising like soot into the air I breathe. He is centered between my eyes, superimposed on all that I see. When I walk through Central Park I see Billy rowing near the boathouse, I see him riding a horse along the western edge of the park, I see him rolling around the grass in private shady crevices where men hide together beneath bushes, behind trees.

My father sees Billy every day at the rehabilitation center, which is attached to the hospital where he does his rounds. Billy has become one more person we pretend does not exist, another forbidden subject. We don't discuss Georgia (too difficult for my father), we don't discuss Lila (too difficult for me) and we don't discuss Billy (too painful for both of us). Conversations with my father are like the white spaces between words on a sheet of paper. There is a yawning blankness, the spotless monotony of the unspoken word.

So we end where we begin. Nigel believed, beneath all the bluster, that he's a poor scrappy kid from Liverpool, and Liverpool is where he's headed, his tail between his legs. Billy believed he was a mistake, a mutant blot on the world, and now his body proves him right, with his useless, atrophied limbs. Georgia believed since the age of three in her own indestructibility. She has survived where others have fallen. She has earned the right to be larger than life. Most sculptors expect their work to outlive them, but Georgia intends to outlive her art.

And where does all this leave me, this fine circular theory? What demon propels me onto that stage nightly, what allows me this professional success tied so intrinsically to personal failure? I was determined from the time I was a child to be nothing like my mother. I thought I would accomplish this not through work, but through love. I thought if I gave my heart faithfully and irrevocably I would grow up not at all like Georgia, who housed her deepest self in only one dwelling: a place of steel or clay or granite, a creative place entirely of her own making.

And here I am, alone with my work, with a growing file of press clips and an increasing number of messages on my answering machine. I hear myself described as having "a gift," the same words which have been used to describe my mother. I wonder, did she pass this gift to me like the wave in my hair or the arch in my foot? Did she silently hand it to me, thinking *Here, you'll need this, because in the end it will be all you'll have?* What I wished for and what was intended for me were two entirely different lives. The possibility for the life I wanted ended with Billy, or perhaps I am fooling myself, perhaps it never existed at all.

In my dream you are standing in the center of a frozen lake beckoning me to follow you. You are wearing a red down jacket— the kind Josie used to wear.

I do not see the fractures in the ice from where I stand, Josephson, so slowly, tentatively I begin to make my way toward you. I do not notice the slivers which extend, razor-sharp, from the smooth surface, the networks of cracks under the ice like wrinkles beneath the skin of a beautiful woman.

I feel a strange homesickness as I watch you in Josie's jacket, your arms reaching out to me, and I walk faster, pounding over the ice until I feel the ground begin to crack beneath me. The freezing water seeps into the soles of my shoes and I realize I am going to die from the ground up. You stand in the center of your island of whiteness. There is nothing you can do to protect me.

It is a slow death, Josephson. You remove your down jacket, you toss it to me; it sails through the air, an inflatable life raft, but your arms are not strong enough, and it falls through a hole in the ice. You strip down to your underwear, hurling a blouse, boots, a camisole, hoping I will be able to create a chain out of your belongings and pull myself out of the numbing cold.

You stand naked on the ice. I am up to my chin in water, but I can still see you. Your body is remarkably like Josie's—and I realize I yearn for her as if she is a birthplace, a country to which I must return—and all I want to do is reach out and touch you once before I die.

We are dining at the Quilted Giraffe—Georgia, Nigel, Billy and I—we are celebrating three graduations and a retrospective. The four of us are brought together only for rituals or tragedies. There is no synchronicity between us; we don't belong around a table such as this one, and we all know it.

We eat in silence. This chewing, this silence is all very elegant, punctuated by the clinking of glasses and the scraping of forks against Limoges. This dinner was Georgia's suggestion. She is the youngest artist to ever get a retrospective at the Whitney, not to mention the first woman sculptor. The museum opening was on the same day as my graduation from Yale, so of course she couldn't make it to New Haven. This elaborate five-course dinner accompanied by an endless stream of wine is my mother's way of making it up to me.

She called the day before graduation, or the day before the opening of the retrospective, depending on your viewpoint.

"Invite whomever you'd like," she offered.

"The only people I want there are Billy and Nigel," I told her.

"Ugh," she said.

I wasn't sure whether she was referring to Billy or Nigel or both.

"Well that's who I'd like to be there," I repeated calmly. "And the celebration is as much for them as for me," I added. "Nigel's getting his master's from the School of Drama tomorrow, and that's a big deal. Billy's cum laude, just like me."

"Also big deal," she said.

"Yes. It is."

I had to brag to Georgia. I felt in some way I had to make her understand that the world was bigger than the structures of her own making. We couldn't compete with the fame which had swept her away, and perhaps we couldn't compete with her endless drive and energy, but we were doing our best. None of us had given up yet.

Tonight, this guilt-offering meal, is a knife that slices through some invisible piece of our young, fragile egos. We are seated at a choice table, in the front room of the Quilted Giraffe, directly across from the front door. There is no privacy; that is the point.

Georgia is wearing jeans and an Italian silk blouse, through which the outline of her bra can be seen. I'm sure that jeans are frowned upon in this restaurant, but they are happy to accommodate Georgia. She is impossible to miss: her mouth is outlined in bright red, a black straw hat rests on top of her head, the brim covered with flowers which appear to be fresh. Her fingernails are painted red to match her lips, and she wears a silver ring on each finger. Only her thumbs are bare, and they look almost naked next to the rest as she spoons her gazpacho. It occurs to me that Georgia has decorated her hands the way a corporate executive might decorate an office, adorning it with minimalist furniture and fancy framed degrees.

I am counting how many bites of food I can manage between visits to our table by other diners.

"Georgia!" they cry, one after the other, these New York wraiths who wear sunglasses at night, these black-clad denizens of the glossy tabloids who never utter a word without the hope it will be recorded somewhere, anywhere, for posterity.

"Darling!" they utter, baring their teeth, these people with small jobs and large expense accounts.

"This must be your daughter," they say, looking at me with a sweep of their eyes, up and down once like the quick click of a camera shutter.

I smile at them through bites of filet mignon. I am Georgia without makeup. Georgia with bare skin and pale nails. I introduce Nigel and Billy.

"This is my boyfriend, Nigel Easden, and my stepbrother, William Overmeyer."

They slide professional glances over Billy and Nigel quickly, taking in the awkward angle of Billy's elbow on the table, the beads of sweat on Nigel's forehead, and in a hawkish, almost imperceptible way, they turn their backs slightly; my boyfriend and stepbrother are perceived as unimportant, and summarily dismissed.

By the time dessert rolls around we are all drunk on Bâtard-Montrachet. Nigel has convinced us that fine wine does not get you drunk, and to prove his point, he has ordered bottle after bottle. The only one of us who is not woozy is Nigel, who sits upright, elbows against the table.

Georgia leans over to Billy.

"See that man at the table over there, the one with the sunburn, against the wall?" she slurs.

Billy looks in the direction of Georgia's finger, which is indelicately pointing.

"No . . ."

"Over there . . . See him? He has those cute horn-rimmed glasses, and he's talking to the woman in the gray-checked suit?"

"I see him," says Billy, craning his neck.

"His name is Truman Bidwell," she says. "He's very well thought of at Sotheby's. Head of antiquities. He's gay, you know," Georgia continues loudly.

"Really," murmurs Billy.

"Georgia!" I exclaim.

"What, dear? I'm just trying to set poor Billy up. He seems rather lonely, sandwiched there between you and Nigel."

"Actually, I rather like it this way," says Billy with a smile.

"What do you see in them, Billy?" Georgia asks. Her left eye droops slightly.

"In whom?"

"In my daughter and that struggler she spends her time with," says Georgia as if Nigel isn't sitting directly across the table from her.

I scrape my chair back.

"You've gone too far tonight," I say.

Nigel pulls me back into my seat. His hand strokes mine. He seems to be telling me he doesn't mind being humiliated, as long as the insult is being hurled from the height of a personage such as Georgia Higgins Hirsch.

"Really," she continues to Billy, "I think I should introduce you to that man. You need to expand your horizons, now that you're going to be living in the city."

"No, that's . . ."

Billy trails off as we watch Georgia rise halfway out of her seat and call across the restaurant.

"Truman!"

I bury my head in my hands, peeking at Billy between two fingers.

Truman Bidwell's head lifts slowly away from his sun-burned shoulders, like the unprotected neck of a snail easing its way out of a shell on a hot pink beach. He looks around the nearly empty restaurant until his eyes rest on Georgia.

He raises his hand in a studied wave.

"Come over here," Georgia insists.

"Your mother," Nigel mutters into my ear, "is four sheets to the wind."

"And whose fault is that?" I hiss.

A shadow casts itself over the table, and Truman Bidwell's hand is out, along with a deep voice repeating the name with which we are, by this time, quite familiar.

"Truman," says Georgia. "I'm sorry, I didn't mean to inter-rupt your dinner."

"We were quite finished," he says solemnly.

"I was just trying to get your attention," she says. "I wanted to introduce you to William Overmeyer, here. You're not mar-ried or otherwise engaged, are you?" she asks, looking at him with her black-streaked eyes.

"Married? No," says Bidwell, taking in Billy, who is blush-ing furiously across the table.

"Why don't we all get a little air," Nigel suggests, rising. Unbeknownst to me, he has slipped the maître d' his credit card; this dinner will take six months of payments to work off. I'm surprised that the amount of the check was not over his credit limit.

We walk outside, Georgia leading the way, as always. She sways from side to side, and is followed by Truman Bidwell, then Billy, then Nigel and me.

Bidwell turns to Billy on the corner of Fiftieth and Second Avenue.

"Which way are you headed?" He seems to have ditched his gray-suited, dressed-for-success companion, who was probably some underling.

"Downtown," says Billy, glancing quickly in my direction.

"So am I. I'll give you a lift," Bidwell says authoritatively. He steps into the avenue, hails a cab, and in a flash of male limbs, which fold easily into black, knife-torn vinyl seats, the slamming of a dented yellow door, they are gone.

I don't hear from Billy for three days. Nigel and I go forty blocks out of our way to drop Georgia at the door of her loft on West Broadway and Broome. She sits between us on the ride downtown like a child stuck between stuffy parents.

"Isn't it wonderful about Billy and Truman?" she cries.

"They're just sharing a cab together," I snap.

"Oh, sure," she says. "Sure."

She looks at me cannily, out of the corner of her eye, and I wonder if she knows. I wonder if she has any idea that, given the chance, I would trade places with Truman Bidwell in the blink of an eye, replacing his hand inching down the inside of Billy's thigh with my own.

I grab Nigel's hand and squeeze hard. We will go home tonight to our new apartment in Hell's Kitchen, and we will collapse on the mattress on the floor; we will talk for hours, dissecting the evening, our knees pulled up around us like embryos in wombs. He will run his fingers through my hair, comforting me as my tears soak our brand-new pillows. Perhaps in the dead of the night we will roll toward one another and connect below our bellies, sliding off the mattress onto the cold hard floor of our new apartment, each of us with our eyes closed tight, each of us dreaming forcibly of places and people farther away than we can imagine.

IX.

*B*illy's voice floats between my ears, up through the yellow plastic-coated wire of my Walkman, which I wear at all times while negotiating the streets of this city. It is part of my armor, as are my sunglasses and the cool, hard line of my lips as I gaze straight ahead, just above the eyebrows of passersby. To look a pedestrian in the eye is to risk contact of any kind: a smile, a wink, a nod, a knife. Last week a woman tried to run me over with her electronic wheelchair. When I jumped out of her way and into oncoming traffic I heard her laugh, a high-pitched, otherworldly sound, a cackle which told me that my bare legs poking out beneath my walking shorts, my sandaled feet, were an affront to her.

Sometimes I lose my bearings as I listen to Billy's words over and over again. I study them as if they are a prayer. I believe if I listen to the tapes enough, the narrow strings of words and sentences will somehow trickle through my aural canals and into my brain, where they will reside like pockets of air, like soft blue chlorine bubbles.

I strap the Walkman around my waist and press the *play* button while on buses, in the back of taxicabs, while walking to the theatre in the late afternoon. I listen to his voice before performances, and sometimes during intermission, quietly in a corner of my dressing room. I have told those who ask that I am listening to inspirational tapes, meditation tapes, classical music tapes from early twentieth-century St. Petersburg, the time and place Nabokov was a boy.

I close my eyes and rest my feet on my dressing table.

Last night I called Truman Bidwell, and you know what that means. I guess I was feeling like I needed to be punished. Yes, Josephson, that's where I received this beautiful shiner on my left eye. Looks like I got into a fist fight, doesn't it? There were fists involved, but for other purposes, I assure you.

Would you like to see my other bruises? They're not as visible. Truman didn't mean to do this to my face; he was quite apologetic afterward. My eye just met violently with the bedpost, that's all. I'll have to stay out of sight for the next few days. Can you imagine what would happen if I showed up at the institute looking like I've been in a barroom brawl? Actually, perhaps I should consider doing just that. It might do wonders for the rumors about my sexual proclivities.

What brought this on?

Why do you ask?

I can never let a year go by without calling Truman. After all, where else would I find someone so good at making me forget? Truman Bidwell is a cure for the vision beneath my closed eyes. For even just a moment he releases me from Joanna.

In Third World cultures don't they use leeches to cure certain diseases?

I felt driven to it, Josephson, the way an abused woman often feels compelled to endure the abuse, or the way masochists, in visiting pain upon themselves, are only covering up previous psychic pain. Isn't that the psychoanalytic theory? By subjecting oneself to whips and chains, the real wounds remain covered. The physical bondage is only a metaphor; the real bondage continues to be buried in the soul.

The pain replaces the fantasy, Josephson. Surely you, of all people, can understand that.

I knew that Billy never crawled with Nigel into a dark place, never whispered his name into the shallow void of his collarbone or the creased sheets of a bed. Their hands never entwined, their stomachs never met in the night like smooth, faceless animals. I now know the silent film which has always been projected inside the lids of Billy's closed eyes, the one which made him both run away from his hunger and embrace it in the form of multiple men at night.

There is the treachery of the body, and then there is the betrayal of the mind. I'm sure Billy would agree with me on this point. Billy's mind was his archenemy. It told him to seek peril: the hard lines of dangerous men, the gleaming eyes and twitching muscles of all the Truman Bidwells of the world. He hoped that in the act of abasement, in the bending over and baring of his defenseless self he would surrender his fantasies, he would offer them like eternal gifts on the funeral pyre of his body, crushing them with every snap of a belt against a bedpost, defeating them with each chafing twist of a rope against his hands held tightly above his head.

Now Billy's harshest wishes have been granted. His body

has betrayed him. His atrophied arms mock him every moment of the day, his legs dangle uselessly off the edge of his wheelchair, his stick of a neck protrudes from the bedclothes around him, pale and lifeless like the disembodied parts inside the cavity of a fresh turkey ready to be cooked.

The first time Billy and I ever made Thanksgiving dinner together, we bought a turkey at a kosher butcher on the Upper West Side, because we had heard kosher turkeys were fresher. Billy held the prickly yellow bird upright on the kitchen counter and turned to me.

"What do I do now?" he asked.

He was wearing an old apron of Georgia's, one she had been given during the days when she still had a mother-in-law; it had never been worn.

"Stick your hand in there," I said, pointing to the cavity, "and clean it out."

Billy stuck his hand into the bird, then let out a scream. He flung something across the room, something pale and prickly, long and thin. It landed on the far wall of the studio and stuck there for a moment before sliding to the floor.

He slid to the floor as well.

"What was that?" he asked. His eyes were shut tight.

I walked across the studio to retrieve it.

"The neck, Billy. It was the neck," I said, gingerly holding it in my hand.

"It didn't feel like a neck."

"Oh?"

"It felt like something altogether different from a neck," said Billy, "a different body part entirely."

"I guess you've felt more of them than I have," I said, dropping the neck into Billy's lap.

He jumped up then, shrieking, and started chasing me. We screamed with laughter like we hadn't done since we were

children together in Morristown, years which had floated by
without the weight of shame or disappointment.

He trapped me at the bed and collapsed on top of me,
pinning me down by my shoulders. We were twenty-two, and
it had been ten years since our first kiss.

He kissed me then, my stepbrother, closing his lips over
mine like a protective shield. It was almost a deferential kiss,
the kind a knight might have bestowed in medieval times on
the coronation ring of a member of royalty. His head gently
rested, for a moment, against my breast.

We looked at each other.

"A long time since I've done that," he said quietly.

He was up in a flash then, and wagging the turkey neck at
me. He threw it at me.

"Catch!"

I ducked just as the door to the studio opened, and the
turkey neck hit Nigel in the chest. He was holding a bouquet
of orange tulips, a paper bag full of clanking bottles.

"Hello, lovey," he said. He kissed me, bent down and
picked the neck up off the floor.

They say when we are born our bodies are vessels housing all
the qualities we will ever attain; that we are, at the moment of
our birth, all we will ever become. Our futures are within us,
unearthed slowly like layers of soil until we reach a rock hard
frontier beyond which there are no more lessons to learn.
When we are finished with our education, we die.

My mother is living two hours northeast of Rome in a
country I have never visited. I have her phone number, a long

series of digits which will connect me to the rectory. But it will not be Georgia who answers the phone.

"*Pronto,*" I will hear through the crackling wire, the voice of Pasca, the caretaker and cook who now runs Georgia's life.

More often than not, when I hear Pasca's voice, I gently place the receiver back on its cradle. My telephone bill is full of one-minute overseas calls to Italy.

Occasionally I try to communicate.

"*Buona notte,* Pasca," I shout, though shouting is unnecessary, "is *la signora* at home?"

She pauses. Since *la signora* never comes to the phone, what should Pasca say to me? She undoubtedly recognizes a thin trickle of fear in my voice crackling through the wires connecting the rectory to a city she has seen only in postcards, where buildings reach like silver blades into the sky and the sun still shines even when it is pitch dark in the Umbrian mountains.

Today I do not hang up the phone. When Pasca answers after eleven rings, I speak slowly, calmly, in English, as if she will understand me better if my voice is soothing.

"Pasca, this is Joanna. I must speak to *la signora* Hirsch."

There is silence across the Atlantic.

"*Mi madre,*" I say, lapsing into Spanish, which is better than no Italian.

"*No,*" she says, "*no la signora,*" she trails off and sits there silently, patiently. She waits, cradling the receiver between chin and shoulder, shelling peas from the garden. I have seen photographs of the rectory in *Architectural Digest: "The European Idyll of Georgia Higgins Hirsch."* A vegetable garden is planted along the edge of her property, which overlooks the hills of Orvieto. According to the article, Georgia bottles her own olive oil, eats her own vegetables, drinks homemade wine.

Pasca and I listen to the sounds of each other's breathing,

thousands of miles apart. A minute goes by, then another. We have made a silent pact, this stranger and I, not to sever the connection. Just as I am beginning to lose hope, I hear a clicking in the background, what I imagine to be the sound of leather heels echoing through the stone arches of the rectory, and I hear my mother's voice.

"Pasca, who was that?" I hear her ask as Pasca holds the phone in her hand, a sleek and dangerous object.

There is a muffled sound as Pasca covers the receiver, a gesture as suffocating as if her hand had reached through the wires and covered my mouth.

In a moment my mother's voice comes streaming to my ear, resonant, powerful, fully capable of destroying me.

"Joanna?"

"Yes," my voice catches in my throat.

"My God, Joanna," Georgia repeats; then, as if leaping off the waves and swells which separate us, I hear the echo of my name through the wire, *Joanna, Joanna.*

"Where are you right now?" I ask her.

I want to create a picture of Georgia in my mind.

"Outside on the terrace. On the portable phone," she says. Her voice is strangely hollow.

"What's wrong?" I ask.

I picture my mother curled up on a wrought-iron chair, long legs tucked beneath her, the heel of one boot digging into her buttock. She leans her head back against the top of the striped linen cushion, and her hair unfurls behind her like a black and white flag.

"Nothing."

"What do you mean, nothing?"

"I'm fine," she says in a monotone.

"Georgia, you don't sound fine. You're not making sense," I say, feeling my heart thud.

"No really. It's beautiful here, Josie. You should see it.

From where I'm sitting I can see vineyards in the distance, orchards . . . Do you know we bottle our own olive oil? You should taste—"

"I'd have to be invited," I say quietly.

She pauses. The line crackles between us.

"I'm sorry," she says, "I've needed to be thousands of miles from everything."

From your daughter, I think.

"Josie, the hills are—"

Her voice cracks, and she stops. I wait a few moments, listening to the silence. I close my eyes, trying to hear her breath, picture the clean line of her jaw nestled against the phone.

"Are you still there?" I ask. My words echo back to me through the line. *Still there, still there* . . .

"You should see the landscape—" Her voice breaks again.

"Georgia, what's wrong? Something's wrong."

"No."

"Tell me."

"No, goddamn it."

She falls silent again, and this time I'm sure I can hear the ocean between us. I am determined to wait her out. Minutes tick by. I listen to the roar.

Finally she begins, almost in a whisper.

"At first there were shades I could see: red, deep green, black and gray spots."

"What are you talking about?"

"Now it's only black and white, shades of gray."

I hear her hand covering the receiver, a muffled sound.

"Georgia, dammit—"

"Shut up and hear me out, Josie. You wanted to know."

"Speak in English, then. I'm not following you."

"Josie, the color's gone! Don't you understand?"

"You're not making any sense."

"Shades of gray, darkness and light—"

"I'm coming over there," I say.

"No!"

"You're scaring me."

"I don't want you here."

"When have you ever wanted me near you? When?" I scream into the receiver.

"Not now," she says.

"Have you seen a doctor?"

This is the way I have always been able to help my mother. I can tell her what to do. When you're sick, see a doctor. When you're hungry, eat a meal. When you're tired, sleep, then sleep some more.

"I can't leave the house," says Georgia Higgins Hirsch.

"What do you mean?" I will keep asking questions until I understand the answers. As the facts sink in, I imagine the worst: a brain tumor, a lesion behind Georgia's eyes.

"Every morning I wake up and lie in bed and pray to God that when I open my eyes colors will be there in front of me," she wails. "The dark stone walls, the reds of the Jackson Pollock between the windows, the pink marble slab from Carrara."

"Georgia . . ." I try to interrupt, but she keeps talking.

"Now it doesn't matter if I open my eyes or keep them closed. I can't work. I don't know what to do if I can't work."

"It's impossible that you would just wake up like this one morning," I say. "There must be an explanation."

"There's something behind my eyes," she says.

Her voice frightens me.

"Josie . . ."

She pauses.

"What?"

"Forget it."

"No. What?"

"It's okay if you want to come here," my mother says. Her voice is low, subdued.

She has never asked anything of me, and she has always expected the same in return. Though she has never said the words, *Please don't love me too much,* they have circled around her like a glowing magnetic field, giving off small shocks to anyone who attempted to get too close.

"Yes." My mouth forms around the word easily.

"You don't *have* to come. Only if you want to."

"Yes," I repeat.

"There's a flight that leaves JFK at eight tomorrow morning, your time," she says hopefully.

Of course it does not occur to her that I have a career, a life. Actually I don't have much of a life, but I do go onstage nightly. I expect this much of myself: I get through the days somehow without the numbing option of alcohol, and at night I walk onstage at my first cue. For the next two hours the words hold me upright; the heady, incalculable words of Nabokov, who would undoubtedly turn in his grave at this staging—at any public spectacle—of his memoir.

I have not missed a performance since opening night of *Speak, Memory*. It has been two hundred and three days since my last drink. This is what I have to be proud of in my life. This is what's left to me.

"I have some things to take care of," I tell her gently, "I'll be there as soon as I can."

"Take Alitalia," she says. Her voice is stronger. "Pasca will arrange for you to be picked up at the airport."

I'm not sure how she's done it, but she's just taken over again. It has been months since I've spoken to my mother, yet in less than five minutes she has managed to commandeer me with drivers, cooks, cosmopolitan emissaries who will carry out her missions. She may be having some sort of nervous breakdown high in the Umbrian mountains, but American dollars allow the outside machinery of her life to run smoothly. She will send her gardener to the telex office with instructions and her American Express card. She will crumple notes and dollars into Pasca's weathered hand and direct her to the next town, where there is a car service which will send a shiny old blue Mercedes winding through the hills and onto the autostrada, all the way to Leonardo da Vinci airport in Rome.

I wonder, does she perceive the great expanse over which she has no control? She can send drivers and cars, she can create a semblance of order with Pasca in the kitchen, shelling peas and picking fresh basil from the garden. Her only daughter will abandon her role in *Speak, Memory* and fly across the ocean in an attempt to save her. But here are some things the great Georgia cannot control: any day now, Nigel Easden will be knocking back three-dollar scotches in economy class on his way back to Liverpool. Perhaps he and I will cross each other's paths for the last time, in the air.

My father and Lila have bought a condominium in Long Island. Their backyard is on the ninth hole of the golf course, and they have insurance for the occasional wild drive which crashes through their glass-enclosed sun porch. Lila has joined the Ladies' Round Robin. My father has cut down on his medical practice, though he keeps his M.D. plates so he can park wherever he wants when they venture into the city for a matinee.

And Billy. She cannot change what has happened to Billy.

Gently I sever the connection between us. Georgia is in the process of telling me about the meals she will have Pasca prepare in honor of my arrival. She is telling me about the bedroom she will provide for me, in a circular tower. She will keep talking for a moment or two into the dark void before she realizes the line is dead.

In the meantime I have work to do. I have to dismantle what remains of my life.

When I close my eyes I see wilderness, Josephson, the hardened mud and worm-eaten leaves of my childhood. In my dreams you stand above me as I kiss Josie for the first time. You watch as she rolls on top of me, our bodies hard and young beneath our winter clothing, our backs grinding into the earth.

What was it that happened on that bed of twigs and leaves? What primeval chain was unleashed between us? Sometimes I feel that night has never ended, Josephson. On this couch I feel the earth beneath me, Josie's hair brushes my face, her breath in my ear.

Sometimes I get an erection lying here, as your pen flies across the paper. I know you are trying to help me. You formulate anagrams, cryptograms, genograms, but you cannot unravel what began in the wilderness nearly twenty years ago.

Here's a fantasy. I want to get Josie drunk, ply her with vodka tonics, force her into a blackout and spread her across my bed. No one would ever know. She would wake up in the morning with a vicious hangover and I would be gone. She would never suspect what had happened, even in her dreams. I would wipe the wetness between her legs with my handkerchief and carry it with me, never to be washed again. I would try to make her come through the psychotropic haze.

I went to the baths last night, Josephson. I think I had about a dozen men. Twelve angry men, as they say. I'm not sure. I lost

*count. I'm bleeding this morning. I'm wearing a sanitary pad, like a
girl. I disgust myself. Are you sure you haven't had enough of this?
What's your personal life like? Are you married? Do you have
children?*

*Josephson. Do you know why I love your name? I imagine you
were named after biblical Joseph, of the many-colored coat—history's first analyst—interpreter of the pharaoh's dreams.*

*Do you think I should ask Joanna to marry me? Are there laws
against that sort of thing? Or perhaps I should join an order of
monks in a foreign country, take my vows and shave my head.
Should I throw myself into my work and discover that my problems
pale in comparison to some of those around me?*

How could someone like me help anyone else?

What's that you ask?

Do I think I can help Joanna?

*The way I could help her best, Josephson, is to fall down and
die.*

We have been invited back to Tipton Academy, Billy and I, to
speak to the students in a special assembly on alternative
careers. Psychology and acting are considered uncommon vocations in a school whose graduates pepper the ranks of Wall
Street, starched and shiny-haired, clean fingernails drumming
against the surfaces of trading floor desks.

We drive to Morristown in my beat-up Volkswagen, the
radio broadcasting the only station it receives, WINS News.
For three cycles of twenty-two minutes, we listen to news,
weather, traffic and sports until the broadcasters' voices become mere background noise, fading into the rattling of the
car's engine, the cacophony of world events transformed into a

jumble of syllables, as meaningless as the low hum of a crowd waiting for a performance to begin.

"It's strange," Billy says.

These are the first words either of us has uttered since leaving the Lincoln Tunnel.

"What's strange?" I ask.

I don't take my eyes off the road. The double line of the highway weaves before me like the manifold yellow ribbons of wartime. We are passing Newark Airport, jets whining and descending overhead.

"Going back."

There is a long pause. We are each lost in our own thoughts, some of which undoubtedly extend to the same images: the dappled sunlight behind the Fiske Garden, the muddy leaves, the sound of reckless feet cracking through dry spring branches.

"Yeah," I say. "Would you ever have imagined we'd be asked back to speak to the students? You and me, of all people?"

We hoot with laughter.

"They actually called me and asked if I would convince you to come," Billy laughs. "I guess they think you're famous or something."

"Or something," I say.

We are somewhere between the ages of twenty-nine and thirty-one. All our lives we have been at the perfect age: when we were children, adults looked at us longingly and told us how lucky we were. When we were adolescents—this was the most absurd, most blindly nostalgic—there were those who told us these were the best years of our lives. When we were in our early twenties, we were self-conscious, embarrassed, aware for the first time of our youth.

And here we are. We have eluded the disasters of early life. We are still here, we are still young. We are suspended in the moment before the physical body begins to reverse itself. When I look closely at Billy's face I can see pale blue shadows beneath his eyes, lines in moments of repose where his dimples used to be. His hands are deeply veined, fully adult hands. They know the shape of grief; these hands which have balled up into fists, groped for an absent body in the dark, clenched each other like separate beings during the hours in which the sky turns from black to blue. These are the hands which have ached to reach out to me, and instead have consented to be tied together, bound tightly, rigidly at the wrists. They say our hands are the first to show signs of aging. It seems apparent why.

It is dangerous to think these thoughts with Billy by my side. He knows nothing of the missing tapes, the missing notes, and I am determined he never will. I try to act normally around him, unconcerned and only vaguely interested in the events of his life. When he doesn't call for a few days, I leave a message on his answering machine: "Hi, it's me. Give me a call today," I say as breezily as possible, envisioning my voice going into a room where his body lies white and naked, arms outstretched, tied to the bedpost.

I've considered arriving at the door of his brownstone apartment late at night, wearing nothing more than a raincoat, wrapped tightly around my waist with an elaborate bow, a human sacrifice, a gift. I would silently hand him a letter, carefully composed earlier in the evening, sealed in an envelope with two plane tickets to an exotic destination and the entire contents of my bank account. "Let's go," I would whisper to him, pulling him by the hand, searching through his bureau drawers for his passport. "Let's go where no one will ever find us."

Billy bumps alongside me in the front seat of the Volkswagen. He is drumming his fingers on the dashboard, keeping time to the theme song of WINS News Radio. He has removed his jacket and rolled up his shirt cuffs. His forearms are veiny and as perfectly delineated as the diagrams of musculature they used to show us in tenth-grade anatomy class.

"Are we there yet?" he jokes.

I don't answer. The radio tells us for the third time about the riots in Tiananmen Square.

"Are we there yet?" he repeats.

"A few more minutes," I say.

"I need to stop at a bathroom."

"Billy!"

"Really, I'm not kidding."

I swerve the VW from the fast lane into the Guy Lombardo service area. I wonder if there are committees that decide which dead Americans are accorded the honor of eternal life in reflective white and green, alongside gas pumps and concession stands on the Jersey Turnpike, rest rooms with graffiti hearts illustrating the current love affairs between teenagers in the state. *Tony & Miranda 4Ever. Sasha loves Jimmy Z.*

I face the stall door at the Guy Lombardo service stop. Directly beneath the heart which surrounds Sasha and Jimmy there is red magic marker in the same handwriting: *Jimmy Z. sucks.* I fish through my handbag for a pen, pulling it out of a leather loophole in my datebook. With it, I scratch the surface of the metal rest room door. *Billy Overmeyer was here,* I scrape into the paint. I go over the letters twice, three times, until I am sure they will stay there forever, or at least until the next coat of paint wipes out a decade of wishful thinking.

I gather my belongings, then throw my ruined pen into the metal trash container. Everything in this public area is metal, unassailable. I stare at my face in the bathroom mirror. There is a banging on the door.

"Josie, let's go! The kiddies are waiting," Billy calls.

I open the door and he is standing there.

"What's wrong?" he asks quickly, looking at me.

"Nothing."

"You look pale," he says. "Are you sure you're all right?"

This is how I will dream of Billy for the rest of my life: he is wearing an Italian suit, his shoes are tassled and perfectly shined. His hair is slicked back from his forehead with some sort of gel which makes it look soft and wet, and his hands are opened slightly as if there is something he is offering me, a small pulsing thing, whatever piece of himself he can give me with all the generosity and bewilderment in his heart.

Billy and I sit side by side onstage in the auditorium. There are four other Tipton alumni seated at the long conference table who are also considered to have succeeded in alternative careers: one man is an editor at a literary publishing house, one works as an art director in an advertising agency, and the two women are legal aid lawyers.

We are the returning heroes. We have it made. Billy has a shingle on the Upper East Side, a book contract for his thesis and a money market account. I have a reel of commercials for various dishwashing liquids, soap opera appearances and the beginnings of a legitimate career. Now, when people ask me what I do and I tell them I'm an actress, I no longer feel as though I'm lying.

For these reasons, Billy and I are seated on this panel of recent Tipton graduates. Our purpose is to illustrate for these boys and girls the promise which has been made to them since they were infants basking in their parents' suburban sunrooms: they will be led through life by some invisible guardian angel, a source of comfort and prosperity. They will move slowly, inexorably, toward futures of accomplishment and grace. And throughout their lives, they will be governed by an unspoken dictum which, if voiced, would tell them they are special, and are entitled—moreover, expected—to live in a world where homelessness, poverty, aberration, failure and loss of courage are simply not possibilities. Their faces are like a string of lights seen on a passing ship at sea, surprisingly bright and uniform. They look at Billy, at me, at the art director, the legal aid lawyers, and they see the glamorous outlines of their adult lives which will unfurl after requisite attendance at an Ivy League institution.

Here are some things they don't know about Billy and me, some truths we have not been brought here to tell them: beneath Billy Overmeyer's Italian suit, there are raised welts the size and shape of beestings. He wears Maxithins to protect his pants. And my body is always in a state of detoxification. The night sweats, the parched throat, the shaking hands. When I have a morning television job I try not to drink the night before, because the alcohol shows up beneath my chin and my cheekbones, emphasized by the camera, adding fifteen or twenty pounds. No one has noticed. I work in a business where excess is expected and encouraged until it crosses an invisible line and becomes dangerous. No one tells us about that line. One day we find ourselves on the other side of it, and we are aware of our fall from grace only by a silence, a terrible silence that hovers above the telephone like a stale cloud of cigarette smoke, or hangs in the static of a hold button, the secretary's lying voice telling us our calls will be returned at some later date.

I know Billy has crossed the line. It has been several months since I have had the tapes in my possession. I wonder if he knows the tapes exist at all. Perhaps Maria Josephson hid the recorder under her leather chair, or attached small wires to her velvet-covered Victorian couch. Is it ethical to tape analysands without their knowledge? In the name of sanity and spiritual growth?

And am I one to discuss ethics in this situation?

I have wondered what to do. I have thought of returning them anonymously to Maria Josephson, leaving them wrapped neatly in brown paper on her office doorstep. I should ring her bell and run, scurrying quickly down Central Park West, dodging pedestrians and baby strollers until I melded in with the crowd. I have thought of calling her and making an appointment. *This is Joanna Hirsch,* I would say, *I have something to discuss with you.* Her voice would rise slightly, but she would express no surprise. A calm, unruffled manner is one of the things they teach psychology students in graduate school. Look at Billy. His exterior is as smooth and polished as any of those walking down Madison Avenue. He buys his decaffeinated cappuccino at Three Guys Restaurant on the corner of Seventy-fourth and Madison, picks up a gourmet lunch at Grace's Market. His wounds are hidden beneath custom shirts and reflecting sunglasses, a good working knowledge of the DSM-III, the PDR, the complete works of Freud.

There is power in this knowledge, a remote belief to cling to: if information can cure, surely he can heal himself.

We do a good job at the school, Billy and I. We accomplish what we were asked to do. We paint the future rosy for these boys and girls; we allow them to believe their prospects are limitless, and in doing so, for a brief couple of hours, we believe it ourselves. We sit in the land of privilege and rolling hills, in the auditorium in which parents and great-grandparents of these students began their own illustrious careers, in these very rows, on this very stage. There are horses in the school stables, a new electronic scoreboard on the lacrosse field, plaques with gold names of sports heroes. We, too, are champions. We have met our early promise. We have done Tipton Academy proud.

X.

$\mathcal{M}$y plane is sitting on the tarmac at Kennedy Airport, where we have been fifth in line for takeoff for the past two hours. A summer storm is passing overhead; although it is morning, the sky crackles white in the dark, and thunder shakes the ground beneath us. The pilot's voice broadcasts through the plane every twenty minutes or so, nasal and resigned, informing us that we will be cleared momentarily for takeoff.

When I picked up my ticket, I was struck by two things: first of all, it was a first-class ticket. No one I know flies first class unless someone else is paying for it. Secondly, it was a one-way ticket. New York to Rome. I searched through the papers, but there was no return flight.

Does she assume I'm moving in with her? Does she think I will guide her gently through the cobblestone streets of Or-

vieto, pointing out bits of color along the way: an orange tabby
cat slipping into an alley, the brightness of a Cinzano umbrella
in a café?

She has another thought coming.

The first-class section is full, and there are two stewardesses for twelve passengers. One of the stewardesses keeps
asking me if I wouldn't like a drink—a mimosa, perhaps, or a
glass of white wine?—while we're waiting. It takes every ounce
of willpower I have to say no, to gulp, instead, from the glass
of mineral water which she keeps refilling in this stifling, pressurized cabin. I play a game with myself, a game which I
sometimes play when real life doesn't seem to be adequate: I
pretend I'm someone else. Now I am a woman who is used to
flying first class, who has never been too interested in a drink,
who fans herself coolly, delicately, with her copy of the *New
York Times;* she doesn't have a problem with newsprint smudg-
ing her fingers and dirtying her clean white pants. She doesn't
feel faint from the cabin's dead air. She wouldn't sell her soul
for a stash of airline vodka bottles.

Unlike me, this imaginary woman would have control over
her life. She would not allow herself to be driven two hours
north on the Autostrada del Sole, deep into the green, mystical
hills. She would not permit herself to be deposited like a sack
of limp laundry at the feet of her mother. She would not be
blinded by the image of a mother looming before her, larger
than life, as if the infant's perception of a lofty giantess hovering above the crib had been maintained in adulthood, so that
as the child grew tall and strong, so the mother grew taller,
stronger, in a race which could be won by only one of them.

They have now informed us that we are going to disem-
bark because of the weather, and may not be departing for
Rome until early afternoon. It is eleven in the morning, and
we have been on the runway for nearly three hours.

For a brief moment I consider abandoning this whole trip

and taking a taxi back to New York, where at least I know I am home. But what waits for me there? I am still surrounded by odds and ends Nigel left behind: dog-eared copies of Ibsen plays, biographies of Olivier, James Dean, Werner Erhard, moth-eaten sweaters knitted by his grandmother, manuscript boxes full of old rejection letters from theatre companies across the United States.

There is nothing for me in New York, in the hissing summer potholes of Hell's Kitchen, the rancid fruit blistering in the sun of Eighth Avenue bodegas, the Lincoln Tunnel leading like a mineshaft underground, burrowing beneath the Hudson River, toward Billy.

An announcement blares over the loudspeakers in the Alitalia waiting lounge. "Boarding for Alitalia Flight 103 to Rome will be delayed until further notice." Amid bilingual groans and a shuffling of luggage and feet, I walk to the back of the waiting area and place my small carry-on in a corner where I am sure no one will be interested in it. Then I amble past the metal detectors and security guards, into the busiest part of the terminal where there are duty-free shops, newsstands and bars. I walk as if I am in a trance, as if I don't know where my feet are carrying me, my final destination.

The sign is lit up in red neon—BAR! BAR! BAR!—just in case those passing by would not be lured inside by the rows of bottles alone, glistening behind the shiny counter, reflected endlessly in the mirror painted with the bold bright labels of different beers.

Beer is not what I'm after.

I plop down on a bar stool wearily, as if by eleven-thirty in the morning I of course deserve a drink. I am already on Italian time. It's cocktail hour in the Umbrian mountains. I order a Bloody Mary with a double shot of Stolichnaya, and silently toast Georgia, raising the glass to my lips as easily as if

I had done this yesterday, and the day before yesterday, as if it has not been a meticulously counted two hundred and fourteen days since my last drink. The thick rim of the airport glass touches my lips and I marvel at how easy it is: I wonder if, across the ocean, my mother is pouring herself a glass of wine. Would she be able to distinguish between the decanters of white and red, or would she require Pasca's help? I know I wouldn't need Pasca in order to find the liquor; I would sniff it out. I have been feeling my way around bottles for most of my life. This act of curling my fingers around a cold ice-filled glass and raising my arm to my mouth in a slow, methodical rhythm seems to have been bred into me, an action I will never forget no matter how long I abstain, like riding a bicycle or making love. It has been many months since I have made love, yet I can imagine exactly what it would feel like to pull the bartender into an airport rest room, unzip his fly, raise my skirt and wrap my legs around his waist in a single motion. I have not forgotten.

The hot trickle of vodka courses down my throat, spreading warmth like orange coils of electric heat through my rib cage, my solar plexus.

I rap my glass on the bar and ask for another one.

"Another double?" asks the bartender, who doesn't suspect that I have just mentally undressed him.

"Yes," I say, "in a plastic cup, please. I have a flight to catch."

$\mathcal{I}$ always believed I would die young. I theorized that I would die in my sleep, a random, unassuming victim of a premature heart attack, a stroke in the night. Although we lived in Hell's Kitchen, I never really believed I would fall prey to a mugger, nor did I worry that a thief would find his way through the iron gates on our windows. I believed my death would be untimely, wasteful, triggered from the inside out. My body was my enemy.

I always made sure Georgia had keys to my apartment, even though she never reciprocated, and I never would have considered dropping by her loft without phoning first. I wanted Georgia to have access to my studio, in preparation for the morning which I was certain would come before I reached my thirtieth birthday. I wanted Georgia to be the one to find me.

Why was it Georgia to whom I accorded this honor, one more image to add to her already overburdened soul? She watched her father gunned down, one of a crowd of worshipers brought to their knees and then to their bellies by boys out of uniform; she nursed Vishna Kripalu until he grew so frail he seemed not to die but rather to fade into the air; and now I wanted her to see her daughter, her most accurate self-portrait, greet the end of her life with arms open and legs dangling over the edge of a bed.

In my imaginary death, why was it not Nigel I wished to find me in my pale misfortune? Why not Billy?

Because it all began with Georgia. I wanted her to scoop me into her arms and bury me with her own hands. I wanted her to feel the dirt beneath her fingernails, to see the animal life embedded six feet below the ground, the clear-winged beetles, the citizenry of the night.

I wanted to shock her into the realization that a life built solely on one's own shoulders—*I have to look out for me,* she always said—may some day come crashing down in splinters and shards beneath the albatross of love.

$\mathcal{T}$wo hundred and fourteen days. A little more than seven months without a drink. Now, today, with a few spoken words, the dispensing of a couple of dollars, the swallowing of the liquid, clear liquid disguised and softened by the spicy blood red mix—I have forgotten in a single instant about the shakes in the beginning, the night sweats, the imaginary cockroaches I used to see crawling up the walls of my studio in the dark.

I am on my way to see my mother who may, for the first time in her life, need me.

These are thoughts I cannot face with the clarity I still possess after a few cups of vodka. I need more of my trusty companion—the cold, clear syrup—the one which has never let me down.

$\mathcal{I}$t is summer. I am performing Shakespeare in Central Park, a Joseph Papp production of *As You Like It*. I am playing the role of Audrey, a country wench, and it is my first big break. It is a small role, but I have several speaking lines, a fact which enables me, after years of futile attempts, to finally become a member of Actors' Equity.

"I do desire it with all my heart: and I hope it is no dishonest desire, to desire to be a woman of the world," I say, my mouth forming elastically around the vowels, four years of training in classical English standing me in good stead.

"I do not know what poetical is. Is it honest in deed and word? Is it a true thing?"

The words still burn into my mind, as surely as if they were branded there. We should have been performing *King Lear* that night, or *Medea*, or any of the great tragedies. Instead we were doing a comedy, playing the fools in the deepest dark of the sweltering New York City summer.

Opening night. Tonight, Georgia has finally decided she is ready to watch me perform. She is not in Paris, or Milwaukee, or Madrid. She doesn't have a more important engagement. There are no gallery openings, no crushing deadlines. Besides, she has known Joe Papp for years.

"I'll call him to get a reserved seat," she said when I invited her. "I don't want to stand on those awful lines."

"Don't call him, Georgia. I'll get you tickets. And I'll ask Billy and Nigel to pick you up and bring you with them. You won't have to wait on line. I'll take care of it," I said.

Papp never knew I was her daughter. I'm sure of it.

The lines that night snaked around the Delacorte Theater and halfway to Central Park West. There were older women standing in pairs, holding shopping bags from the Silver Palate, college-age couples wearing shorts and tank tops, carrying blankets and bottles of wine. There was a threat of a thunderstorm in the air, and collapsible umbrellas could be seen poking from the tops of picnic baskets.

Concerts and theatre in Central Park are summer mainstays of life in the city, great equalizers, times when Fifth Avenue families blend with those who usually open doors for them. At first these people in their light summer linens barely recognize their doormen out of uniform, lolling on the burnt brown grass waiting for tickets to the evening's performance.

Complementary tickets doled out to cast and production staff members are more coveted and valuable than any ticket to a Broadway show. We are each allowed two advance tickets for opening night. I give mine to Georgia and Billy. Nigel knows the man at the box office, who used to wait tables at Pacific Rim, so he'll be able to slip in any time he wants. Nigel hasn't told me whether he'll be coming to opening night. He's barely spoken to me since I got the part, at which time he muttered something about my "weakness at Shakespearean dialect," something we both know to be untrue.

We are living in the days before *Speak, Memory,* shortly before my career begins to fall into place, adjusting to a track which leads to larger audiences, the money to buy a living room couch and countless white lies in the pages of glossy magazines. Nigel is beginning to despise me—the slow, clinical result of envy—but he has not yet let me know it. Or perhaps I am blind. He has not yet walked out of my life.

No matter.

The show was a blur, as it always is. When I perform I am in a time warp. When it is over I can't tell you what happened. I lose consciousness on stage. I black out. The applause, I remember, was loud and enthusiastic. It was before the review came in the next day's paper, condemning the production of *As You Like It.* This audience was caught up in the moment, the bows of the movie stars playing Orlando and Jaques.

When I took my curtain call with the whole cast, our sweaty palms joined together, our hands raised in fists above our heads then lowered as we bowed simultaneously, I looked into the audience. My mother was in the third row, front and center, as I had always imagined her to be in every performance since I was an eighteen-year-old drama student. If actors could dedicate performances the way authors dedicate books, mine would all be for Georgia.

She was sitting erect, between Billy and Nigel. Billy was clapping wildly (I even thought I heard him whistle). Nigel was sitting with his arms crossed, squinting into the stage lights, his mouth a grim line. Georgia was leaning slightly in

Billy's direction, her hands moving together and apart in slow motion. I saw her whisper something to Billy, and he leaned his head back and laughed. I wondered what she was saying, my charming mother. I flushed, fearing she had said something about me, disparaging and cruel. Would Billy have laughed, then? I like to think he would have turned away from her angrily. He had always been able to protect me, to wrap himself around me like a shell. I sometimes wonder if all his sheltering of me left him somehow exposed to the elements.

But I can't think about that now. The captain has turned off the Fasten Seat Belts sign. We are free to move about the cabin. If I follow the path of assigning blame, I will force myself against the emergency exit of this jet, I will twist the various knobs and handles in a motion so fast that no one will be able to stop me. I will be inhaled by the wind out of this pressurized cabin and into the sky. I wonder if I would be enveloped by the sea on impact, or whether the moment of death would be brutal, like crashing at an impossible speed into a solid blue wall.

This is how I will always remember Billy: he is sitting in the third row of the Delacorte Theater, next to the other person I love most in the world, my mother. His hair lies limp against his head in the humid August air, then is blown across his forehead by a strong summer breeze (the breeze which will later bring with it the white flashes of lightning, the thunder louder than any Harlem night). His arms are raised above his head and he is clapping. His teeth—perfect, even, white— glimmer in the dark. There is a light emanating from him: the shock of blond hair, pale rosy skin, gangly limbs which I had always been able to spot from far away on a soccer field, now call out to me, a beacon among hundreds of faces, strangers in this night. He is wearing a light pink oxford-cloth shirt with a white tee-shirt beneath it, faded jeans held up by a belt too large for him, the leather strap hanging down like the lolling tongue of a dog. He is wearing thick white cotton socks and good loafers. On his wrist there is a braided rope bracelet, given to him by a lover who tied it on his wrist, telling him that the bracelet had ancient Indonesian powers, that Billy must allow it to unravel—to remove it oneself would bring the worst kind of luck.

Later in this night I will rip the pink oxford cloth away from Billy's chest. I will tear my own white tee-shirt from neck to waist, I will wrap it around his head like a tourniquet. I will hold his head in my lap and feel his blood seep through my pants, onto my skin, dark and slick as oil. I will rock him back and forth, closing his ears to the sounds of shrieking, of sirens, of bottle-necked ambulances on Central Park West.

We left the Delacorte Theater in Central Park, Georgia, Nigel, Billy and I. The crowd had dispersed during the time it took me to remove my heavy stage makeup and change from my Edwardian outfit into street clothes. There were a few straggling audience members near the makeshift stage door, waiting for autographs from some of the stars. Janitors were sweeping up, and two lighting technicians were standing on-stage, discussing a mechanical problem which occurred during the evening's performance.

"Let's get something to eat," said Georgia, "I'm famished." She didn't say a word about the show.

"Where to?" asked Nigel. "Des Artistes? Café Luxembourg?"

I mentally kicked him. He had just mentioned two of Manhattan's expensive restaurants. We certainly didn't have one hundred dollars for dinner. As it stood, our telephone was dangerously close to being disconnected. Did he think Georgia was going to treat us? Or Billy? I didn't enjoy being taken out to dinner. It reminded me of how poor we were, and Nigel always ordered the most expensive thing on the menu, starved for excess. We saw it at Pacific Rim every night, the expense account dinners replete with caviar and Veuve Clicquot, desserts which were left almost untouched on the plate.

"No, I'd like to walk a little," I said.

I was high from the performance, from a few glasses of champagne backstage with the cast, and I was also angry. Angry with Georgia for not being another kind of mother, the Lila Overmeyer variety, the kind who would sweep me into her arms and look into my eyes, her voice breaking as she tells me she's proud of me.

"The park's empty," said Billy. "Let's just go straight over to Central Park West."

"I want to walk down to Seventy-second Street, Billy," I said. "We can eat something at Dallas Jones Barbecue."

I didn't turn around, but I knew Nigel was wrinkling his nose. Dallas Jones was a cavernous place where they served chicken and ribs. But the reason I liked it was the size of the margaritas, served in huge, potent tubs.

"No, really, Jo. Let's just walk out here," Billy said, and I began running, following his directions, running down the exit ramp out to Central Park West, sprinting over the cobblestones with all the adrenaline at my command, daring them to follow. The air was heavy that night, the trees still. There were few cars, only a remote bleating of horns in the distance. My feet carried me through the darkness unseen, as if kicking through water, and after a moment I heard footsteps pounding behind me. I was grabbed around the waist, then there was Billy's breath in my ear: "You were wonderful tonight," he said.

I sometimes wonder if I imagined these words: "I love you so much," he whispered, "I'm proud of you." It never struck me as odd that these words were coming not from my mother, not from my lover, but from my stepbrother, his blond hair shining in the black of the night, his pink shirt already soaked through the back with sweat.

We stood there for a moment, Billy and I, his arms still around me. Nigel and Georgia caught up with us.

"Hey, Overmeyer, take your hands off my woman," Nigel half-joked.

Billy released me.

Sometimes, when I can't sleep at night, I can still feel his arms around my waist, the stubble on his chin tickling my neck.

We began to walk in one straight file, soldiers striding next to the stone wall which separated Central Park from the street. Nigel was to my left, Billy to my right, and Georgia next to Billy. There were no cyclists that night, no joggers with reflectors on their ankles and wrists. The air smelled of horse dung and leaves on the trees rustled in the wind which was beginning to surface.

"It's going to storm," said Nigel flatly.

"Marvelous," said Georgia.

I remember how she relished the idea.

"Isn't the fellow who played Touchstone a character on 'thirtysomething'?" Billy asked.

"No, you're remembering him from 'The Partridge Family,' " I say. "Don't you remember, he played one of the kids on 'The Partridge Family'?"

"No!"

"Yes. From the ridiculous to the sublime," I say.

"Those sit-com actors always need to prove themselves," said Nigel, "and they invariably fall on their miserable pansy asses."

"What did you just say?" asked Billy, leaning forward so he could see Nigel.

"Beats me. What did I just say?"

"Pansy is a derogatory term used to describe faggots," Billy said. "Kindly take it back."

"You just called yourself a faggot," Nigel said. "Why can't I?"

"Ah! Only the persecuted can refer to their own persecution."

"Bullshit!" snapped Georgia.

After this exchange we were silent for a few paces. We passed a family sleeping on a park bench, a mother and two children wrapped together in a poncho probably fished out of a trash can, the red nylon fabric enveloping them, a precautionary measure, a brightly colored raft at sea.

"Georgia, what did you think of tonight's performance?" I asked, finding just the right tone of voice, a reed thin, fluty honk through the dark, a general question which required no more than the vaguest of answers.

She did not disappoint me.

"Very nice," she said.

"Very nice!" sputtered Nigel. "Very nice? It was a piece of dog doo. No offense, Josie."

" 'No offense'? 'Very nice'? I can't believe you people," said Billy. "Can't you once, just this once, find something decent to say to Josie? Do you know how many actresses auditioned for her role?"

Awkward silence.

"How many, Joanna?" Georgia asked.

"Forty or fifty," I mumbled.

"Are you ready for a lifetime of that kind of competition? Because it will only get worse," said Georgia. "It takes a heart of stone."

"Listen to you!" cried Billy. "To both of you!"

And at that moment the shadow appeared. I heard it before I saw it and knew from the sound of pounding feet that there were eyes darting quickly over us, assessing us through a haze of pale powder-scorched lungs. A hand reached out and pulled with more force than I thought possible in such a skinny needle-tracked arm. It snapped Georgia's bag from her shoulder and pushed her across us. She grabbed my hair as she fell, and I went down with her in a tangle of hips and elbows.

Heat lightning had begun and as I felt my own shriek die like bile in my throat, I lifted my head to watch the mugger run, lit every few seconds by a white flash which made it look as if he were moving in slow motion, an actor in an ancient film perhaps, full of jerky movements.

Georgia's body was shaking, and I wondered if she was in shock. I looked down at her for a moment, her chattering teeth, then up again at the receding back of the man, two men running now, the shadow had a shadow like the paper dolls we used to cut from construction paper as children, one stick figure following another: Billy had taken off after him.

Nigel stood there breathing heavily, as if it were he who was running.

"He's insane," he muttered, "he's going to get us all killed."

Georgia moaned, a primordial sound, as if in sleep.

Sometimes my mind plays tricks on me. A clear plastic shower ring becomes a hospital bracelet in my mind's eye, the ring of a telephone pierces the night like a siren, and anything red appears to be blood.

There is a man who sits on Madison Avenue and Seventy-sixth Street, on the sidewalk. He holds a sign: *I am homeless and have AIDS (I have proof!). Just need $16.37 to get back to Florida. Please help me. (I have proof!)*

The man has been there intermittently for at least a year. When I passed him last week on the way to Georgia's travel office to pick up my plane ticket to Rome, he was still there. Open sores stare at passersby like the waxy eyes of the dead.

They cover his shins, neck, forearms. His sign is the same. He still needs sixteen dollars and thirty-seven cents. And it is possible, in this city, that a year may have passed without a single penny being tossed, from a vast distance, into his paper cup.

On the other side of this stately avenue, street vendors who have set up their wares near the entrances to the park begin to take cover, wheeling their squeaky apparatus into nearby vans with gates on the windows and hand-printed signs (*no radio, no nothing*); those headed home after late office hours quicken their pace, eyes fastened to the dark birdless sky; rubber runners are placed by doormen inside the marble lobbies on Central Park West.

But on this particular block, in the shadows cast by old trees and stone walls, just across the street from civilization, Georgia Higgins Hirsch lies in a heap, and now she is writhing. I feel something move beneath her light summer sweater, and realize her shoulder—yanked away from her neck by the pull of a leather strap—is dislocated. I hold it in place, willing her to stop moving, feeling the bile rise again in my throat. The sculptor in Georgia would appreciate this sensation, this bony knob of human frailty moving in my hand like the head of a hot, newborn pup.

In the few seconds which, in memory, stretch into hours, Nigel has been crouching next to Georgia, as still as one of the bronze war heroes which populate the park. His eyes are invisible to me, trapped behind the glare of the street lights. His hands clench and unclench as he watches Billy sprint—legs splayed out like a hurdler—the way he used to run when he was captain of the track team at Tipton.

Georgia begins screaming, and Nigel clamps a hand over her mouth.

"Stop it," he hisses.

There is now the sound of pounding feet in the asphalt, like thunder through the night. There are people coming to help us, I think.

Help! I try to scream, but not a sound comes out. *Someone help!*

They come out of the bushes, from behind trees, and they have not come to help us, but to help the shadow. The mugger turns when he sees them, eyes dark as the baseball bat he holds in his hand, and this is what I remember of him, like a black-and-white photograph seen only once, an image so stark it remains forever in the eye: white tee-shirt, black jeans, thick orderly lines painted on the roadway, white high-top sneakers, and the bat so dark it almost fades into the night until the instant he sways toward Billy's head and, with a *crack* like a home run, swings it so fast it is impossible to see Billy jerk back, the way he falls against the concrete barrier of the exit ramp, blood dripping against graffiti and stone.

The rain has begun. It hisses on the steaming asphalt, it makes slapping sounds as the mugger is surrounded by his friends. The blood pouring from just above Billy's left eyebrow is diluted with rainwater. They stand over him with their bats, with damp branches, and swing at him, kicking him in the ribs.

"Do something," Georgia groans. "Nigel—"

But Nigel has turned his back; he is hunched over, vomiting.

"Can't you—"

"Sssshh." He turns. His chin is wet. He presses a finger to his lips. "They don't know we're here."

They are rolling Billy back and forth. First there are four of them, then five, then six. They kick his back so hard I hear the thud of impact from where we stand, motionless. His hair is matted, eyes swollen into slits. *C'mon, man, we better get out of here,* I hear one of them call in a high voice, a boy's voice. *Let's leave this faggot to rot.*

I feel Georgia behind me on the ground. She has reached her one working arm around me to hold me still. She places her palm over my eyes, closing them. We are in the Rambles, the part of Central Park where men come alone in search of other men, and packs of boys lie in wait for moments such as this one.

I break away from Georgia and run toward the gang, my voice returning, screeching, an inhuman sound. I flail my arms madly, pedaling through the air, and somehow I frighten them; they scatter into the darkness, back into the wilderness, the low stone walls.

I am kneeling by Billy, his head in my lap.

"Don't move him!" someone says.

Suddenly there are people, a whole damn crowd of people.

"Keep his head still!"

"Wrap his head!"

"Keep him warm!"

I rip my own shirt open, buttons flying, yank it off my body like an animal caught in a trap. Under my blouse I am wearing a cotton tee-shirt, which I pull over my head, then tear a panel down the front, and wrap the thin white cotton tightly around his head once, twice; immediately the fabric is red. Not just in spots, but all of it. I cover the makeshift tourniquet with anything handed to me: my blouse, paper towels, handkerchiefs. I feel someone place a jacket over my bare back.

There is an ambulance in the distance, and for the first time in my life I understand why the sound of the siren is described as a wail. It is steady, a sound the human ear cannot bear as it moves closer.

I begin to whisper, and my voice seems to be louder than

the approaching siren. I bend my head and murmur steadily into Billy's ear, as if my words will somehow keep him conscious, keep him afloat until the real work begins.

I say anything that comes to mind.

"Are you with me?" I ask him.

He moans. His eyes are turning to glass.

"Everything's going to be all right," I whisper, shutting my eyes tightly as I say it, pained by my own lack of authenticity or vision. These are television words, Marcus Welby words. "Everything's going to be all right," I drone again and again.

Billy looks at me then, and I see his eyes go in and out of focus.

"No, Josie."

When he opens his mouth, blood spurts out, a solid mass, covering both our faces.

These were the last words Billy Overmeyer ever said to me.

"No, Josie," he said, his voice bubbling up from a foreign dwelling, his eyes focusing on me for a split second before he lost consciousness. And in the months following, in a bed made daily with colorless sheets, in a room filled with flowers which he could neither see nor smell, in days indistinguishable from nights, I wonder whether there was an image gliding through the blackness, my face smeared with blood, my hair, my bare breasts hanging over him like a lover's, my lips parting, moving soundlessly, telling the biggest lie I had ever told him.

Ah, Josephson, Josephson. Don't you see? I'm a hybrid, a hunchback, half-man, half-beast. I'm a medieval cartoon, I'm what

mothers always warned their children would happen if they mas-
turbated, or in twisting their features into a grimace—their faces
would become frozen forever with eyes crossed, gums pulled back
from teeth.

Guess what, Josephson, hold onto your seat. I met someone this
weekend, someone I actually like. His name is Eric and he's in the
research department at Merrill Lynch. He looks as straight as they
come, Josephson, as straight as I appear to be, I'm sure, in my
brand-new Eames chair where I sit and nod sagely at people who
are crazy enough to pay me $100 an hour for my acute psychologi-
cal expertise.

Eric wants to get married. He wants to be with the same man
at the end of each day, sliding into restaurant banquettes, meeting
in the aisles of video stores, ordering Chinese food delivered by fast
boys on bicycles on dim, rainy nights.

It seems he wants me, Josephson. He wants this lonely fellow,
this poor specimen who spreads out before you each weekday
morning on this couch and tries to heal the echo chamber which is
his heart.

He's already told me he thinks he's falling in love with me.

After only two nights!

Can't he see?

Oh, physician, heal thyself.

Dinner has been served, the movie is over, the shades have
been lowered to block the sun. There are pinpoints of light
scattered through the cabin, small overhead beams aimed at
books, legal pads, laptop computers as passengers work,
oblivious to the speed at which they are traveling, crossing
time zones, racing into the night.

It is safe to say I am drunk. I have been drinking for almost seven hours now, a full day's work. I bypassed dinner, which even in first class looked uninteresting, particularly when compared to the choice of red or white wines meant to accompany the meal.

I drink my dinner, and have been drinking my dessert as well. I took a breather for a few hours and slept during the movie, which I gathered from watching the beginning without the sound is about a career woman who chucks it all and moves to Vermont to raise a baby. She trades in her silk separates for perfectly faded flannel shirts—this fashion statement being indicative of a spiritual change—and she buys a storybook house. In my dream I move to a house in the middle of nowhere, and Billy and Georgia come to visit me. The house is surrounded by many flights of stairs and a body of water. Billy and Georgia climb and climb to see my beautiful new house, then Georgia slips and falls into the deep water. In my dream I stand there screaming as Billy dives in to rescue her; as she plummets he grabs her hair and begins to pull her to the surface, but it takes much longer to come up than it did to go down. It is always faster to go down.

I have switched from vodka to white wine to red wine to cognac, and as the captain turns on the No Smoking and Fasten Seat Belt signs, and informs us in several languages that we are beginning our descent to Rome, I hold my glass of cognac in my lap beneath my blanket, so the stewardess will not take it away.

I wonder what the odds are that my mother will be there when we land in Rome. I look through my wallet, fingering two hundred American dollars, half the contents of my savings account. I hope it's enough to get to Orvieto.

As the plane circles and begins its descent, I clench my fists together, press the arches of my feet against the floor, squeeze my eyes shut, harden the muscles of my stomach as if

I'm about to be punched. I am doing a body check, going over each limb and muscle the way the pilot inspected the jet's gauges in the cockpit before takeoff. It seems logical to me, somehow irrefutable, that at any moment some significant part of my body will fail. It is possible to be running one moment and paralyzed the next; it is conceivable to wake up to a black-and-white world. I imagine somewhere in my body there must be a lurking time bomb, an atavistic gene, a blood clot lodged in a sinew beneath my right shoulder, a microscopic malignant cell.

Across the aisle there is an older gentleman, hands crossed and resting against his substantial belly. Perspiration stains have soaked through the fine blue cotton of his mono-grammed shirt, and he has been smoking thin brown cigarettes most of the way across the Atlantic, orange embers glowing like car lighters in the dark. When he breathes in, I can hear him wheezing three feet away, and I see the red veins tracking across his nose like a map to all the hotel bars in London.

I believe it is no more likely that I will survive the next twenty-four hours than my fellow passenger, this man who already looks like his obituary photograph, smoke billowing above his head, spiraling, evaporating like the memories which die with us. I hear my heart pounding in my chest, thudding once, followed by a light-headedness which may have something to do with the amount of alcohol in my system. I weave to the bathroom and look at myself in the yellow-ish light reflected against the tinny washbasin. I look horrible, ill, yet somehow more like my mother than I have ever imagined possible. For a moment it seems my eyes are playing tricks, that Georgia is staring back at me through the mirror, the thin blue skin beneath her eyes, the faint lines in her cheeks where dimples appear on the rare occasions when she smiles; but mostly the eyes, the blackness of them, the pupils filling up the gray irises, dark and glittering, radiating a distorted image back at the viewer like the silvery lenses of mirrored sunglasses: whoever looks into them sees himself as smaller, diminished.

"Georgia?" I whisper to the mirror.

"No," the image replies.

"Is that you?" I ask.

And I hear Billy's voice in front of me, behind me, floating through the intercom system, the air vents in the door.

"No, Josie," the voice says, echoing around me. But unlike an echo it grows louder instead of softer: "No, Josie, *no, Josie, NO, JOSIE!*"

The back of my blouse is drenched, my palms dripping when I finally manage to get the bathroom door open and collapse against my seat.

XI.

$\mathcal{T}$he table is set for two at either end like a nineteenth-century painting of a wealthy couple dining. There is a pewter bowl in the center of the table, overflowing with vegetables just picked from the garden. The mahogany furniture is piled with heavy white cotton throw pillows, the wood moldings are polished, gleaming, the antiquities are grouped in corners—small clusters of Buddha heads—and the Moroccan rugs are tasteful, thrown together with a sort of threadbare elegance. There is nothing transient about this place. Georgia has clearly made a decision to sink her roots here in the Umbrian mountains, far away from anyone or anything that she knows. The silver, the mahogany chairs, the frayed rugs all seem like family heirlooms, the legacy of some fine ancestry which does not exist, extinguished before a dry-eyed three-year-old in a small Lithuanian village.

There were probably some estate sales in Rome or Florence. I can envision my mother gliding from table to rug to gilded mirror, pointing a finger at this, at that, purchasing the remnant shards of another family's pain.

She has escaped what little family she has left, and yet has dragged me here as surely as if she had pulled me across the ocean by the roots of my hair, screaming.

I have been here two hours, and have yet to see her. I have met Pasca, taciturn Pasca, who greeted me at the door with a finger to her lips and a small glass of grappa in her hand, an offering. Her eyebrows meet across her forehead in one straight line; whether or not she is, by nature, stern, she certainly appears to be.

"Tua madre sta dormendo nella sua stanza di sopra," she whispered, pointing a finger up a winding staircase wedged into the pale gray stone interior walls of the rectory.

You could bury a person within these rectory walls. The outside of the structure is weathered, the stone boulders surrounding the base of the building are buffed smooth, the way wrinkles in an old woman's face can become so plentiful they create a whole new surface, flat and placid, erasing any hint of what came before.

When life is allowed to run its course, by the time we die we are, I think, ready to die. Age prepares us, erasing our prior selves slowly, so quietly we are never aware we are mourning them. Sickness readies us as well, changing the shapes of our brain cells until the will to live alters itself relentlessly; when death becomes an inevitability, we find ways to embrace it.

It is nighttime. The rectory is dark, illuminated only by translucent white candles dripping from wall sconces. I watch Pasca light each candle with a long kitchen taper in what seems to be an evening ritual, cupping the flame around her tanned fingers as she walks from room to room, the orange light licking her face, casting shadows across the grim lines of her mouth and eyebrows.

She has apologized for my mother since I arrived at dusk, shrugging her shoulders, shaking her head, pointing upstairs vaguely, to a room where I saw light streaming from beneath the door when I passed, thinking it was just like Georgia to fill a room with a blaze of light.

I wish my Italian were proficient enough to tell Pasca not to worry, that this is along the lines of what I expected from my mother. Pasca would not be able to understand, even if I were to find the words to tell her. She is probably from a family of twelve, a family in which relatives who arrive from great distances are greeted with breath-defying hugs.

I fall asleep without laying eyes on my mother. The bedroom in which Pasca has left my bags is on the third floor of the tower. It is a circular room, just as Georgia promised, and the walls are the same smooth gray stones which can be found outside the rectory; the effect is tomblike at this hour of the night. The tile floor is cold beneath my bare feet as I pad into the bathroom and arrange my toothpaste, shampoo, toiletries and birth control pills in one orderly line. I stare at the pink case of pills for a moment, wondering at the habit, or the hopefulness, which makes me continue to pop one into my mouth every morning, though it has been many months since I have had need for them.

From my window, shutters open into the night, I see the hazy outlines of vineyards, olive groves, mountains in the distance. There are ledges to this property, giant man-made steps in the earth which lead to the tower, visible from a mile away. *La nordamericana*'s rectory is one of the signposts to travelers, rising above the hills, glimpsed from the railway line or from cars speeding along the Rome-Florence autostrada.

As I fall asleep, my train ride rumbles through my head. I see a Gothic cathedral, medieval towers and palaces, severe stone houses which have not changed since the Middle Ages. As the train's brakes screech I see Orvieto looming in the distance, high up on a six-hundred-foot plateau, huddled around its majestic cathedral like a family surrounding a matriarch dying, the sheer brown walls floodlit in the night.

I am awakened by the smell of eggs frying, bacon, a nauseating smell for someone in my condition, someone who has spent the better part of the night on her knees on the cold tile of the bathroom floor. Blood pounds in my head, my eyes seem to be permanently stuck together, my mouth is parched.

Sun pours through the open window, and beneath my closed lids I see a swirling of red, a figure moving back and forth in front of the window, blocking and releasing the light, which pulses against my eyelids as intensely as a disco strobe.

"Pasca?" I croak.

"No," my mother's voice answers.

I am silent for a moment.

"Hi," I say softly, a tentative offering.

I feel her sit on the edge of my bed. I keep my eyes closed, as if eliminating sight altogether might create a balance between us.

She says nothing. I feel her moving closer, then, as if it were the logical thing, one hand rests against my face. Her fingers brush along my hairline and tremble across my temples, passing over my eyes gently, ending at my jaw, cupping my chin lightly between her thumb and forefinger.

"I'm glad you're here," she says under her breath.

I feel her stretch out next to me, the silky fabric of her robe, the smell of her—faintly metallic—I don't need to open my eyes to see Georgia.

There is a physicality between us in this morning-bright room, each touch weighted and conscious, as it would be between timid lovers. Georgia has held me so few times in my life that each is imprinted in my memory like scar tissue, a small epileptic gash which brings with it the horror of a complete, flailing loss of control.

The morning the movers came she held me to her breast, and the next hour she was gone. The purple dusk seen from halfway across the Brooklyn Bridge, her arms covering me: *this is all I have to give you,* she had murmured, her eyes sweeping the sky. She did not know that the blue lights of the East River Drive shining in the night would have meant nothing to me wrapped in anyone else's arms; what caused my tears that night was not the beauty of what was seen, but the beauty of what was felt.

And now I can barely feel.

"I'm here, Georgia," I say quietly. "I'm right here."

"How long are you staying?" she asks.

"I just got here and you're already wondering when I'm leaving?"

"Jo, that isn't what I meant, I—"

"I can't believe you."

"No. You don't understand. I want you to stay," she says. Her lips brush my forehead.

"I just got here. Can't you be happy with that?"

I feel her stiffen.

"Don't make me do this," she says.

"Do what?"

"I'm reaching out to you, Josie. It isn't easy."

I open my eyes. My mother's face is inches away from mine, and I look at the whiteness of her, the thin blue veins throbbing at either side of her forehead. *I'm reaching out to you.* Georgia has never wished to carry the heavy burden of a daughter's love. Now that she needs it, I am trying to dredge it up like a hand of cards, a flush of hearts.

I think of her self-portraits, the distorted images, the seemingly random pieces of trash, and wonder how far away from herself Georgia ever really managed to run. The four-poster bed in this room is covered with pale gauze netting, a cloud of fabric resting just below the ceiling. There are sconces on the walls with half-dripped candles. I wonder if anyone else has slept in this bed, in this room, or if the candles have been burned by Georgia herself, walking alone through the twenty-three rooms of the rectory, lighting candles and blowing them out.

"Have you seen a doctor?"

"No."

"We'll go this afternoon," I say, relieved. This is something I can handle. It is a task, an assignment which has a beginning and an end. There undoubtedly is an answer, a medical answer buried deep within a physician's desk reference book, and with the comfort of numbers and the spouting of multisyllables, we will uncover the cause of this grayness which has descended upon Georgia like a cloud cover.

"Let's go downstairs," I say, "and have some breakfast. Then I want to call the doctor. We have to get you to see someone today. Do you have a doctor here?"

"Just a family doctor. And Italian, to boot. He doesn't know anything about eyes," says Georgia. "Whenever anything's wrong, they always say it's the liver."

"How are we going to find a good doctor in Rome?" I ask.

"That's an oxymoron."

"Do you have a gallery in Rome? Can we call them and ask for a recommendation?"

"I don't want them to know, Josie."

I realize she is frightened.

"I'm afraid this is just the beginning," she whispers.

"What do you mean?"

"First the color goes, then everything will fade to black. No shapes. No light. Nothing. I want to kill myself when I think of it."

"That's not going to happen."

"What?" she asks dryly. "That I'll lose my sight or that I'll kill myself?"

"Either."

"How do *you* know?"

I smell fresh coffee wafting all the way up to the third floor, and the heavy odor of eggs, butter, bacon. I imagine I should drink juice mixed with raw egg, or quinine water, or any kind of elixir for my pounding head.

"Come on. Let's go downstairs," I repeat, pushing myself up on my elbows. The sooner I can procure medical attention for Georgia, the sooner this need to take care of her will disappear. I will be able to crawl back into my shell, back into my bottle. The bond I once felt with the rest of humanity disappeared into the hole in Billy Overmeyer's head. It resides there, in central New Jersey.

"No. Let's stay here," Georgia whispers, holding me tighter. I wrap my arms around her, trying to stop the tremor which runs through her arms and legs, the slight quake of her body.

"*Signora! Signorina! La prima colazione è servita!*" Pasca's voice travels upstairs.

"She wants us to come have breakfast," Georgia says. "Jesus Christ. I don't think I can face another day like this."

She buries her head in her hands, and I marvel at the gesture. When we bury our heads in our hands, is it not to shield our eyes from seeing? Through the web of her fingers I see a tear fall from her left eye. She angrily swipes at her face.

"Stop it! Stop it, stop it!" she mutters. "You know I see you in black and white? Though I'm sure you don't have much color to begin with. Your face is pale gray. It reflects light like a freshwater pearl. You must have a hell of a hangover, judging from the smell. Alcohol is seeping from your pores. My sense of smell, you see, is still firmly intact."

She holds my chin, turning my head this way and that, inspecting me. She grasps my jaw so hard I flinch.

"You're looking a bit puffy, you know."

Now it is my turn.

"Enough." I hold her wrists. "Cut it out, Georgia."

"Georgia. Goddamn Georgia. You don't even call me Mom. I've never heard you call me Mom," she says.

"You've never been a mom," I tell her. The words slip through my lips inadvertently.

She rolls onto her back and stares at the ceiling. She hugs her arms to her chest. Her body begins trembling again, the bed creaks, and in her silence I hear a fissure, a crack so deep and bottomless I cannot imagine what might be required to repair it.

"Rilke says . . . something like . . . that poets write in order to harness images, that images left unharnessed can turn sharp and wound you. That's how I'm beginning to imagine color, Josie."

I reach out and cradle my mother in my arms. I imagine that somewhere between us there is strength, that in our combined molecular structure there is the courage which propelled me here on yesterday's flight, the boldness which allowed Georgia to sell all of her belongings and create a new life for herself on a continent which held no painful memories. She does not remember: the soul knows no geography. And she does not know—or perhaps she is learning—that outer vision is a poor relation, a black sheep cousin of the inner eye.

I've ruined everything, Josephson.

We were on Fire Island. It was Saturday night, and everybody wanted to go dancing. Eric was there, and about six art world guys Truman had introduced me to—you know the type—wire-rimmed glasses and shoes made from the skins of endangered species. We were getting ready to go out, and Eric was lying in bed, wearing the shorts he had just gone running in.

"Come on, Eric," the others said, "let's go," coaxing him, walking in and out of our room as they got ready for the evening.

"No," he said, "you all go ahead. I'm just going to stay in and rest."

He smiled and turned on his side, away from them. The next thing I knew, there were four guys in the room and they had pinned Eric on his back. One was holding his legs down, two held his arms, and the fourth one held the special K in the palm of his hand.

"Come on, Billy, help us," they called as I stood there.

I walked over to Eric. I forced myself not to look at his eyes, which were pleading with me, as I held the Special K beneath his nose with one hand, and used the other to clamp his mouth shut so he couldn't breathe.

What's Special K, you ask?

I can assure you it's not a brand of breakfast cereal. Or perhaps it is to you. Perhaps you eat it every morning, seated in your Central Park West breakfast nook, overlooking the joggers circling the reservoir. Perhaps your housekeeper picks it up at the Food Emporium. Is that it, Josephson? Do I have your number?

Special K. Ketamine.

Ah, now I see the lift in your eyebrows. You're familiar with it? You read about it, perhaps, in one of your medical journals, a brief skimming of the PDR? It's an animal tranquilizer.

We held the powder beneath Eric's nose and I watched as he held his breath as long as he possibly could, but then he snorted it, Josephson, he had no choice. The granules burned the inside of his nose, blasting through his sinuses all the way past his adenoids and into his brain.

He was up in a flash, dressed within minutes. We convinced

him to borrow a turquoise muscle tee and a pair of ripped denim shorts, and lest I forget, an earring. The hole we punched in his ear that night will take a while to heal, but he can't very well walk around with an earring in his ear, can he, on the trading floor of Merrill Lynch?

Ah, your eyebrows lift again. Can't picture the Eric of my description flitting around Fire Island dressed like a queen, can you?

Well, neither could he. The next morning he was gone. Gone forever, Josephson, after three months of the first decent, monogamous relationship I've ever had with a man.

I guess I just couldn't stand it, the simplicity of it, the normalcy, the lovely parallel desire. The leather banquettes, the video store, the sesame noodles eaten straight out of the container, rain pounding against the air conditioner outside his window. Every night, Josephson, every night he curled around me like a hard, protective shell. And every night, in my sleep, I pushed him away. I ruined it, Josephson, just like I ruin everything I set my hands on.

Let me ask you a question.

Get ready, prepare your blank face, your impassive mask.

You collect my dreams like gold coins. My words congregate on the ceiling, prisms of light. They must form a pattern for you. When will my illusions provide you with the answers?

𝒲e are in Florence, Renaissance city, where pale yellow buildings refract the light of the western sun, and earth-colored rooftops rise like a natural landscape beneath the sky. One could climb these rooftops, scamper over them as if they were the olive groves or orchards of the Tuscan countryside. The Duomo and the Baptistry soar above the ribbons of pavement clogged with motor scooters and bus fumes, the clay-colored dome ascending to a gilded ball at its peak; this is what the eye is drawn to when seated near the Piazzale Michelangiolo in early evening, or on the steps of the thirteenth-century Romanesque Church of San Miniato al Monte.

Georgia cannot see the color of the sun setting over the red-domed cathedral, or the golden Arno punctuated by the Ponte Vecchio. She is wearing dark glasses which perch on the bridge of her nose; if she can only see gray, it will be the darkest gray possible.

Our day's journey begins with a two-hour cab ride into Florence, a stop at the United States consulate at Lungarno Vespucci, and an arrival, finally, at the door of an iron-gated mansion which houses a suite of doctors' offices.

In all the American cities I have visited, the neighborhoods which are filled with doctors' offices are inevitably the sheltered havens of the rich: the tulips on Park Avenue, the townhouses of Beacon Hill, the sparkling glass structures lining Lake Shore Drive—wherever you look the bronze plaques are discreetly scattered as if they were simply bricks in the facade, as if they had belonged there always. Billy's office was in a neighborhood such as this, his newly minted degree shining among brownstone windowboxes.

The address of the ophthamologist given to us by the consulate is a Florentine version of Park Avenue or Beacon Hill. The villas are set back from the street, pebbled courtyards with ancient stone fountains, wood-slatted windows closed against the mid-afternoon sun, private homes surrounded by black iron gates which seem to discourage announcing oneself without prior appointment.

The secretary at the consulate has called ahead, and Dr. Abbruzzese, a bilingual ophthamologist, is expecting us, forgoing his usual break from two until four in the afternoon.

It is three o'clock when I ring the buzzer. We are admitted into the courtyard, and through the heavy wooden door, which looks to be centuries old. The building itself has been modernized, and after checking the list of names in the foyer, I lead Georgia into a tiny elevator which takes us to the third floor.

"What the hell are we *doing?*" she mutters.

"Almost there," I say.

"I don't want to do this."

"I know."

"What can he possibly tell me that I'll want to hear?" she asks.

"I don't know, Georgia."

"You're making me do this."

"You asked me to come here."

We have been bickering for the past hour, since leaving the consulate and negotiating our way to the other side of the city with a cabdriver from Orvieto who is unfamiliar with the winding streets of Florence. Below her dark glasses, which cover half her face, her mouth crumbles like an old woman's.

"I hate you," she says, "you're mean."

She turns away from me in the tiny elevator, and I make obscene gestures behind her back. I stick both my middle fingers in the air, waving them back and forth.

"You can leave, after this," she says.

"Leave, as in go back to New York?"

"Yes."

"Fine."

The elevator doors slide open and we are in a modern waiting room, furnished in leather and chrome, tables scattered with copies of *The New Yorker* and Italian *Vogue*. Behind a glass partition there is a receptionist who is on the telephone. She gestures to a leather couch in the center of the room.

I place a hand on Georgia's back and guide her toward the couch.

She shakes my hand away.

"I'm not a cripple, Joanna," she says. "You're really enjoying this, aren't you."

I am silent.

"Aren't you?"

"What—precisely—about this experience do you think I would find enjoyable?" I ask quietly.

She looks at me angrily, and I am reminded of the day she first met Nigel. *What are you doing with him? What's my daughter doing with a waiter?* she asked, as if what I did, as her daughter, reflected more clearly, more harshly on her than it did on me.

"I'm here because you need me, Georgia. Let's just keep our facts straight," I say. "You asked me to come."

"You called and called. For months. You wouldn't just let me disappear. Don't you think Pasca told me?" she says.

My hands curl in my lap, and I realize I want to slap her. I want to feel the sting of my hand across her cheekbone, the sudden crack which would come with no warning. It would hurt both of us; my hand, her face.

"Hello," a voice says from behind us.

I swivel, as does Georgia, and see a white-haired man wearing a doctor's coat over a blue and white pin-striped shirt. He is standing in the doorway leading to the inner offices.

"I'm Dr. Abbruzzese," he says. "Please come in."

He leads us into a paneled room which contains his tools, from rudimentary eye charts to elaborate gleaming machines. He looks at Georgia, then at me.

"Tell me what I can do for you," he says kindly in Georgia's direction. Her dark glasses in this shuttered room are a dead giveaway; her shielded eyes, trembling hands, instruments of survival. I imagine if Georgia were told she needed a double mastectomy, a hysterectomy, it would incite less terror than this.

I am reminded of what she told me earlier today: of Rilke, who once said that poets write in order to harness words, words which otherwise have the power to destroy us. Georgia has always attempted to harness what she sees: the blue of the Sabbath sky in Lithuania, twilight setting over the Brooklyn Bridge, a single balloon floating against an East Houston Street ceiling—blue, fugitive blue, which starts out a clear color, but begins to bleed and eclipse all that surrounds it, hemophiliac blue, which keeps on bleeding.

"Thirteen days ago I woke up and the color was gone," she says.

The doctor is writing on a chart, a spanking-new white page for Georgia.

"The color?"

"Yes."

"Do you see reds and greens, or blues and yellows?" he asks.

"No color at all."

"But you can discern shapes, features on faces?"

"Yes."

I hear an echo, a sound thousands of miles away in a New York City theatre: Nabokov's words in *Speak, Memory*, spoken onstage as I drift in the background . . .

What I mean is not the bright mental image (as, for instance, the face of a beloved parent long dead) conjured up by a wing-stroke of the will; that is one of the bravest movements a human spirit can make. Nor am I alluding to the so-called muscae voli-tantes—shadows cast upon the retinal rods by motes in the vitreous humor, which are seen as transparent threads drifting across the visual field . . .

"So I doubt we're dealing with macular degeneration," he murmurs, focused on his notes.

"What's that?"

"Come," he rises from his desk, patting a seat which is part of an elaborate steel machine, "let's take a look."

"Doctor, what does this sound like to you?" I ask.

He glances at me.

"I can't answer that yet. It could be a symptom of a number of different things," he says. "But I don't want to play guessing games. I've never seen a case where total color vision simply up and disappeared."

"So you're saying—"

"I'm saying I'd better examine this lady here."

"My daughter will sit in the waiting room," Georgia answers.

Dr. Abbruzzese looks at me, smiles, inclines his head toward the door.

"She'll be a little while," he says.

What would happen if I were to simply leave her here? I imagine she would find her way to safe ground, and eventually would search for me. My doorbell would ring one night. She would step out of the shadows of Times Square.

An hour goes by before Georgia appears in the waiting room, casting a shadow over the Italian fashion spread of a model whose naked body has been spray-painted entirely in silver. I look up. She is standing in the center of the doorway, turning her head from side to side.

I stand quickly, the magazine sliding off my lap to the floor. I bend down to pick it up and catch the receptionist's eye as she glances at it, then at me, and sniffs as she turns back to the typewriter. She doesn't have much use for these American tourists who are referred from the consulate, soft, pale people with minor ailments. She types up their bills as they sit in the doctor's sanctum, her nimble fingers translating lire into American dollars.

"The doctor wants to talk to us together," Georgia says.

This time, as we walk back into his offices, I make no motion to help her.

He places his hands together beneath his chin, elbows on his desk. Through this tent of flesh, crisp cotton, gold flash of wedding ring I see the patterned silk of his necktie and realize the design is made entirely from a repetitive formation of eyes. Blue, green, blue, green. I wonder whether the tie was a gift from a patient, a daughter, a wife. I wonder if he wears it every day. Perhaps he has a whole slew of them in different colors: gray, brown, hazel, even the pink of an albino.

But he is talking, and I must focus on what he is saying. After all, this is the purpose of my visit, this long, drawn-out day. Georgia is next to me, slumped in her chair, her dark glasses sitting on the desk, lenses down. She closes her eyes, pinches the bridge of her nose.

". . . as I was telling Ms. Higgins Hirsch, I really don't know what to suggest. There's absolutely nothing wrong with her sight," the doctor says.

"What do you mean?" I ask.

"Exactly what I said. These devices," he waves at a whir-ring bank of computerized testing equipment, "measure brain-wave activity picked up through sensors attached to the pa-tient's head. The machines don't lie. They *can't* lie. When you look at the images of shifting checkerboards on the screen, what the eye sees registers in the brain. Now with Ms. Higgins Hirsch, brain activity shows up, and we know she has light perception, which would mean that there's no medical reason why she wouldn't be seeing color."

"This is gibberish," snaps Georgia. "Kindly speak English."

The doctor blinks.

"I am speaking English. You just don't like what you're hearing."

"Nonsense! I can't even see the color of your tie," says Georgia.

"I didn't say you're faking. I'm just running through possible causes."

"Such as—" I pipe in.

"Your mother could have an inflammation of the optic nerve which could be causing this, but I can't detect it."

"Any other possibilities?"

"Well, she could have had a transient ischemic attack—"

"Speak English!" Georgia interrupts sharply.

"A stroke, Ms. Higgins Hirsch," he blinks at her. "You could have had a mini-stroke."

She gasps.

"Jo, let's get out of here. I don't like it here."

"I'm just laying out the possibilities," Abbruzzese says. "I don't think, in a case such as this one—"

"Cases like what? I'm not a case, I'm a person, an artist, and I'm sitting here seeing in black and white, and you're talking about fucking textbooks!" Georgia yells.

"Please sit down. I didn't mean to alarm or insult you. I realize how frightening this must be for you. When you came here today, I knew who you were. I've been a great admirer of yours. Forgive me. I know little of the art world. I only know medicine, this small, specialized field. Sometimes I can only rely on what the machines tell me."

Georgia sits down, mollified for the moment.

"Dr. Abbruzzese, what are you telling us?" I ask.

"I'm not sure. But I have a hunch. Ms. Higgins Hirsch, may I ask you a few questions?"

"Certainly," says Georgia.

"They may seem a bit personal."

"That's all right."

"First, let me tell you why I'm asking. Actually, no, I think I'll explain afterward, if that's all right."

"All right," says Georgia faintly. I can see her brow wrinkling. "Let's get on with it."

"Have you recently undergone any kind of crisis in your life?"

"Recently?" Georgia draws the syllables out slowly. "No."

"Let me rephrase the question. Has there been anything you have witnessed which has upset you, visual in nature . . ."

He trails off. Georgia doesn't answer him. I know what she is thinking. I imagine if you placed transparencies of our thoughts, one on top of the other, they would form the same image: the trees, the white flash of lightning, the blood pouring from every pore, splashing to the ground as if from a spigot.

"What are you grasping at, Dr. Abbruzzese? This is ridiculous," I break the silence. "My mother has lost her ability to see color. There must be a medical reason. If you can't find it, we'll go to someone else. We'll fly back to the States."

"Miss Hirsch, I assure you there are stacks of research to back me up. Bear with me." He clears his throat every few seconds.

We both look at Georgia. And Georgia looks inward.

"Yes, there *was* something . . ." she says finally.

"When was it?" asks the doctor.

"The month before I moved here permanently."

"And when was that?"

"I moved to Orvieto in September. The night I mean was August 9."

"You barely even knew him!" I hear myself say. I bite the words off. There are spaces between each word, spaces which could be filled with whole paragraphs. I have swung myself around so I am facing her, my hands gripping the sides of my chair. All my life she has taken away from me what I needed most; now she is trying to fill the cavity which has been created in my own life, the one which corresponds with the hole in her memory.

"How can that be?" I sputter.

"What's going on here?" asks the doctor.

Through it all, Georgia sits calmly, almost peacefully, her hands folded, motionless in her lap. She has the dreamy, unburdened look of a woman exiting a confessional booth. The surface has momentarily been wiped clean by the expulsion of words; the illusion is maintained that disclosure will heal, that the spoken word carries with it a salve for the soul.

"I saw Joanna's stepbrother beaten nearly to death last August," Georgia states flatly, "during a mugging."

"I'm so sorry," the doctor says. The words fall into a well-worn groove; he has said these words many times in his professional life.

"He has been hospitalized ever since," she continues.

An image rises to the surface of my mind as if through the darkness of a dream: Georgia moaning and turning her head, cradling her shoulder in one hand as Billy ran after the mugger. When the mugger multiplied and became a gang of six, when Billy's body was kicked through the air, folding like a mannequin dismantled in a store window, her breathing remained steady, as if this were nothing unusual, as if she had anticipated an event like this all her life. I remember her breath, the expulsion of air. The staunch, ceaseless in-out of it.

"What did it have to do with you?" I ask. I have no patience for this dramatic display, her motionless hands, the mournful nodding of the doctor's head. *I saw Joanna's stepbrother beaten to death.* She has managed to make this tragedy self-referential. Is there nothing Georgia sees which she doesn't try to own?

Something snaps.

"That's it. You're on your own, Georgia," I say, getting up from my chair. I plan to take a taxi directly to the train station, a train directly to Rome, and a flight home. My American Express card and passport are waiting agreeably in my wallet.

I walk to the door but am stopped by foreign words, an unfamiliar language pouring from my mother's lips. The sounds are guttural—harsh and muted, like the sound of someone wretching behind a closed bathroom door—and the voice is not Georgia's but an echo.

I turn around.

The doctor and I both stare at her.

"What is she saying?" he asks.

"I don't know."

I walk to where she is seated; she is slumped forward, hair hanging around her face, enclosing it like the curtains which surround the critically ill in hospital rooms. I kneel in front of her and put my hands on her shoulders.

"Georgia?"

The language continues, now reduced to a mumble.

"Should I call for help?" the doctor asks.

I wonder who he thinks he should call.

"Georgia?"

Her shoulders are rigid. If I closed my eyes I would not think I was touching flesh. How little difference there is, I think, between a twig and a finger, a rib cage and a discarded egg carton left on the street.

She is keening now, her body moving back and forth as if in prayer. I look at Dr. Abbruzzese and realize he is frightened. I am frightened too. The fear in this room sucks language from the air.

"Mom?"

I wrap my arms around her.

"Mom?" I repeat again and again. A mantra, the easiest word in the English language; it is soft on the tongue, requires only the opening and closing of the mouth, the emitting of a slight sound through the throat, and there it is: *Mom, Mom, Mom.*

The keening stops. Her body stops rocking, her shoulders sag, and she looks at me through a tangle of hair.

"Let's go," she says in English. "I want to talk to you."

"I don't know if that's such a good idea," says the doctor.

"Ah. What can you do for me, Dr. Abbruzzese?" Georgia asks.

"Well, there is therapy which can be helpful, for patients with hysterical symptoms, group therapy for psychosomatic . . ."

"Is there anything you can do for me right now?" She rears herself up.

A pause.

"No," he says, "but I don't think you should leave. You're in no kind of shape . . ."

She is already standing, holding out her arm to me.

"Come on, Josie. There's a place I want to take you. Quickly, before it gets dark."

Here's a breakthrough. Sorry to say it didn't happen in here, on this torture rack of a couch; it came to me as I was hanging onto a subway strap, as if one of the dark-eyed poster children began speaking to me in a new and mystical language.

I realized that all we were ever trying to do, Josie and I, was to chisel a world for ourselves, a place where we could survive. We were trying to create order out of chaos, a kind of animal serenity, love out of the anarchy of our childhoods.

You think the root of it is incestuous, Josephson. You carry my words to your supervisor and surround yourself with textbook answers, but what about a more creative possibility? What about an instance—inconceivable to a clinician, perhaps—when passion is borne out of an essential benevolence, a reaching of the human heart?

XII.

We are headed for the Church of San Miniato al Monte, near the Piazzale Michelangiolo. Georgia asked the taxi driver to let us off at the Ponte alle Grazie, a replica of a thirteenth-century bridge which spans the Arno. Beyond the bridge is a steep hill, and we are hiking up to the church, its marble and gold facade rising in the distance.

"This is the highest point above the city," Georgia pants.

"I should imagine so," I reply. "Why are we doing this?"

She stumbles over a small rock.

I steady her.

"I want you to see it," she answers.

I think of the Brooklyn Bridge, of my twelve-year-old self wrapped in Georgia's arms with the Manhattan skyline spread out before us, the purple river, bridges hung like Christmas lights in the night. I remember the November wind blowing her cape, her long hair whipping against my face.

This is all I live for, she said, *if I don't live for this, I will die.*

It is twenty years later.

When we reach the piazzale, Georgia stops for a moment, breathing heavily.

"Do you see the bell tower?" she asks.

"Where?"

"Over there, to your left, next to the church," she says.

I see the charred walls of a tower which looks to have been built a few centuries after the church.

"The bell tower burned during the sixteenth century," Georgia says, "during the invasion by the Spaniards. Michelangelo and a small band of soldiers piled mattresses and bales of wool around the tower to protect it, but the mattresses were set on fire by a cannon blast and the tower burned. Thank God the church was left standing."

She is impassioned in her speech. The preservation of history is infinitely more important to her than any individual life.

"Sit down, Josie," she says, "I want to talk to you."

We sit side by side on the steps. In the distance the sun turns the Duomo red.

I am as motionless as possible, feeling Georgia next to me, a jumble of unsaid words in the air. If I am very still, the words will come slowly, they will perch serenely on my shoulders, and I will be able to recall each syllable, each silence.

My mother takes off her glasses and rubs the bridge of her nose. She closes her eyes and begins speaking in the harsh language of an hour ago. A gleeful agitation enters her voice as she speaks faster, more expressively. Blood vessels flare in her cheeks. She rocks back and forth as I begin to detect a cadence, a measured beat. She is reciting something.

Kol Nidre, or a peasant *Kaddish,* perhaps, the prayer for the dead.

I am silent, dry-eyed, staring at her.

"What's the matter?" she asks as she turns away from me, out toward the city. "You don't understand?"

I say nothing.

"I am trying to explain it to you."

"What are you trying to explain to me, Georgia?" I ask bitterly. "What, exactly, are you trying to explain? The best I can tell is you're trying to drive me crazy, and I've got to tell you, you're succeeding."

I crave a drink. I look down at the city and imagine all the bars, the outdoor cafés becoming busy as night falls, waitresses balancing trays filled with cappuccino cups and glasses of Campari.

"This is the language I learned in my parents' home," Georgia says.

Rarely have I heard her say the words, "my parents." Georgia does not speak of her mother, her father. She has never referred to a brother or a sister. I don't imagine she had any siblings, or if she did, that they survived the pogrom. Pogrom is a word I learned from textbooks. It has never, to the best of my knowledge, passed my mother's lips.

We are a family of only children, of quiescence, of ghosts.

"I think it is a combination of Lithuanian and Yiddish," she says. "I thought I had forgotten it."

"Where did it come from?" I ask.

She shakes her head.

"They say there's a part of the brain where language is stored," she says; "perhaps the words have always been trapped there."

She doesn't say it, but I know we are both wondering if her eyesight is trapped there as well. I know the place; it is the bloody, hollow locus of her brilliance. For what is genius if not the use of the unconscious as a tool? A small, careless carving knife whittling, forming by reckless slips and slides what is inaccessible to the self.

"Do you want to tell me about it?" I ask her.

Silence.

I try again.

"Tell me about it," I say, trying to keep all inflection out of my voice, all desire. "I've always wanted to know."

"I can't tell you much," Georgia says.

"Please."

"I can't, Josie. I don't remember."

With this, her shoulders begin to shake. After a lifetime of never having seen my mother cry, it seems now she can't stop.

"I'm sorry," she gasps, "I just don't remember."

"Tell me what you do remember."

She closes her eyes, and I wonder if she is trying to summon memory, or if all that's left to her are the photographs of Calvaria, curled around the edges, black and white.

"We used to play in the back lot behind the hardware store," she closes her eyes, "the smell of metal. Dust."

"Dust?"

"There was dust everywhere in the village. It covered the clothing of children whose fathers mysteriously disappeared, the ones who were escorted quietly from their homes by two S.A. men, the ones who were known to be Social Democrats, who passed out illegal leaflets and newspapers. Everyone knew who the Jews were, and there were certain limits. The limits were understood. It was before the war, before the yellow stars of David," she says, as if she is telling me something I don't already know, as if the clues have not been scattered through her work; all my life I have stumbled into them, feeling my way around in the darkness until I achieved at least a rudimentary understanding of her life.

"And the smell of metal?"

"My father was a welder."

As she speaks, her tone and affect change imperceptibly from her well-cultivated accent, a way of speaking which carries with it the weight of its own defense, a story without a sense of place, a tale without a history. Now her words carry images. Dark-capped children. Burning streets.

"My father was a welder," she repeats softly, "and a member of the Communist defense organization. He had his own store until the day the S.A. smeared red paint on his windows and stationed two men outside his front door."

The heat swelters as the sun sets, creating waves in the air, mirages, and in the distance I watch citizens scurry home from work, women carrying mesh sacks filled with yellow and red peppers, loaves of bread. To my left are the scarred remains of the bell tower, standing after four centuries.

"You think you've had a rough life, Joanna?" my mother asks.

I look at her profile, the aging planes of her face, and say nothing. I assume she is asking a rhetorical question.

"Do you?" she repeats.

"I haven't lived as long as you, Georgia."

She draws in a breath sharply, through her nose.

"By the time I was ten years old I had been through more than you'll ever know in a lifetime."

"Is that what this is about? Did you bring me here to have a competition: who's had it worse?" I ask her.

By *here* I mean this country, this city, these marble steps far from home. Some define home as being near a family, but home for me is a place fifty-seven steps above West Forty-sixth Street, a door slammed shut with three locks and bolts, windows barred against a fire escape which leads to the avenue below. Home is a place where my desk is littered with photographs. My face appears in many of these photographs as the one common denominator. If a stranger were to look at the assortment we would all look supremely interesting, privileged and optimistic. Look closely at our smiles: see the strain in our jaws, see the backs of our molars, all ground down. Look at our eyes: in some, you will see dilated pupils, the residue of street drugs. Look at the lines in our faces; we all have them if you look close enough. Can you see the future embedded somewhere—a concentration camp number, or ash on a forehead—the gray and white newsprint which will some day condense our lives into three small paragraphs?

"My mother's sister took me to Germany, and eventually across the German border into Switzerland," Georgia says. "I remember the beauty of that day. I remember the sun as we passed through the Black Forest on the train, and I remember I didn't know where we were going, or why my mother wasn't with us. Then we got to the station. We waited all afternoon until darkness fell. Once it was nighttime, my mother's sister held my hand as we walked quickly through the woods. Quickly, quickly. I heard her teeth chattering so loud I thought the trees would hear them. Then there was the searchlight. It swept the forest with a precise, dazzling rhythm. When my mother's sister saw the searchlight she picked me up and started to run, and every time it glared she fell to the ground, cradling me, crushing me beneath her. When we crossed the border she didn't know it, she kept running, running until she heard our names called again and again by the friend who had come to meet us in Switzerland."

She stares straight ahead, past the twilight sky over Florence, beyond the Duomo and Baptistry, into the recesses of her own mind, as gnarled and dense as the Black Forest, and as full of ruthless illumination.

"You're soft, Jo," my mother says. "You've always had money, you've always had opportunity. No one's ever said no to you. You're—how old?—thirty-two? Have you ever failed at anything in your life?"

"Yes," I say, but she is not listening.

"You drink too much," she says. "You look for solutions outside yourself."

"You're right," I say quietly, "I do drink too much. I stopped for a while, but—"

She interrupts me with the foreign, thick-tongued language, then lapses into English, and I begin to wonder about her sanity, about the place in her mind where the language has hidden all these years, where the sight has gone, where the rage toward me spills from. The place is like a cellular memory, a scar which has been torn open, skin tougher than any other until broken.

"Was I such a terrible mother?" she asks, another rhetorical question. "Was it unbearable to have me in your life?"

"I never had you in my life," I say.

"I did the best I could!" she screams. Tourists on the piazzale turn to stare. Their cameras hang from their necks, witnesses, shuttered eyes.

"I wanted to leave something behind!"

"What are you talking about?" I ask. I am afraid to know the answer.

"My work, Joanna."

"What about a daughter? Did you want to leave a daughter behind?" My voice rises to match hers.

"I never thought of you that way," she says.

"How did you think of me? Did you think of me at all?"

"I brought you into the world. I figured you would make your way," she says.

"Like you did?"

A pause.

"Yes, like I did."

Another pause. I imagine her as a child, a heavy bundle being held, eyes shut tight.

"Why did you get married?" I ask her.

"I don't know."

"How can you not know?"

"I was young, Josie," she says with a shrug, "and I thought your father would protect me. Who was it who once said an artist has to choose: passion in life, or passion in work?"

"Whoever said it was wrong."

She snorts.

"I've lived a lot longer than you have, Josie. Trust me on this. You can't have it all. Look at you! You're beginning to really make it in your career. What's the first thing that happens? Nigel walks. Men like Nigel have fragile egos. They need easy women. You and I aren't easy."

I turn her words over in my head, approaching them from different angles: *You and I aren't easy.*

"Josie, listen to me," she says as gently as possible, "it's love or work. Unfortunately for an artist."

"What about Vishna?" I ask her.

"Vishna was wounded. I am able to care for the wounded."

I am wounded, I want to say.

"And what happens now?" I ask.

"I don't know. I feel like I haven't even begun my work. I haven't done enough," she says grimly.

What about me? The words, pathetic echoes, remain unsaid. *I've traveled thousands of miles, real and imagined. Am I, just for this moment, enough? Was there a hole in you, Mother, bigger than a bullet would make, a hole you didn't even know you had until I filled it for nine months?*

"Tell me, Jo. Have you ever wanted anything enough to trade your whole life for it? Have you ever wanted anything you can't have?"

"Yes."

Night has fallen over the city.

"What?"

"I'd rather not say."

"Does it have anything to do with me?" she asks.

"In a way, yes."

"What is it?"

"Don't push, Georgia."

"I have to push. It's the only way I'll know."

"After all these years, you really want to know?" I ask. "Why?"

The pitch of my voice rises; a group of German tourists seated near us gather their belongings and move away.

A shadow of a smile crosses my mother's face.

"It's selfish, I suppose," she says, "but when I see you in my mind's eye, Josie, I see myself so clearly that sometimes I think if I can just find a way inside you . . ."

There is a law of humanity, an atavistic law that hangs from every family tree. In the womb we are imprinted not only with the genes which determine our hair color and the strength of our bones, but also with an invisible cryptograph, an edict which coats us like plasma when we are born. In our lives we believe we make our own choices, but in fact our actions have been laid out for us over hundreds of years. The very paths we attempt to avoid are the ones which, one way or another, we will end up navigating.

"Do you love me?" I ask my mother.

My eyes are squeezed tightly together, holding back tears, because I think I know the answer.

"Of course I love you," she says, as if love is commonplace, an emotion akin to a cool regard, a tolerance.

"I love you too."

Our words sound hollow, counterfeit. We are actors in a drama, my mother and I, a tour de force on which the tenuous chords connecting us depend.

"Then tell me. Where does the emptiness come from? What would you trade your life for?"

"I already have," I answer quietly.

"What do you mean?"

I turn, facing her.

"When I was a child I used to make paper dolls while I waited for you to come out of your studio. I would cut the shape of a figure from paper folded like an accordion, then I would unfold the paper and what would be left would be the holes, the shape of what was missing."

"What's missing, Jo?"

I look at my mother. She has always seemed so dauntless to me, so immutable that I have somehow missed seeing her physical decline: now I see the fine lines around her eyes, the age spots on her hands, the smear of lipstick on her teeth which I haven't mentioned to her all afternoon.

"Just for a moment," my voice shakes, "for a moment I'd like to know what it might be like to live without absence; to feel the shape of a life defined by its substance, not by what is missing."

"Your life has substance," Georgia says.

"I suppose we learn to live with what we're given," I say. "And I'm not so sure, after all these years, that you ought to look for yourself in me, Georgia. You just might not like what you find there."

It was the most magical night of my life: I had just turned seventeen, and I spent from midnight until six in the morning in bed with Joanna.

Have you ever been held, Josephson, just held close by a person whose limbs matched your own as if you were twins, as if you had shared a womb, legs wound like tree roots, arms wound together like branches rising in the sky?

We didn't make love. It was never really a possibility, though I was hard, and pressed up against her. We both knew desire was something to be understood, not spoken about, not acted on.

Earlier that evening she had disappeared behind a bedroom door at that party, and I knew what was happening in there. With my knee I could feel her thigh, sticky with blood. I assumed it was blood. Anything else was unthinkable. It felt to me like a sacrifice. She offered herself to some Tipton lacrosse player because she knew she could never be with me, and she knew she had better get on with it. It was the same motive, several months later, which led me into the woods at Todd Wanamaker's heels.

What would have happened, do you think, if we had changed our names and disappeared one night, becoming another statistic in the thousands of missing children who vanish? Who are never found again, alive or dead?

I never experienced with a lover what I felt that night with Josie, that perfect blend of safety and desire. I have looked for it my whole life. I have looked for it in the arms of countless men. I never touched another woman.

Did I say touched?

I didn't mean that.

I didn't—didn't touch her.

Am I sure? How can you ask me if I'm sure?

Allow me, please, to turn the tables.

Are you sure, Herr Doktor? Or do you think, perhaps, that I sleepwalked into her room each night, adrift, in a dream, and ran my fingertips down the curves of her body as if it were my own second skin?

Answer me, Josephson. Shatter my illusions, I beg of you.

We are somewhere over the Atlantic when Georgia removes the headphones and leans back in the soft leather seat of the Alitalia jet. A box of cassette tapes lies open on her lap; it is the box I carry with me everywhere like a diary, the story of my life folded into sound bites, wound tightly on sprockets. I play them over and over again. The tapes are always with me, in the large black shoulder bag I carry, jumbled together with my wallet, checkbook, pills, postcards printed with my photograph, an airbrushed headshot of me with bare shoulders and excessive eye makeup.

The stewardess comes by with snacks and drinks, the last service they will offer before landing at Kennedy. We shake our heads in unison. I have had no alcohol on this flight. I have turned down Bloody Marys, white wine, red wine and a laminated list of after-dinner cordials. Handing Georgia the tapes was an act that, for me, is not unlike taking a drink; an unpremeditated gesture whose end result is unknown.

"My God," says Georgia. She rolls her head toward the window, the endless sheet of clouds below.

She says nothing for a long while. She rewinds part of one tape and listens again. I watch her. A muscle flutters beneath her eye.

Finally she takes off the headphones.

"Why did you share these with me?" she asks.

"I—"

This is my holocaust, Mother, insignificant and private though it is.

"How could you possibly let me listen to this?" she interrupts.

"I think I—"

"My God, Josie."

She reaches across the armrest which separates us and gropes for my hand. I put my hand in hers, and she squeezes tightly, cramping my fingers with all the strength she possesses, the sinews extending from her wrists, the bones rising up like a topographical map.

"How long have you had these tapes? Since after Billy was—"

"No. Before."

"How did you—"

"Never mind that," I say quickly.

"You're right. It doesn't matter," Georgia says, patting the tapes on her lap.

We are quiet as the world hurls beneath us, whirling, splendid. I lean back and watch my mother with this new luxury of time, of appraisal. She is dressed in her usual black, enveloped in soft cashmere, fine wool, an elegant alligator belt. On the floor beneath her seat, wedged under the flotation cushion, lies a supple leather overnight bag. In her private life, Georgia is an aesthete; she surrounds herself with splendor, she brands herself with it, relating intimately to objects, more moved by an African mask, a jade ax head than by anything alive.

"I thought you, of all people, would understand," I say softly. "After all, you're an artist."

"But you're an artist too, Jo."

"I've never been anything when I compare myself to you."

"That's not true!"

"Have you always known how gifted you are, Georgia? Have you always known, deep inside yourself, before anyone else told you?"

"Deep inside myself, yes," Georgia answers.

"Well that's not true of me. I've never had that kind of

faith in myself. Billy always knew that about me. And so did Nigel."

"Nigel preyed on that knowledge, in fact," Georgia says dryly.

"But he was right."

"He was dead wrong, Josie. You *are* gifted," Georgia says.

"How do you know? You've never really seen my work, except for that night in the park, and that hardly counted . . ."

"But I have seen your work."

"You have?"

"I came to see you in *Speak, Memory*."

"You did? When?"

"The night before I left for Orvieto. Late September. It was a Saturday night. The show was in previews," she says.

"Why didn't you let me know you were there?" I ask. "Every night I looked for you, Georgia. Every night until I knew you were gone. And even then . . ."

"I didn't want to ruin it for you. I thought you'd be terrified if you knew I was there. I never wanted you to compete with me, Josie. I just wanted to be able to do my own work. I never wanted to get in your way. And I certainly never wanted to hurt you," she cries. "I did try to do the best I could."

Between us, in the pressurized air of this cabin, the words, *the best I could,* hang in the air, toxic gray, the terrible ultimate defense between parent and child.

I glance at the tapes spread across a blanket on her lap. *B. Overmeyer,* they are lightly labeled in pencil, with dates showing the month and year.

"What do you make of these?" I ask, sweeping my hand across the tapes, gathering them together. I should make copies. I should ensure that nothing will ever happen to them, that they will not burn or get tangled; they are the last remnants of Billy, his soul captured, in his cracking, cajoling, desolate voice.

"I know one thing: it's amazing nothing happened to him sooner," Georgia says.

"What do you mean?"

"My dear, he was committing suicide by erosion. The baths, the drugs, the violence . . . Oh God. Truman Bidwell," she says with a shudder, "I can't believe I introduced him to Truman Bidwell."

"You didn't know."

"No, I didn't, but if I had thought about it . . ."

"When did we ever think about each other? When did we ever really think about anyone but ourselves?"

It occurs to me that we are physically polarized, my mother and I, with the leather armrest immovable between us, this silver capsule hurling us through the sky. We are distinct from each other as we are distinct from the world which curves below us. I think of the night she came to see me in *Speak, Memory*. It has always been inconceivable to me that Georgia could be in a room without my knowing it. Every night I saw pieces of her from the stage when I took my bows: a mass of curls, a length of neck, an elegant wrist. Every night I saw parts of Georgia, but when she was there, actually seated in the audience, I didn't know it. I could not smell her from the stage, I could not hear the clink of her bracelets, or sense the sharpness in the air around her, as if she extended larger than her actual physical self.

"I'd like to try again," she whispers.

"Try again at what?"

"I have no idea what it would be like to be a mother," she says. She has not let go of my hand. "I never had one myself."

"Yes you did," I say.

I am fighting back tears. I feel all of us here at this moment

—my father, Lila, Georgia, Nigel and most of all Billy—their names all in the tapes scattered across my mother's lap, their spirits somehow hovering in the air of this cabin, swirling through the thin blue sky outside this oval window. When I was a child, Georgia used to paint faces in the shapes of clouds. Now, when I look at Georgia's profile, her dark glasses and squared shoulders, beyond her to the plane window, I see them dancing. Billy's face floats way above the earth. I see him using the white cottony clouds as a trampoline. *Higher, higher!* I scream in my head, a twelve-year-old's voice. *Higher, Billy!*

The soccer fields, Katz's corner deli, bicycles ridden without hands with the grace of children and angels. Cicada shells lined the suburban streets. *Wait for me! Wait for me, Billy! Me too!*

I no longer feel the urge to hurl myself through the emergency doors, a jumper with no parachute. The miles I would fall through the thin air to the ground—the moment of impact —plays through my mind for an instant, an idle daydream, and I realize the uneasy truce, the tightrope my mother and I are negotiating. Bottles clink in the galley kitchen behind me. I know that, with one single act, I can eradicate the pain, and along with it, the joy, the hope, all potentiality.

I reach my hand out and gently stroke my mother's face. I brush my fingers across her temples. I don't want to frighten her. Then slowly, carefully, I remove her dark glasses.

ACKNOWLEDGMENTS

Every book has guardian angels. Here are mine: Peter Brunell, Hallie Gay Walden-Bagley, Seymour Reit, Robert Brownstein, Ellen Geist, Loretta Barrett, Laura Van Wormer, Shaye Areheart and my family.

And my two *guiding* angels: my editor, Nan A. Talese, and my agent, Esther Newberg. It is not possible to be in better hands.

ABOUT THE AUTHOR

Dani Shapiro received a B.A. and M.F.A. from Sarah Lawrence College. Her first novel, *Playing with Fire,* was published by Doubleday in 1990. Ms. Shapiro teaches creative writing at Columbia University in New York City, where she lives.